The Man Who

Vanished

Charles Dayton

Published by Foothill Associates
Nevada City, CA 95959

First Edition, 2023
Imprint of Record – Create Space

Also by Charles Dayton

In the Lew Travis Mystery Series:

Come Hell or High Water

Hell Hath No Fury

Hell to Pay

Hell's Angel

There But For Fortune: A Novel

Is That All There Is: A Novel

Time Passages: Ten Stories

For more information about the author
and his books:

charlesdayton.net

Dedicated to

Laurie Harrison

1945-2022

My wife of 44 years

The Sienna Sentinel

The *Sienna Sentinel* is a small local newspaper in the city of Sienna, an old gold-mining town in the foothills of the Sierra Nevada Mountains of northern California. The following item appeared in its police blotter column on the morning of Saturday, September seventh.

> A caller from Chestnut Street informed police that a neighbor, Robert Campbell, hadn't been seen for several days.

Two days later, Monday, September ninth, a story appeared on page three of the paper under the headline: *Local Man Missing*. It read:

> Robert Campbell, a long-time resident of Sienna, has apparently been missing since early last week. A neighbor noticed several newspapers lying on his front porch and decided to investigate. The neighbor, who alerted police, reported that Campbell's house was unlocked, and a brief inspection suggested he hadn't been there for several days.
> Fearing foul play, police searched Campbell's house the next day for possible clues to his

disappearance. According to Police Chief John Christiansen they found nothing suspicious. The house was open, but nothing appeared to have been disturbed. Campbell's pickup truck, his only vehicle, was parked in the garage. Currently police are at a loss to explain his disappearance.

Campbell, sixty-two, is a retired high school English teacher who lived by himself. The friend and neighbor who noticed his absence, Philip Palmer, noted that several newspapers were lying on his porch, untouched, which is what alerted him to Campbell's disappearance.

Palmer said he'd known Campbell for a long time, that they were fellow teachers at the high school who were the same age and retired the same year. He described Campbell as thoughtful and likable, an easy-going type who he couldn't imagine anyone wanting to harm.

A waitress at the Coffee Roasters Café in downtown Sienna, Crystal Hampton, said Campbell was a regular customer there. She said 'Rob' was a quiet and engaging man who was friendly to everyone and a generous tipper.

Police are now seeking information from his next of kin. They are also inviting anyone with relevant information to contact Sergeant Tony Gonzales at the Sienna Police Station. Christiansen said Gonzales has been put in charge of the investigation.

It was now September thirteenth. No additional stories about Campbell's disappearance had appeared in the *Sienna Sentinel*.

The Sienna Police Station

I'd just finished the report on the drunk I'd arrested last night, a man so inebriated he could barely stand. I'd noticed him on my routine circuit through town as he was staggering into the driver's seat of an old beat-up pickup. When asked to produce his driver's license, registration, and proof of insurance he leaned over toward his glove box and collapsed on the passenger seat, passed out. So technically he hadn't tried to drive in his condition, but the intent seemed clear. He's still drying out in a cell.

I hate the paperwork. No incident, however minor, can be left unreported. I didn't get into this to be a damn stenographer. I wanted to catch the bad guys, further the cause of justice, and help those in need. I enjoy the drives through the neighborhoods. Many residents wave at me and I think have come to see me as a friend.

I don't mind the walking beats through the small downtown either. There are just a few square blocks, where merchants know me, and I think also view me as an ally. I don't even mind it when I'm called out into the surrounding countryside for some emergency, given the beautiful mountain terrain and endless deciduous and evergreen forests. It's just the damn paperwork that drives me crazy.

But I shouldn't complain; Sienna is a nice place. I grew up in Los Angeles and resisted moving to the middle of nowhere, but my wife Sarah convinced me it would be a better place to raise our kids, and it turns out she was right. The schools are good, the pace relaxed, the crime rate low. We do have our share of homelessness, marital disputes, and drunken driving accidents, but none of the gang warfare, street shootings, and murders common in big cities.

At least we never have, up until now. But this one feels different. Why would a guy who everyone describes as quiet and likable, who has no criminal record or history of mental problems, who had a long career as an English teacher at the high school, where he was apparently popular with both other teachers and students, simply vanish? It's been four days since that last piece in *The Sentinel* and almost two weeks since he was last seen, and I don't have a single clue.

As far as we've been able to determine he doesn't own anything of much value. His most valuable possessions seem to be a computer, a TV, and an old pickup truck. Maybe he has money stashed away on an offshore island somewhere, who knows. Or had a secret life no one knew about. But come on, what are the chances?

Whatever happened, I can tell you this: it's not good. I've read a little about disappearances. Most of those that aren't resolved quickly turn out bad. It's a simple rule: the longer the person isn't found, the worse the statistics get. Two weeks? It's highly likely this guy's a goner. We just have to figure out how, and why. And who did it. It's not going to be pretty.

Which is a damn shame, because he seems like a really good man. In my interviews with people who knew him I've tracked down three of his ex-students. All describe him as a genial and supportive teacher who encouraged their participation in class and graded them fairly. I've also talked with two of his former teaching colleagues and they both say he was friendly and likable, and well regarded in the English Department.

His parents are deceased and his only living relative is his brother, James, who I've talked with. He lives in Florida and has had only occasional contact with Robert for a long time. He says while they weren't particularly close, they'd always gotten on well. He said Robert—who he referred to as 'Rob'—had been a little 'spacy' as a kid, spent a lot of time in his room reading. He'd done well in school, then college, and had gotten a teaching credential. He'd taught for almost forty years here, retired just three years ago, and has been living on his pension since.

I'm just a deputy in the Police Department here. I don't pretend to be any kind of authority. I just try to do my job, keep a clean record, call things as I see them. The Chief is John Christiansen. He's been here thirty years and knows everyone and pretty much every bit of history on the place. He's a bit of a troglodyte, says good police work still comes down to establishing motives for a crime, opportunities to commit it, and working from there.

John could stand to lose a little weight; I'm glad I'm not one of his belts. And a better haircut wouldn't hurt, the comb-over is hard to look at. When you have thinning blond hair, it makes it worse. But I'm not unsympathetic to his position; as the chief he's under a lot of pressure to solve this thing. He's not in a great mood these days.

Here he comes now. God, he looks awful, bags under his eyes, sagging cheeks, a hangdog expression. He's a little out of his depth with this one.

"Hey, Tony." Christiansen's voice is low and raspy.

"Hi, boss."

"Any leads yet?"

"Nothing, boss. I've tried everything I can think of. As soon as we got the warrant from the judge, I searched his house. The front and back doors were both unlocked. A neighbor told me he hardly ever locked them, said it was too much trouble to carry a key around and no one has ever broken in. His pickup truck was in the garage, the keys to it lying on the kitchen counter.

"There was nothing out of place, no evidence of any kind of struggle, nothing broken or messy. His bed was made. His clothes were hung up. There were a couple unpaid bills on his desk, but they weren't overdue. I don't have permission back yet to examine his bank records, but just from talking with friends there's no reason to suspect we'll find anything there."

"What about fingerprints?"

"Tom dusted everywhere in the house he thought they might be. He hasn't gotten back to me yet, but I hope to have that information soon."

John stared at Tony, sighing. "Okay. Well, keep at it. Something's got to turn up. A man doesn't just disappear for no reason."

Port Le Claire, Florida

I keep remembering our childhood in that little town in Ohio. Rob was four years younger, so we weren't all that close, but we were always brothers, family. There's a bond there that endures. We haven't been all that close as adults, since I moved to Florida and Rob to California. Especially after the folks died. They gave us an excuse to see each other when they were still around, visits home to Ohio during the summer, the little place where we grew up, Alloro. You don't really want to be in Ohio in the winter.

I haven't been back in what, twenty years? Nor as far as I know has Rob. Looking back, those days of growing up in a little town in the nineteen-fifties in rural Ohio were idyllic. Eisenhower, the first Interstates, hoola hoops, Ford and GM and Chrysler putting out new models every year. Rock and roll a new thing, Elvis and all the others. Not to mention sports. Baseball was huge then. We were Indians fans of course.

I'm still not sure why he moved to California and I did to Florida. I suppose Gloria was part of it. She never liked California. Said it was too Hollywoody. Plus she was terrified of earthquakes. I must admit, they kind of freak me out too. Can't imagine the ground shaking under me and not knowing what might fall on my head. Not that I'm fond of hurricanes either. Wish we'd thought about those a little more before we picked Florida.

It's not clear to me why he liked California so much, though. Some weird stuff goes on out there. I guess it's not like that up where Rob lives, some old gold-mining town in the Sierra Nevada foothills. Although he said even it has its problems, drinking and bar fights, illegal weed being grown, homelessness.

Rob was always up there in his bedroom reading something. Mostly science fiction: Isaac Asimov, Arthur C. Clarke, Robert

7

Heinlein. And crime fiction: Sherlock Holmes, Agatha Christie, Erle Stanley Gardner. Or just thinking. Things that weren't the way they should be got to him. He'd hear about some troubling thing on the news and get depressed. Or a friend in school would tell him about a problem at home.

He asked me once what our purpose was. I said something like, "We need a purpose?" And he said, "If we don't have a purpose, what's the point of it all? We're just born, hang around a few decades, and depart? Aren't we supposed to have accomplished something during that time? And if not, what does it matter what we do? Good, bad. It's all the same." I didn't know what to say. Who asks questions like that?

One time we found a dead cat on our doorstep. Its throat was cut; it had been deliberately killed. We never knew who did it or how it got there. Rob denied doing it, but I was never sure. He was strangely quiet when we talked about it. Which could have been just because it was another example of the uncaring nature of the world. But I always wondered.

I think the teaching helped. I know he loved it; it gave him a sense of purpose. He had an unusual ability to connect with young people. I suspect he would have liked to have a kid or two of his own, but sadly that never happened.

As much as he loved it, it was also hard on him. He'd talk about the problems his kids faced: four or five of them crammed into some hovel, not having enough to eat, or living in a camper, or not knowing *where* they were going to sleep. And the usual struggles with growing up, trying to figure who they were and what they wanted to be.

And sex. Boys, girls, he told me they both confided in him. Said he often talked with them during his off periods, lunch breaks, maybe after school. Sometimes even let kids sleep at his house, just so they'd have a warm safe place to stay. Which felt a little strange to me. Being devoted to your job is one thing, but giving up your own home for it?

There was also all the work of teaching: preparing lessons, leading discussions, grading tests. He told me once the number of papers he had to read every year; it was staggering. He said the hard part wasn't grading, it was providing useful feedback, helping kids improve, wherever they were on the curve. He said if he couldn't make at least three constructive suggestions on every paper he wasn't doing his job.

Which took it out of him. When we'd be together at the folks' place in the summer, it took him days before he'd really get relaxed. I kept telling him to ease off, kids are resilient, it wasn't his sole job to help them grow up. He just ignored me.

I know he suffered from depression sometimes, even as an adult. I've read it's a chemical thing, neurotransmitters out of whack. But a lot of the serious writers and philosophers we admire had that problem. The deep thinkers among us. Rob was one of them.

I'm not even sure retirement helped. He didn't have the daily reminders of kids suffering. But he missed the positive stuff, seeing them learn and grow. And he never married. I had Gloria to give me a kick in the ass when things got out of focus, bring some perspective. He must have spent some long, lonely days. He's been a little different the last three years; quieter, more introverted.

Speaking of Gloria, I think there might be a clue there to why he never married. He liked girls, I knew that, even though he was four years younger than me. I used to sneak *Playboys* into our room, and I caught him looking at them a few times. He'd ask me about girls, whether I'd seen them naked. I didn't really know any more than he did, but I'd heard stuff talked about in the locker room and there was nothing wrong with my imagination. Or his.

He had that one girlfriend in high school. It was after I'd graduated, but sometimes he'd bring her to family events. She was a knockout; I was jealous as hell. You could tell she wanted to marry him, have a family together. I think one side of him wanted to also. But there was always that other, deeper, side. He wondered if he'd be a good father or have the wherewithal to support them like they deserve. Kids were a big responsibility, especially your own. I suspect he regretted that decision at times, not having kids.

I haven't talked with him in a couple of months, and then just the usual: travel, health, what we were watching on TV. Rob always asked the right questions—how was Gloria, how were the kids, how was retirement going—but somehow it always felt kind of pro forma. I never really knew what was going on inside that head. I just knew there was a lot, whatever it was.

The Coffee Roasters

My name's Crystal. I'm just a waitress in a café, trying to get by. Seems like it's getting harder every year, and there's been a few of them. But the job is good, you meet a lot of people, get to know the repeaters. They pour in for their morning hit of joe. I see all kinds in here. And we've had some doozies.

But this town is not like New York City. If a goddam bicycle gets stolen, it's news for a week. And half the time it turns out to be some idiot who just forgot where they left it, and when they remember and go back to look, it's still there. Unlocked. We don't have serious crime.

We have arguments, sure. Everybody has those. I have them all the time myself. And, okay, some of them get heated. We're normal. We have our political differences, like anywhere else. But it's still a great place.

In fact, it's idyllic. We're only ten minutes from the Tahoe National Forest. You just have to head east up Route 20 and you're there in no time, driving through endless evergreen trees. If you keep going it's just an hour to Lake Tahoe. Prettiest place you've ever seen. Being out on that incredibly deep clear lake—it's like being in another world. Plus there's great hiking in summer, great skiing in winter.

If you don't like mountains, you can go the other way, down into the Sacramento Valley, which is also pretty. A big farming area, all kinds of fruit trees: cherries, peaches, apricots. Plus the vineyards. Seems like there are more of them every year. Not to mention Sacramento itself. Every kind of restaurant imaginable, theaters, music, sports, art museums, a classic train museum. It's where the the Sacramento and American Rivers meet, then feed into that vast delta that goes out to the San Francisco Bay.

I've lived here my whole life. Went to school here. Got married after graduation. Greg, my husband, worked for the phone company. Which was good until people started dropping their land lines for cell phones. That's when things went south. He got laid off after thirty years, didn't know what to do with himself. Turned to beer. He wasn't exactly skinny to begin with, but it got worse. He was a hundred pounds overweight at the end. One of those massive heart attacks. So I've been alone for the last five years.

This job helps, all the regulars. It's like one big family. They walk in with that look on their face, bordering on desperation, *give me some coffee*! I pour them that first hot one, get them a donut or bagel or whatever, watch them begin to relax, ease into the day, start talking and joshing and having fun. After two or three they're ready for the day.

Rob is one of them. A true gentleman, that man. "How's my sunshine this morning?" Always says that when he comes in. And then the same question, every time: "How's the drug supply holding out?" The coffee never changes. He knows that, but we go through the little ritual every morning. "Let me check with our syndicate rep." Then I pour him a cup. And the tips? God, he's generous. I'm as likely to find a twenty-dollar bill under his mug as a couple of ones. For a three-dollar cup of coffee and a donut. He's the best.

I do wonder if maybe he's lonely. It's never been clear to me why he isn't married. I know a lot of women who would jump at the chance if he showed any interest. Like me, I suppose. He's always well dressed—casual, of course—still trim, keeps his waistline in check. Still has his hair. He sure rings my bell.

Velma—she's the other morning waitress—used to tease me. Sometimes she'd spot him as he was coming in and say something like, "Crystal, let me get this guy, he looks kind of interesting." Of course she didn't, she always left him for me, knew I had a little thing for him. She's still got a husband. Not that she's all that happy about it. We've talked.

At first, I was devastated he'd disappeared. Especially after talking with Tony, who seems troubled but already half resigned. Says they don't really have a clue what's happened, and the longer it goes on the worse the chances are it will turn out well. He's seriously down about it. So am I, really. But now I can't help thinking there's something going on, something we have no clue about, that maybe it's not going to be as bad as we fear. It just can't be. Not Rob Campbell.

Two-thirty-seven Chestnut Street

I don't know a single person who doesn't like Rob Campbell. He just never rubs anyone the wrong way. It pisses me off sometimes, no one's that perfect, everyone has their flaws. But he could always sense where you were if something was bothering you. He'd gently probe, try to listen and help, never tried to push your buttons. He was above that kind of thing. Made of different stuff.

I've known him for forty years. He taught English, I taught history. We live just a couple blocks apart, so we sometimes shared rides to school. Ate lunch together most days in the teacher's lounge. Swapped stories about our kids. I'm the one who noticed he was missing. Phil Palmer.

The students were something. Half the time a pain in the ass, the other half they'd amaze you with what they'd learned or thought or wondered about. I don't deny it, sometimes they'd piss me off, any teacher will tell you that. But Rob always seemed to love the kids, and they seemed to love him. Worshipped him, more like.

We retired the same year, three years ago. We'd both taught for nearly forty years; we were ready. Takes a lot of energy, teaching. Always up there in front of the class, having to cover the curriculum or oversee an exercise or lead a discussion. Not to mention the tests and papers. Endless work in the evenings. Takes it out of you. Rob seemed to thrive on it. Oh, he'd be tired sometimes. Those could be long days. But he always seemed reenergized in the morning.

He had an affection for his students, however strange they might be. He had this one kid who loved baseball. Every time he wrote a paper analyzing a story, he'd compare it to baseball. Say the story was about a guy who had spent ten days at sea with no food, exposed to the elements, on the point of starvation. And at the last possible moment there's a miraculous rescue. He'd say it was just like a batter coming up in the bottom of the ninth, two outs, two runs down, two guys on base, and he'd pound a home run over the outfield wall. Rob just found it amusing.

Wasn't just the kids; the other teachers and the administrators liked him too. When some school conflict would come up it was Rob they would go to for help. Once there was this fight about whether kids could bring cell phones to school. The administrators were searching kids when they arrived and taking their phones away. Half the teachers agreed with this, they didn't want kids surreptiously playing some video game in their class. The other half thought it wasn't fair, that if we wanted the kids to behave like adults, we needed to treat them like adults.

Rob suggested we needed clearly-defined rules for what they could or couldn't do with their phones. Set limits, enforce them, and otherwise leave them alone. The rule he came up with was they could use them between classes, or if there was an emergency, but not otherwise. If they were visible during class they'd be taken away for the day, then returned before they left for home if they went to the principal's office and agreed to follow the rules from then on. Problem solved; it worked like a charm.

Then there was the time a kid brought his dog to school with him. The school had a 'no pets' policy. Which made sense. If all the kids brought their pets it would be crazy. The administration got on the kid, told him he couldn't do that. I saw him leaving the office that day, big tears running down his cheeks.

Word got around to Rob. He sought the kid out and talked to him, found out his mom had just died in a car accident and his dad had disappeared years earlier. He was staying with an uncle he barely knew. The dog was the only link he had to anything familiar. So Rob went to the principal and talked to him, and they agreed to make an exception, let the kid bring the dog to school if he behaved. Fortunately it was a calm, friendly dog. And it really helped—the dog became kind of a school mascot. Even helped the kid make new friends.

Probably doesn't hurt that Rob's also a handsome SOB. I knew at least two of the teachers there had a crush on the guy. They would bring him snacks for lunch, find excuses to visit his classroom after school, hint around about not having anything on the calendar for the weekend. He was always friendly to them, but he never picked up on their hints. It was like he lived on another plane, just didn't get tempted like any ordinary guy.

When we retired, he suggested we form a book group, meet every month or so. He thought it would give us a little focus, motivate us to keep reading and thinking about things. He rounded up a couple of other guys, as did I, and for three years now the six of us have gotten together every month to talk about a book we've read. Which has turned out to be a lot of fun. We have different interests: historical fiction, literary fiction, popularized science. For Rob it's science fiction and crime drama.

I suppose there is one shortcoming I should mention: he's not a yard guy. His yard is frankly an embarrassment. He doesn't water it, which means it dries up in the summer. And he doesn't rake leaves, they just lay there all winter, rotting away. His fences are half falling down. Probably annoys his neighbors. But who cares.

Anyway, when I hadn't heard from him for almost a week I decided to go over there and investigate. I noticed a little pile of newspapers on his front porch. So I knocked, and when he didn't answer, I just turned the knob and went it. I knew he never locked the place up. Everything looked normal, there was just no sign of Rob. That's when I got worried and called the cops.

I waited at the house for the officer, Sergeant Gonzales. When he arrived, he asked me some questions. Then he conducted a search. I asked if I could watch and he said okay. So I followed him around. He looked in every room, pulled out drawers, opened cupboards, checked the waste baskets. When he was finished he called some guy named Tom to come over and dust for fingerprints. Then he went out to the garage and looked around there. Rob's pickup was still there, like I'd told him.

One thing he asked me was about Rob's weekend activities. I mentioned that he loved to go hiking up in the mountains, head off for a day, explore new trails he didn't know. I've gone with him a few times. He's an adventurous guy, didn't always stick to trails. If he saw what looked like an interesting peak he'd just start climbing, making his own trail. So my theory is he got lost up there and died of exposure. I told Gonzales they should institute a search, but I don't know if they will.

The Sienna Police Station

Well, another day gone by and I'm not making much progress. But I have done some research. So many people go missing every year in the United States that there is a national organization devoted to the sole purpose of keeping track of them. Its website describes the organization as follows:

> NamUs is a national information clearinghouse and resource center for missing, unidentified, and unclaimed person cases across the United States. Funded and administered by the National Institute of Justice and managed through a cooperative agreement with the UNT Health Science Center in Fort Worth, Texas, all NamUs resources are provided at no cost to law enforcement, medical examiners, coroners, allied forensic professionals, and family members of missing persons.

According to NamUs, over 600,000 people go missing in the United States every year. Many are found alive and well, often quickly. However, tens of thousands remain missing for more than a year – what are called cold cases. About ninety percent of missing people are recovered every year, either alive or deceased. Meaning the rest aren't. Do the math: ten percent of 600,000 people is sixty thousand people. What happened to them? No one knows.

NamUs says some are lost in national parks and forests, people who get lost hiking or encounter a mountain lion or bear or fall off a cliff. Maybe they experience a night too cold for the preparations they'd made. Maybe they run into a psychopath who gets off on killing hikers and hiding their bodies. Ultimately, no one knows.

Anyway, that all got me to thinking. His neighbor Phil told me that Rob liked to go on hikes by himself, explore new trails. Even bushwhack if he saw what looked like an interesting peak or wondered what was over a horizon. He said Rob liked to depend on his native skills to find his way back, that it sharpened his senses, made him feel alive. So maybe he got so lost he *couldn't* find his way back and expired out there in the wilderness.

I suppose that argues for getting a search party together to start combing the trails up there, like that guy who discovered Campbell was missing suggested. But Jesus, there are thousands of miles of such trails. Not to mention millions of acres, if he decided to go off trail. There's no way to search all that, not if we had an army of help. Which we don't, it's just the five of us, the chief, me, and the three other deputies, plus a couple of people who hold the office down.

It's been another day of phone calls and emails and texts, everybody asking whether we've made any progress in the investigation. What am I supposed to say? I wrote a standard response a few days ago, and now simply send it out to each new inquirer.

```
     We're doing everything in our
power to locate Mr. Campbell. We are
ignoring no lead offered by the
public. Should we find anything that
offers new clues or avenues of
investigation we will follow up with
them. Meanwhile, we ask for your
patience as we continue our efforts.
As soon as we have any new
information we will make it known to
the public.
```

Poor John is going nuts. Speaking of the devil, here he comes.

"Hey, Tony."

"Boss."

"I know you're tired of this. We all are. We need to find some new course of action. Something that will at least show the public we're doing something."

"Right, boss."

"So let's put our thinking caps on. Have you gone back and searched the house again?"

"I was pretty thorough the first time."

"I take it that's a no?"

"Sure. I can go again."

"I know you have a good eye for this but let's go over it again. There was nothing out of place, nothing messy, bed made, clothes hung up, normal amount of food in the frig, nothing that looked suspicious? The doors were unlocked, and his pickup was in the garage. Right?"

"Right."

"This is the strangest thing that's happened in this town since I've been the Chief. People everywhere are talking about it. You been in a restaurant or bar lately? I can't go out anymore; everywhere I go I'm accosted by worried residents. They're afraid we've got a kidnapper on the loose. They won't let their kids out to play. The principal has hired two new school guards to keep an eye out. We've got to come up with *something*."

"I know, boss. I've been wracking my brain since it happened. I'm wide open if you've got any suggestions."

"Okay, so there was nothing out of place in his house. Here's a thought: What was *in* place?"

"*In* place?"

"You know, that might offer a clue. Something subtle that you might have missed."

"Like what, boss?"

"Was there any reading material around? Something that might tell us what he was thinking about?"

"I think there were some magazines on the living room coffee table. And there was a book on the bed stand."

"What book?"

"Jeez. Let me think. A science fiction book maybe? I vaguely recall a picture of an alien on the cover."

"Okay. Good. What does that tell us?"

"He liked to read science fiction books?"

"Come on, let's think about it. If he had his head into science fiction, something involving aliens, maybe he...went looking for evidence of aliens?"

"How do you look for evidence of aliens?"

"No idea. But maybe he did."

"So you're saying...the question is...how might he have gone looking for evidence of aliens?"

"I know it sounds a little crazy. But, hey, we've got nothing, Tony. We've got to try everything we can think of, even if it sounds a little crazy."

"Well, *I've* never looked for evidence of aliens. How do we do that?"

"Let me think here." He hesitated, brows furrowed. Then cocked his head, and nodded, eyebrows raised.

"How about this: maybe look at that book he was reading and see if *it* says anything about looking for evidence of aliens!"

"You want me to read that book?"

"Don't you think it's worth a try?"

"Sure, okay, boss. I've not nothing better. I'll go back over there and pick it up. See what I can learn."

"And, Tony."

"Yes."

"While you're there, see if there are any other clues along the same lines."

"The lines of looking for evidence of aliens?"

He frowned, shaking his head. "No. Just look around. See if anything comes to you. We've got to find *something* to go on."

"Right, boss."

The Sienna Sentinel

The following item appeared on page three of the *Sienna Sentinel* the morning of Saturday, September fourteenth. No details were provided other than a brief statement that followed the note.

> Police shared with this newspaper
> that late last evening there was a
> new development in the
> disappearance of Robert Campbell. A
> ransom note was received by an
> unidentified local resident. Police
> summarized the note as follows:
>
> > We have Robert Campbell. He
> > is alive and well. He will be
> > returned within seventy-two
> > hours, assuming we receive one
> > million dollars within the
> > next forty-eight hours.
> > This is a demand, not a
> > request. Should our terms not
> > be met, we will provide
> > directions for the recovery of
> > Campbell's body.

Below this notice was a picture of a man holding up the previous day's issue of *The Sentinel*, a concerned look on his face. The caption below it read: "Picture of Robert Campbell accompanying the ransom note". Police thanked the resident who received the note for providing it to police, and repeated that they were doing everything in their power to solve this case.

Offices of the Sienna Sentinel

As in every other corner of Sienna, the offices of the *Sienna Sentinel* were abuzz. Three men sat around a conference table conferring. A smallish young man with dark curly hair, Tim Royce, was rubbing his face. Tim had moved to Sienna several years earlier from New York City, shortly after graduating from college, for reasons no one quite understood. With a degree in journalism, he'd been hired as a reporter for the *Sentinel* and had adapted quickly to the considerably less cosmopolitan ambience of Sienna. His obvious intelligence and friendliness had moved him quickly up the 'corporate ladder', and when the old editor had decided to spend his waning days in Hawaii, and no one else wanted the job, he'd reluctantly taken over. Not one employee of the paper was younger than Tim, but all had come to respect him.

A six-foot tall man with straight black hair and a muscular build sat across from him. Walter 'White Cloud' Harvey was one of the few full-blooded Nisenan Indians still alive. Everyone called him Harve. His tribe, nearly ten thousand strong at the time of the gold rush, had been almost annihilated by that event. Now generations removed from that travesty, Harve still carried scars, stories his grandfather had told him about the horrors his parents had faced when they were small: hiding from bounty hunters, avoiding diseases they had no defense against, and simply trying to survive in the remote mountain region they'd had to retreat to.

Tim spoke with a slight New York City accent. "At least the police *are* sharing news," he said. "It's the first thing resembling a break in the case in nearly two weeks."

"It's that last sentence that worries me," Harve said. "The 'everything in our power' part. I don't question their motivation, but when's the last time the men in blue here had to investigate a kidnapping?"

The third man, older, with wispy white hair and a thoughtful, alert expression, nodded. "Hasn't happened in the fifty years *I've* lived here. I'm also not particularly impressed with the statement about sharing any information they get."

"What do you mean, Lew," Tim asked.

"The person to whom the note was sent wasn't named. Nor the method of delivering the note. Nor the directions for delivering the money."

"Well, jeez. Do you expect police to share that kind of information? They have to protect their sources."

"Understood. It would just be interesting to know these things."

"Why?"

"How was the person who received this note selected? Might he or she be known to the kidnappers? Known to Robert Campbell? What might they be able to contribute in the way of clues? And the method of delivering the note? Was it by US mail? Courier? Electronically? An audio recording? Any of those might provide a clue. And the money? Did they specify cash or check? If a check, it seems like banks could be alerted; not all that many checks for a million dollars get deposited. If it's cash, that's a lot of cash. Where and how do they want it delivered? A mailbox? A remote location? A hollow tree?"

"A hollow tree?"

"Okay, probably not a hollow tree. But you get my point. So far the cops appear to have no clues at all. Sometimes the clues are there and you just don't see them."

Harve stared at him, his head cocked, eyebrows raised. He said nothing more. A pregnant silence fell over the group.

Finally Tim said, "I know you've wanted to stay out of this, Lew. But I'm not sure you have a choice. They're clearly out of their depth. They need help. Who else is going to provide it?"

Lew frowned. "I really don't know what I can do. I mean, I've kept up with what's in the paper, but that isn't much. I don't know anything more than anyone else. And with less than forty-eight hours in which to learn enough to be helpful?" He held out his hands, palms up.

Both other men stared at Lew. Neither spoke.

Lew sighed. "Well, if you're going to give me no choice, I'll need help. I can't do it alone."

Tim: "What do you need?"

"There is way too much we don't know. We need to learn a lot of things. Quickly."

"Such as?"

"To begin with, everything the police know. As we just discussed, they have more information than they're letting out." He looked directly at Tim. "As the editor, you're the public face of the paper. You're the one with contacts in every corner of this community. And you know John Christiansen, the Chief."

Tim stared back. "Okay. I can talk to John. Or perhaps better, Tony. He seems to be the lead guy on this."

"Okay, Tony."

He turned to Harve. "Don't you guest teach at the high school?"

"Once in a while. The journalism class."

"That's where Campbell worked. Other teachers there must have known him."

Harve frowned. "Yeah."

"Go find one. How about that guy who noticed his papers hadn't been picked up? Didn't he teach with him?"

Harve nodded.

"Go talk to him. Find out who else Campbell was friends with. Did he have any enemies? Angry women from his past. Students he'd flunked. We need to learn everything we can about this guy. Who knows if any of it will prove useful, but we've got to start somewhere."

"Okay, Lew. I can talk to Palmer." His tone was sober.

"So what do *you* plan to do, Lew?" Tim asked.

He shrugged. "Think."

The three of them looked at each other, silently, like a team of soldiers preparing for battle, knowing the odds were stacked against them. Then they nodded, stood, and went their separate ways.

An Old Cedar Bungalow

He sat at his desk, sipping another cup of coffee, still trying to wipe the last of the cobwebs from his head. He knew he should drink less, but somehow, ever since his wife had been killed by a drunk driver in a nasty accident ten years earlier, he hadn't found another way to get through a lot of evenings. His fingers drummed on the keyboard as he looked out at the clear blue sky, the leaves turning red and yellow and brown, branches stretching over the old half-collapsed six-foot wooden fence around his back yard.

He'd returned from the *Sentinel* offices in his old blue Honda Accord, now in its twentieth year and just past the two-hundred-thousand-mile mark. He'd come to view it as a friend. It still ran fine; it was all he needed.

His large black cat had greeted him at the back door. Judging from the tone of his meow, Lew could tell Earl wanted something, and he had little doubt what. He let him in, shook some kibble into his dish, and watched for a bit while he began crunching away. "You're nothing if not predictable, old man."

Lew didn't know exactly how old Earl was. He'd gotten him from a rescue center and his history had been a mystery. He'd proven to be a welcome companion, no replacement for Mary, but with his own charms. His daily schedule, other than regular meal times, consisted mostly of roaming around the neighborhood, where Lew suspected he either had some female friends or begged still more food from lonely old ladies. Earl did not lack for motivation, or intelligence. But when he was home, he pretty much confined his time to eating and sleeping. Were he a philosopher he'd have been classified as a hedonist.

Lew turned to his list of questions. It was divided into three columns. The first one read: "What information would be most helpful?" He already had a lengthy list here. The second column read: "What's the best way to obtain this?" Some of the questions had notations here and some didn't. A third column read: "Who could best provide help?" He'd jotted down the names of Tim and Harve alongside "Local Police" and "Teaching Associates". He was trying to think of others when the phone rang.

"Hello."

"Hi, Lew." Soft feminine voice.

"Violet." Violet was in her early fifties, still thin and attractive, with soft brown hair and a quick wit. She had been hired by the *Sentinel* as a secretary following the death of her husband several years earlier. She had proved to be so adept at researching information for reporters she'd been promoted to a new position, created just for her: "Research Associate". For reasons still not entirely clear to Lew, but which he was loath to question, she'd exhibited a friendliness toward him beyond that of just a work associate, and they had become close companions.

"Good morning?" she asked.

"No."

"Well, that's a cheery greeting. You get up on the wrong side of the bed?"

"I had a meeting with Tim and Harve."

"I thought you liked them."

"I do, unless they're pushing me to do something I don't want to do."

"You mean like write an actual story for the paper?"

A brief pause. "Have you looked at today's paper?"

"Yeah."

"So you saw the development in the Campbell disappearance?"

"Yes. What's that got to do with anything?"

"They think the men in blue need help. And they want me to provide it."

"They have a firm command of the obvious. Is that a bad thing? Couldn't you use some excitement in your life?"

"Not that kind."

"Hey, you're the paper's so-called Investigative Reporter. This is right up your alley. What's the last story you've written? I can't remember anything for weeks."

"I'm retired. Given what I get paid this is practically volunteer work."

"Doesn't that imply volunteering occasionally?"

"Thanks for the support."

"Am I wrong?"

A moment of silence. "Yes and no."

"Don't be abstruse."

"I'm not working on any other stories at the moment. But this one will be a gigantic headache."

"So?"

"You like headaches?"

"As long as they're somebody else's."

"Well, brace yourself."

She waited.

"If you guys want me to do this, you're going to have to help."

"Unlike you, Lew, I *have* a full-time job."

"Okay. Forget it." He started to hang up.

"Well, *jeez*. Can you give a lady a minute to think?"

"This is not an obligation, Violet. We don't *have* to do a damn thing. Of course it might result in some unpleasant feelings when this guy's body turns up and we haven't even tried to help. He sounds like a nice man."

"You put it so gently."

"Who can ferret out information on damn near anything better than you?"

"And look at the recognition I get."

"You're well paid."

"For an eight-hour day. Not for evenings and weekends. Unless you want to negotiate with Tim to get me off the forty-seven things I'm already trying to do. My title should be CSL: Chief Support Lackey. Like women most places, I have to do twice as much as men to get half the recognition." She paused. "Of course, that's not hard."

"Are you done with your comments on our society's gender disparities? Our time here is limited."

"Forty-eight hours, if the paper was accurate."

"Beginning last evening. We're down to about thirty-six."

She sighed. "Okay, Sherlock. What can I do?"

"Did you know Robert Campbell?"

"Not really."

"What does that mean?"

"I knew who he was."

"How?"

"I think Harve mentioned him a couple times when he was guest teaching in the journalism class at the high school. And I've seen him at the Coffee Roaster's a couple times."

"You go to the Coffee Roasters?"

"I get up before noon, Lew."

"How do you know it was him?"

"Because one of the waitresses there always calls him by name. It's one of those shrewd female things."

"Do you know the waitress?"

"No. I know who she is."

"There you go."

"There I go *where*?"

"Your first assignment. Go talk to that waitress. See what you can find out about Robert Campbell."

"Like?"

"Whatever. His likes and dislikes. His habits. Whatever she knows about him. They're called leads. You know, like newspapers get. Clues. Things that will give us a toehold on this."

"Sounds a little vague."

"I've been thinking about this for roughly an hour."

"Doesn't sound like you got very far."

There was a pause.

"Okay, Lew. I'll go talk to the waitress. Want to join me there for lunch?"

"I've got too much to do."

A longer pause. That went on. Finally his brain kicked in. "How about dinner…um, tomorrow?"

"Dinner *tomorrow*?"

"Time is of the essence here. We need to figure out what we can do, and start doing it, ASAP."

"Okaay, dinner tomorrow. You sure know how to make a girl feel important." There was a click.

He sat there, alternately staring out the window and glancing down at his list. Then he picked up the phone and dialed a number he knew by memory. It rang five times.

A sleepy voice answered. "Yo."

"You sound like I woke you up."

A moment of silence. "It's ten o'clock. On Saturday." An audible yawn. "Is that you, Mr. T?"

"Morning, Zane. Sorry."

Zane was a senior in high school. Lew had run into him at a restaurant a couple years earlier. He'd been there with a girl. They had just finished lunch when Zane had realized he didn't have enough money to pay for it. Lew had overheard their conversation from the next booth. He'd surreptiously handed Zane a twenty-dollar bill. It had led to an enduring friendship.

One that had had a substantial payoff. Zane wasn't a very good student. He found high school boring. Except for one subject: computers. He loved everything about them. And he'd proven to be something of a genius in using them. Not always limited to what was legal. He also seemed to always have uses for the payments that came his way from helping the less-skilled portion of the population. Like Lew. In short, it had become a mutually-beneficial relationship.

Lew explained the situation.

"Yeah. Heard."

"You still in that computer class?"

"I help the teacher when he gets stuck, if that counts."

"Kind of like you help me?"

"I suppose."

"Want a challenge?"

"Like?"

"Think you can get into Campbell's email?"

"I can get into anybody's email. You already know that. What are you looking for?"

"Whatever might provide a clue to his disappearance."

A pause. "I suppose I could do that."

"I'll make it worth your while."

"You always do."

"Still got the same girlfriend?"

"Yeah. She wants to get married."

"Really?"

"I keep telling her she's crazy."

"Want me to talk to her?"
"About what?"
"To convince her she's crazy."
There was a click.

Three-forty-two Chestnut Street

Robert Campbell's address was a matter of public record: 342 Chestnut Street. Lew decided to go have a look. He knew the cops had conducted a search there and had concluded there weren't any clues to go on. And they might be right. But it never hurt to look for yourself. He pulled up in front of Campbell's house in Old Blue, checked to make sure the address was right, and turned off the engine.

People sometimes asked why there was a Chestnut Street in a place like Sienna. Everyone knew the chestnut trees disappeared a long time ago, wiped out by a pestilence unmatched in tree history, a fungal spore likely from a Chinese specimen imported by the New York Botanical Garden. The most predominant tree on the east coast for centuries, an estimated three to four billion trees, went nearly extinct within five years in the early nineteen-hundreds.

But not quite. The trees had survived on the west coast. They weren't a big presence, but they comprised a thousand or so acres in California, mostly grown on small farms. They were a variety called Colossal, and as it happened, every one had come from two that stood just outside Sienna, next to an old Victorian house. Thus the presence of a Chestnut Street in Sienna.

But at the moment Lew was more interested in the present than the botanical past. He sat there for a bit, looking over the place. It was a cute house, an arts and crafts bungalow, one-and-a-half stories, cedar shingles, open front porch. A lot like his own. It was also a pleasant neighborhood. Some big two-story houses along with well-kept one-story ones, all set back from the street. Big shade trees. Tidy lawns.

Except for this one, now that he looked at it. Apparently

Campbell wasn't much into lawns. Just some wispy dried-up foot-high brown grass. No sprinkler system, apparently. There were nice trees however, big maples.

As he sat studying the house it appeared that Campbell was into upkeep of his house about as much as he was his lawn. The roof had missing shingles. The fence was leaning so much it looked like it might collapse. There was a gutter hanging loose on one side. Whatever Campbell was, he wasn't great on home upkeep. Unlike the neighbors.

Speaking of whom, Lew noticed a guy across the street mowing his lawn. Lew had never seen greener grass this late in the season. This guy must water it every day. And fertilize it. And aerate it. Nor better trimmed. Given the length of grass, it looked like he mowed it every day. It was the shortest grass Lew had ever seen outside a putting green. Did he really need that giant riding mower for that much yard? It was flat, and unless there was something Lew couldn't see, not all that big. Looked like he could do the whole thing in about three minutes on that monster.

Lew got out, headed for Campbell's house, ducked under the yellow police tape, and walked up toward the front door. He was about halfway there when his eye caught something in his periphery. Something white, under an untrimmed hedge. He bent over to look closer. Tugged at it and pulled it out. A wadded-up tissue, stuck together with something dark. He looked at it more closely; dried blood. Should he take it? He *could* be a good citizen and tell Gonzales about it, even give it to him for analysis. He tucked it in his pocket.

Then he continued up to the front door and tried it. Sure enough, locked, as he'd expected. You didn't keep a potential crime scene open for just anyone to barge in. He thought for a moment, then decided his best option for getting in was around in back somewhere, where the driveway led. It was a short walk.

He tried the back door; same result--locked. So, how was he going to get in? He wondered if they'd locked all the windows. He peeked into the kitchen, noticed the window was above a counter. Got his finger into a crack at the edge of the screen. Popped it out. Tried the window, which moved. Voila!

He put on a pair of gloves he'd brought, opened the window the rest of the way, pulled himself up, and scrambled in. Which took some strength; he was getting a little old for this stuff. Seventy-two, to be precise. But what the hell, he could still do most of the stuff he used to, if maybe a bit slower. He was nevertheless glad for the counter, which made it easier to climb in and get down. He took a deep breath and looked around.

The kitchen showed no signs of recent activity. Just a teakettle on the stove and a toaster on the otherwise empty counter. He looked under the sink for the garbage. Couple of used tissues, trail mix package, a receipt from a grocery store for a little over fifty dollars, mostly for fruit and salad and dairy stuff.

He wandered into the living room, where his eye went to the coffee table and the magazines there. *Scientific American. Astronomy.* There was a story about aliens on the cover, based on recent congressional records released related to government research into UFOs. And a… *National Geographic.*

He wondered what station he'd had on TV last, looked around for the remote. Not on the coffee table. Not by the TV, which he noticed wasn't very big, maybe thirty inches. He felt between the cushions. There it was, right where he usually found his own. Clicked on the TV. And it was on…the travel channel. He clicked the "last" button and it switched to the history channel. There was a certain consistency there. He'd already learned something of interest about Robert Campbell.

Okay, on to the upstairs. One bedroom and a bath, just like his own place. His toothbrush and toothpaste lay on the sink counter. Wouldn't he take those with him if he went on a trip? Soap dish and bar of soap. He pulled open the medicine cabinet: practically empty, just ibuprofen, acetaminophen, Benadryl, and a multi-vitamin. No prescriptions? For a man sixty-two years old?

Okay, the bedroom. First the nightstand. A Bill Bryson. He liked Bill Bryson, all those travel books, unfailingly amusing and informative. He picked it up to see which one it was: *The Body: A User's Guide.* He hadn't read it, but it sounded interesting. Bryson always did his research, made the topic interesting and fun.

Another one: *Deacon King Kong,* by James McBride. That one he knew, a story set in a down-and-out neighborhood in New York City. McBride had won a National Book Award. Well, Campbell *was* an English teacher, so it made sense.

And one with what looked like an alien on the cover, must be science fiction. He noticed a bookmark about halfway through. Why wouldn't Campbell have taken that, a book he was in the middle of?

The closet was small; bungalows didn't have a lot of storage space. There were a couple pairs of jeans, khakis, some sport shirts, pullovers, hiking shirt and pants, a couple pairs of loafers, two pairs of running shoes, slippers. But no hiking boots. He pulled out stuff so he could look behind. Definitely no hiking boots.

He headed back downstairs. There was a den which could double as a second bedroom, and a bathroom. He glanced into the bathroom. A toilet, sink, and upright shower. Couple of small guest towels next to the sink. Couple bath towels next to the shower. Bar of soap and container of shampoo in the shower. Toilet paper role next to the toilet, half used. He lifted the toilet lid: a couple urine stains on the rim. Nothing in the waste basket. That was about it.

He moved to the den. The desk was a little messy—computer sitting on top, pens and paper clips, a stapler, papers scattered around. He checked the top drawer, stared for a moment at a picture lying on top of some pads. Some babe in a skimpy blue dress. Really skimpy, almost see-through, even blowing a bit in the breeze. Look at those legs. She wasn't young, but man. Blond hair, blue eyes, enticing smile. And it looked like it had been taken out and looked at a fair amount, two of the corners were bent up.

He pulled out the other drawers: nothing unusual, just more pens and paper and paper clips, white out, scissors. Tried the file drawer at the bottom: taxes, insurance policies, owner's manuals. He shoved it closed and leaned back.

Wherever Campbell was he hadn't taken his computer. He wondered what might come up if he opened it. Might there be a clue there? But that probably required a password. Unless he hadn't turned it off. He lifted the top and waited; bingo. It opened to a page of scribbled notes. Dates. Times. Dollar figures: Six hundred sixty-two, r.t.; seven hundred fourteen, r.t. Looked like travel information. But there were no locations.

Would the times provide a clue? OB—six forty-five a.m.; ARR—seven fifteen p.m. Twelve and a half hours. Somewhere on the east coast? It didn't take that long to get anywhere in the west, but with the time change—three hours—and maybe a layover somewhere, that would be about right for the east coast.

He leaned back, reflecting. When, to his alarm, there was a knock at the front door. Lew froze. Sat there holding his breath. Another knock, three loud raps. Whoever it was sounded determined. Did he have time to make it to the kitchen window and back out before they got in? But then he thought: how could they get in; the door was locked. He waited, fearing the sound of a key in the lock. But there was nothing.

He didn't move for another minute, just waited, breath shallow. There were no more knocks. Was it possible someone was snooping around, looking in windows? The den window, where he was, would be the last if they were, it was furthest from the front door and on the other side from the driveway. He quietly closed the computer. Stood and moved stealthily to the door. Peeked around the corner. Quick movements attracted attention; it was how human perception worked. However unfavorably their eyesight might compare with certain other species, humans were particularly good at picking up movements.

He had a clear view out the side window toward the driveway: no one there. He slowly stepped out so he could see the front door. It was solid wood, but there were windows on either side someone could peer in. But no one was. He walked tentatively back to the kitchen, which had windows toward the back. No sign of anyone there either.

He waited a few more moments, then carefully unlocked the back door, making sure the knob was still in the locked position, and stepped out. He tested the door; locked. He slid the window shut, picked up the window screen he'd popped out, and popped it back into place.

As he turned to head back to his car, he noticed the garage. Maybe it would be better not to get out front too quickly. He quietly walked over and tried the door; locked. He walked around to the window on the side and peeked in. A pickup truck, partially oxidized red paint, looked like an old Tacoma. He couldn't see much else, there wasn't enough light. It did seem curious, his truck being there.

He tried to think of an excuse he could use if there was someone still in front. Claim he was the yard guy, there for the weekly trim?

Not if whoever it was bothered to look at the yard. But what were the chances anyone would still be there? When someone knocks and there's no answer, what do they usually do? Leave. What the hell. It could have been anyone, a salesperson, the mailman, a Jehovah's Witness.

He walked quietly around the side of the house and looked out toward the street. All quiet. Old Blue was sitting there waiting for him. He continued around to the front sidewalk, out through the gate, ducked under the police tape, and climbed in. Took a deep breath. When he noticed a woman walking toward him from across the street. Waving for him to wait. He was trapped.

She hurried up to him, a little breathless. She was wearing jeans and a pullover shirt, her hair short and a bit disheveled. He rolled down the window.

"Hi. I saw you parked over here; thought you might be inside. Are you with the police?"

He shook his head. "No, just a common snoop."

"Oh. I thought maybe you were investigating Rob's disappearance."

"I am. But not in any official capacity."

"What capacity?"

He pulled a business card out of his pocket and handed it to her.

"You're an investigative reporter?"

"With the *Sentinel*."

She frowned, glanced back up at him. "Aren't you that guy who's always solving mysteries?"

"Lew Travis, at your service."

"I've heard about you."

"I'm not as bad as you've probably heard."

She smiled. "No. It was good." She hesitated. "So, can I tell you something, Mr. Travis?"

"Tell me what?"

She sighed, looked away, then back. "This is hard. But I need to tell *someone*."

He sensed he was probably at the bottom of her list of desirable possibilities.

"It's about my husband."

"Your husband?"

She glanced back at the house across the street. "You might have seen him out mowing the lawn?"

"Oh. Yeah. Lawn looks great."

"You don't have to say that. I know Don is a little…obsessive. Didn't used to be." She took a deep breath. "He was in a terrible industrial accident a couple years ago; a heavy beam fell on his head. They didn't know if he was going to make it for a while. But after weeks in a coma he finally pulled out of it. Mostly."

"Mostly?"

"He's never been quite right since. He went on disability, and he'll probably never work again. Which he resents. He says he's fine. And he has a lot of time on his hands."

"Okay."

"Technically it's what the doctors call OCD. Obsessive Compulsive Disorder. He gets focused on certain things and can go a little...overboard."

"Sounds like OCD."

"And…one of the things he's focused on is Robert Campbell."

"Why?"

She nodded toward Campbell's yard. "Don is really into keeping the yard nice. You saw him on that mower?"

Lew nodded.

"He does that almost every day. He's completely obsessed with it. And he hates it when neighbors aren't."

"You mean like…" He nodded toward Campbell's yard.

She sighed. "Exactly. I don't think he'd actually *do* anything. I mean anything…you know. But he gets really upset about it. And he's gotten in a couple fights since the accident." Again she paused, sighing. "Look, I don't want to get Don in any trouble. He has enough problems. But I just thought someone ought to know…about this yard thing. And Campbell."

"Are *you* safe?"

"Oh. Yeah. He's actually very affectionate. He wouldn't do anything crazy."

"You're sure?"

"Yeah." Spoken slowly.

Lew waited a moment. "Did something happen around the time Campbell disappeared?"

36

Her furrow deepened. "I don't think so."

"But you're not sure?"

"Sometimes Don can't sleep, so he gets up and goes for walks. Sometimes early in the morning." She hesitated. "I tried to feel him out about it, and he vehemently denied he had any contact with Mr. Campbell." She looked away. "I want to believe him. And I basically do. It's just…well, I thought I should say something. Since the cops seem at a loss."

"And one of those walks was when Mr. Campbell disappeared?"

She rolled her eyes. "I think so. He's usually back by the time I wake up, but I heard him coming in, I think it was around five a.m. He just got back into bed, didn't say anything. But I'm pretty sure he never went back to sleep. And he seemed really antsy that morning."

"Do you remember what morning that was?"

Her brows furrowed. "I'm not sure. It was a couple weeks ago. I think it might have been a Monday morning?"

"Okay. Thanks. What's your name?"

"Peggie. Peggie Thompson."

"Thanks, Peggie. So it's Don Thompson?"

She nodded. Wiped her forehead with her arm.

"Well, my number's on that card. If anything comes up, give me a call?"

She nodded. "Okay."

"Hey, you be careful, eh?"

"Oh, he won't hurt me. He's basically a big old teddy bear. It's just that damn accident."

"I hear you. You take care."

She stepped back, nodding. "Good luck. We want this solved as much as everybody else."

"Of course."

He pulled out slowly, gradually rolling up his window, and headed home, feeling the crusty tissue in his pocket.

The Sienna Sentinel

The following news bulletin was sent out electronically from the *Sienna Sentinel* on the morning of September fourteenth.

A ransom note demanding one million dollars for the return of Robert Campbell, to be delivered within forty-eight hours, was received last evening by an individual in Sienna. Given the critical time factor in the situation, we felt we needed to provide this bulletin as soon as possible.

The person who received the ransom note has agreed to put up half of this amount on two conditions: 1) that his name be kept anonymous; and 2) that this amount be matched by other contributors. Thus a GoFundMe account has been set up in the name of Robert Campbell. If you wish to contribute you can do so online at "RobertCampbellFund.net".

Should the goal be reached in time, namely by tomorrow evening, the Sienna Police Department has agreed to act as intermediary and deliver the money to the kidnappers. Should the goal not be reached, or should the kidnappers be captured, all funds will be returned to contributors.

The Sienna Police Station

Tony Gonzales was back at his desk, sipping cups of coffee between phone calls, jotting notes, trying to make two and five add to eleven. His thoughts kept going in circles.

He wasn't sure if the ransom note had helped or hurt. At least they now knew what happened to Campbell. That was progress of a sort. But it added to the time pressure.

Plus they still didn't have much to go on. The note itself was really of little help. It came as an email, so anyone could have written it. There were no fingerprints to help. He'd concluded these guys weren't idiots; in fact, they were probably professionals.

The directions about the money were also a little confusing. The note had specified it must be paid entirely in small bills: fives, tens, and twenties. Also, that the money was to be left next to a big redwood tree with a huge scar on the trunk a mile up a trail into the Tahoe National Forest. And it must be left in a suitcase that couldn't be traced. If there was any indication of either a tracking device or observation of the drop site, it would be the end of Campbell.

Why they'd picked Robert Campbell was a complete mystery. The only reason Tony could think of was because everyone liked him, which would create more pressure for contributions to cover the demands of the ransom. To add to the problems, the damn newspaper was now asking for more details about the note. They were even specifying the kinds of details they wanted: what form the note came in, how it had been delivered, and directions for delivery of the money.

Both John and Tony were frustrated: these damn newspaper guys were never satisfied. But they were reluctant to cause a full break with them; they could sometimes be helpful. Like when they needed help from the public, the paper was good about getting the word out. Or when it was obvious something needed to be kept quiet because of the danger involved, they understood. But it still seemed like they always wanted more.

It was one more pressure in the face of all the problems they were already facing: some guy everyone liked had been kidnapped by a bunch of evil bastards; he'd been gone for almost two weeks with no clue where or why; now there was a million-dollar ransom demand, delivered in such a way and with directions for delivery such that no one could learn anything. It was a goddam nightmare.

John seemed like he was about to disintegrate altogether. No one ever thought about the cops in these situations. The pressure they were under. What it did to them. It even seemed like Ros, the receptionist, was going to have a breakdown with all the damn calls from frustrated people, or kooks with some wild theory.

Tony was trying to decide, in the face of all this, just how much to tell that kid from the paper, Tim Royce. He *was* their top guy, the editor, even if he looked about fifteen and was from New York City. And he had always shown respect for John and himself, complied when they asked for cooperation. They needed to stay on his good side. So he wanted to at least keep up the appearance of being cooperative.

That damn part-time investigative reporter made it harder. *Lew Travis*: God, he'd stick his nose in anywhere. No respect for protocol. *We* are the official presence here. *We* have the authority to conduct investigations. Not some old codger who thinks he's Sherlock Holmes.

The worst part was the old bastard was good at it. He'd embarrassed them before. And the public loved him because of that. Half the questions they were getting were whether they were involving *Lew Travis* in the investigation. Hell, no. They hadn't and they weren't going to. Not that they could stop him from doing whatever the hell he decided to do. One more headache to add to all the others. He buried his face in his hands, wondering how much longer he could take this.

The Coffee Roasters

It hasn't been one of my better mornings. The damn coffee machine went kerflooey in the middle of rush hour. No apparent reason, it just stopped working. It's a good thing we have a backup in back, but that meant even more walking, and no way could I keep up.

I don't blame them; you *need* that coffee in the morning. It is an addiction, after all. Sure, people like their donuts or bagels or ham and eggs, whatever, but the first thing you give them is that cup of coffee. That's what they're dying for when they walk in. It's a little amazing how much of it some of them drink. One guy has five cups every morning. Which, frankly, is kind of taking advantage of our policy of free refills. He drank practically a whole carafe himself this morning.

I wasn't in the best of moods to begin with. I got in a few minutes late. Sam, the owner, was a little pointed, asking me where I'd been. I can't really blame him, he's an even-tempered guy, and for whatever reason the crowd seemed to get here early. He was running around like a squirrel on Red Bull when I arrived. So was Velma. Had to be this kind of morning on the exact day I had a little trouble getting started?

Then this lady came in and sat down at the counter and started asking me questions. She wouldn't leave me alone: Crystal this, Crystal that. I didn't even know her; she just saw the name on my badge. Don't get me wrong, she seemed like a nice enough person. Had a soft voice, pretty face, nice clothes. She left me alone when I was busy, but when I wasn't, there she was, wanting to know what waitressing was like, whether I liked working here, etc., etc.

I've seen her in here before, but she never tried to talk to me before. She was kind of shifty. At first, she just seemed interested in me, but after a while she started asking me about Rob. Like I was some kind of expert on him. I do see him every morning, but it's not a topic I want to talk about; it's none of her damn business. We have a special bond, Rob and me, just between us. Not something I want to share with anyone, especially a complete stranger.

He's always friendly, cheery, seeing the good side of things. If the stock market is down, he'll say something like, "Hurting those fat cats, Crystal, not people like us." If there's a big fire, he'll mention how incredible the fire fighters are. When there's a blizzard in the east, he'll comment on how glad he is we live in California.

When he's around—ten months a year, he disappears over the summer—he never misses. It began the day he retired, I think. Which makes you know there's more than coffee involved. We've had a lot of conversations, and some of them are even surreptitious, whispering about some new customer we've never seen before, trying to figure out who he is or what he's doing here. Maybe pretending he's some kind of agent, secretly spying on the place. We have that kind of connection. Who can blame me, a single lady about the same age. A handsome single guy. No wonder I have a sense there's more to it.

He's a cautious guy, hasn't taken the next step yet. Not that I don't give him hints. Not much on my calendar this weekend. Good movie playing at the cinema. I pour his refill really slow, kind of linger there. But he never bites. Actually, I think he's shy. Lot of men are. Scared to ask a woman out. But he cares about me, that's obvious. One of these days....

Port Le Claire, Florida

I had this dream last night. It was horrible. I can't get the images out of my head. Rob was lying out in a field somewhere, under a hot sun, his body white and unmoving. There were scavengers circling overhead, those huge ugly ones, turkey vultures. They're gigantic, nine or ten-foot wingspans, bigger than eagles. Just circling around and around, looking down at Rob. It brought it all rushing back.

I was the one who found him. Rob hadn't gone to school that day, said he didn't feel well. The folks had gone to work and left him home alone. He was in high school; it wasn't like they were being irresponsible. He didn't have a fever or anything, they checked before they left. He just seemed to be in one of those down moods, and they didn't like to push him when that happened. I think Mom had some of the same problems when she was young.

I was the first one home. I fixed a little snack and went up to his room to see how he was. He was flat on his back, head tilted to one side, eyes closed, completely inert. There was an open bottle of pills on the bedstand. I shook him, tried to bring him around, but nothing. I thought he was a goner.

I really didn't know what to do. I'd only graduated a couple years before, and I'd sure never had to deal with anything like this. I kept shaking him, shouting his name, but it became obvious I wasn't going to get anywhere. He wasn't dead, I could see him taking slow, shallow breaths. So I called Mom at work.

She immediately called for an ambulance. Which got there in only ten minutes, it was a little amazing. They took one look, checked his pulse, and gave him an injection of something. Then they loaded him on a gurney, put him in the ambulance, and whisked him off, sirens blaring.

I didn't see him again for three days. It took him two to come out of the coma. He came really close. Not like those fake attempts: he really tried to do it. If I hadn't found him when I did, he almost certainly *would* have died. He didn't go back to school for a month. The doctors wouldn't let him. They wanted to give the shrink time to work with him, and the antidepressants time to take effect.

Rob was different after that. He'd always been kind of withdrawn, off in another world half the time. Spending time alone in his room, reading or listening to music. While I'd be out playing a pickup game of baseball or flag football or whatever. He was like that for months.

He was on antidepressants for a long time. I don't think he stopped taking them until he left home. The folks made sure of it. They were really traumatized. And everybody kind of gave him a wide berth after that. Which I think he kind of liked. He'd never been much into the social scene—it became almost a badge of distinction. People don't want to be around someone who does that, it's too disturbing. I think he kind of reveled in that status.

He did seem to get better eventually. I don't know whether it was the therapy or the drugs or just growing up. He lost a few credits that year, had to make them up, but he was a good student. Teachers liked him. So by halfway through the school year he was pretty much back to normal. He was still quiet, thoughtful, considerate. Still read a lot, thought a lot. He liked to analyze things, like the characters in stories he read, what made this one do this or that one do that. I thought maybe he'd become a shrink himself. I've read that happens; kids who needed help growing up sometimes become shrinks.

Anyway, there is a corner of my mind that never really stopped worrying about him. Especially after he retired. He was all by himself. He didn't have the daily structure work brings, the kids he'd see every day, being focused on *their* problems. Or the other teachers he'd see regularly.

There were a few guys he did stuff with, like his book group members. He mentioned some guy named Phil once that sometimes went on hikes with him. But at the core he was by himself.

I have to say, that cop who called didn't sound encouraging. He didn't say it in so many words, but I could tell he thinks it's bad. I feel bad I haven't tried to visit him. I mean, I'm his big brother. I'm supposed to be there for him. I know we haven't been all that close for a while; quite a while, to be honest. Living on opposite coasts, me married, him not. But we're family. He's my only brother.

Two-thirty-seven Chestnut Street

This ransom demand? Don't know what to say about it. Someone trying to make money off his disappearance? That's low. They're scumbags, whoever they are. Someone needs to track them down and give them what they deserve. Can't tell you how much scorn I'm feeling toward them. But I don't know if there's much chance they'll be caught. Everybody knows this town's police force doesn't have the sharpest knives in the drawer.

Anyway, the book group guys and I talked about what we could do, since I was the one who discovered he was missing and they're all concerned about him. We came up with nothing. Wade had actually called the police station. It took him four tries to get through it was so busy. And when he finally did, he never got past the receptionist. Of course she couldn't tell him anything. She just said they're doing everything they can, and when they had more information they'd share it. He said she sounded tired and stressed.

We thought about trying to send Rob a text, on the outside chance he had his cell phone with him. Then we remembered he doesn't have a cell phone. Said he got by most of his life without one and didn't particularly feel a need to be always available to be contacted. He likes his peace and quiet. And while he likes researching things on the Internet, he said he didn't need to do that with a little screen he kept in his pocket, it worked fine from his computer. That's the way he is; he doesn't just automatically go along with every new invention that comes down the pike, he thinks about whether it will improve his quality of life or not.

I got a call from a reporter at the *Sentinel*, some guy named Walter Harvey. I looked him up after we talked. Turns out he's a full-blooded Nisenan Indian, the tribe that lived here before the gold rush. I vaguely remember him guest teaching in the high school journalism class a couple times. Once he asked his students to conduct research for a story that incorporated historical background information. Some of them came to me for help.

When he called, this Harvey guy asked my thoughts on Rob, what he was like, what kind of interests he had. I told him about our teaching together for almost forty years, sharing our lunch hours, sometimes commuting together. And about the book club, his fascination with science fiction and crime mysteries. How he loved trying to figure out who the perp was.

I also mentioned that he was an outdoor guy, liked to go on hikes in the Tahoe National Forest. I've gone with him occasionally. There are some amazing trails up there, not to mention endless evergreen forests and pristine mountain lakes. Place gets a little crowded over the summer when school is out and families go camping, but it's pretty empty once school is back in session.

Harvey asked me how Rob spent his spare time, other than reading and hiking. I told him he didn't have a lot of spare time during the school year with all the prep work and papers to read and grade. That's hard work. People don't appreciate it enough.

As for summers, I have no idea what he did. He'd just disappear. Whenever I tried to ask him where he'd gone, he'd just clam up. Said that was when he recharged his batteries, got away from school stuff. Where he went or what he did is a mystery. Only clue I ever got was that he always came back with a great tan.

I must admit I've wondered if he had a babe stashed away somewhere that he spent summers with. I think he would have liked having a girlfriend, at least. We'd sometimes talk about one of the girls in our classes. They weren't trying to appeal to us, they had their eye on some basketball star or football hunk. But we're not blind, those revealing tops and short skirts—whoa. I may not be a teenager, but there are still a few juices flowing in there.

The cop asked me if Rob had any enemies: old girlfriends he'd dumped or students he'd flunked who might be carrying a grudge? I told him I didn't think so, he was always supportive of students. All they had to do was show him they were putting in an honest effort. Didn't matter how good or bad they were as students. He tried to help them all.

It wasn't clear to me why this Harvey guy was so interested. Not really the newspaper's business. Ultimately, I suppose, it's a business strategy: people respond more to bad news than good. Ever see a report on how there's been no hurricane or wildfire or earthquake for a long time? But let one happen and it's headlines for days.

An Old Cedar Bungalow

Lew didn't know how long it would take for Zane to get to his attempts to hack into Robert Campbell's email, but if history was any guide, he'd probably do it sooner rather than later. Zane seemed to like these challenges. It kind of depended on which email service Campbell used; some were easier to hack into than others. But Zane was good at this whatever it was.

He considered texting—that was Zane's usual mode of communication. He didn't like email, said it was too slow and cumbersome. Exactly what young people a generation earlier had said about written letters, 'snail-mail', when email showed up. How quickly things evolve.

Lew wasn't all that fond of texting himself. True, it was quick and usually resulted in a quick response. But it was also a limited form of communication. The whole point was to convey the essence without the details. He wanted as many details as he could get.

He dialed Zane's number. It rang four times. He was getting ready to leave a message when he heard: "Yo. Mr. T."

"Zane. You busy?"

"Nah. Sorry for the slow pickup. Just out on my bicycle. Had trouble getting the phone out of my pocket. What's up?"

"You're talking on the phone while on a bicycle? Isn't that dangerous?"

"Do it all the time."

"Well, be careful. I need you around until we've got this thing figured out."

There was a small chuckle. "What's up?"

"I was just wondering if you'd been able to get into Robert Campbell's email."

"Didn't I tell you I can get into anyone's email?"

"You did. I just thought that stuff was more well protected these days than it used to be."

"It is. They keep us on our toes. It took a while. But nothing is *that* well protected."

"So?"

"I found a couple exchanges with a guy in Florida, guy named James Campbell, his brother I guess?"

"Yes, he has a brother there."

"Ordinary stuff. Wanted to know how the kids and grandkids were. What he'd been up to. Didn't say much about himself."

"Okay. What else?"

"He's got an email thing going with some woman in Ohio."

"Oh?"

"These were more frequent, about one a week. Sounded like they were old friends. Maybe more than friends."

"What do you mean?"

"Veiled references to stuff they did in high school. I guess they must have had a thing going then."

"Sounds like maybe they still do?"

"Hard to tell. In one of the recent ones she asked him if he'd consider coming back for a visit, touch base with some of his old high school buds."

"And?"

"He said he'd think about it, that it had been a long time. There were things he'd rather forget. But maybe."

"You think he was planning to go?"

"He sounded reluctant. Couldn't tell if it was something to do with her or there were other matters he didn't want to revisit. She said she could 'make it worth his while', I believe was the phrasing. And if he'd like a place to stay, she had room. He said he'd think about it."

"Where is this place in Ohio?"

"No idea. But it sounded like a lot of their old friends were still around. There was mention of a park by the lake they used to go to, which could be Lake Erie. So maybe near Cleveland?"

"Anything else?"

"He must be in some book group. There were a couple exchanges about picking a book for the next meeting. And there was one that sounded like it was from an ex-student who wanted to talk to him about something."

"An ex-female student?"

"Not sure, but I think so. He was kind of a counselor to students who needed help."

"How do you know that?"

"I was in his class my freshman year. He invited that. Good teacher. Everybody liked him."

"Did you get her name?"

"No, she didn't sign her name, just 'you know who'. And her email address was just a code. Which he obviously knew."

"Why do you think it was a girl?"

"The language sounded female, kind of soft and emotionally."

"Soft and emotionally?"

"You know, how girls are always talking about their feelings."

"How did he respond?"

"Said he'd be glad to talk with her."

"Okay. Good work. Want to tackle another one?"

"Like?"

"His financial status. How much money he has invested, size of his checking account, recent credit card activity."

"I don't know, Mr. T. That's kind of dangerous territory. If some guy finds out I hacked his emails, I've got one guy mad at me. If a bank finds out I hacked someone's account, I've got the law on me. There are severe penalties for that."

"Okay. Didn't realize that. No problem."

There was a pause. "Although I suppose there might be another way around that."

I waited.

"He might have something in his email account. You know, like he attached a form to an email he sent to his CPA or something like that. People can be sloppy with what they attach to emails."

"Whatever. But don't put yourself in any danger."

"You talked to the cops about this? They have legal access to such information when there's a crime they're investigating."

"Good thought. Tim is talking to the lead investigator, Tony Gonzales. Let me mention it to him."

"Yo."

"Okay. Thanks, Zane. You're going to have a nice payday."

"My girlfriend thanks you."

The phone clicked. Lew leaned back. Zane was a find, no question. In addition to his computer skills, Lew liked having someone he thought of as a friend who was that young. Strange how as the years go by that becomes unusual. He didn't feel like he'd changed all that much inside. But the outside sure had. The thin hair, the wrinkles, the slower pace. They create a barrier for young people. Not that seventy-two was ancient, but it was a lot different than, say, twenty-seven, or worse, eighteen. Zane was eighteen.

It's strange how life moves on. How a stage you're in at one point becomes a memory after a while, and then a distant memory after another while. He glanced around the room, looking at the pictures of Mary and the kids. That warm smile he'd always found intoxicating. Those blue eyes, which to his endless gratitude and wonder had somehow lighted on him. The kids little, Kate leaning in on one side of her, Nick on the other.

Now, looking back, he hadn't sufficiently realized at the time what magical years they were. Ended ten years ago, in a heartbeat, on a rainy night, on a narrow country road, by a drunk driver in a huge gas-guzzling car, which had veered into Mary's lane on a curve and totally wiped out her little Toyota. And her. He'd found her, when she didn't come back from visiting a friend or answer her cell phone calls. He knew he'd never get the images of her twisted, broken body out of his mind. The thought occurred to him he needed to check his gin supply.

Offices of the Sienna Sentinel

The next morning the four of them sat around the table in the newspaper's small conference room: Lew, Tim, Harve, and Violet. They each had a cup of coffee, and Tim and Harve had half-eaten donuts. The clock on the wall read nine-thirty.

"You going to offer one of those to your crack investigative reporter?" Lew asked.

"You eat junk like this?" Harve said, his eyebrows raised. "I thought you were the smart one."

"The brain requires a lot of energy to function, Harve. So the bigger your brain, the more calories you need. Where are they?"

Harve looked at Tim, frowning. "I think I might have gotten the last one." He took a bite out of his, smacked his lips. "You see any left, Tim?"

"I thought *I* got the last one, Harve. Either way, I'm sure they're gone." He shrugged.

Lew sighed. "I don't know how I put up with you guys. Okay, I'm going to assume they're in the usual place." He stood and headed for the door.

"They're on the coffee island," Violet said quietly as he was leaving.

He nodded. "What I figured. You want one?"

She shook her head.

"At least one of us here has good sense," Harve said.

"Why is it women are supposed to worry about this stuff, but men hardly ever do?" she said.

"Because women are more complicated creatures," Harve said. "Men are basically quite simple. Satisfy our basic needs and we're happy. Women have more complex standards."

Lew returned with two donuts. He was licking the frosting off his lips from a bite he'd taken out of the first one. He held the second out to Violet.

Violet rolled her eyes. "You guys. Okay, Lew, I'll split the second one with you."

"It's my understanding that anyone who takes two has to buy donuts for the whole office the next day," Harve said to Tim.

Tim nodded. "Hard and fast rule."

"Well, since I'm only half-time, my math says I'm only half responsible," Lew said.

"Au contraire. Bad math. If you're half-time you should only get half a donut. You should also be contributing articles half the time. Can't remember the last one." This from Tim.

"Nature of investigative reporting. Takes a *lot* of research. Following up clue after clue. Sorting them out, careful analysis, follow up questions. I have to put a ton of research into every one of my stories."

Tim sighed, shaking his head. "I hate to bring this discussion around to the topic at hand, but can we maybe talk about what we're here for? We don't have a ton of time." He turned to Lew. "I believe you called this meeting?"

Lew nodded. "Good point. Let's get focused. We're investigating a possible crime. A *likely* crime. And if the ransom note is to be believed, we absolutely don't have much time. Each of you had an assignment. Let's see where we are. Who wants to go first?" No one spoke. "Okay, I can begin. I decided to actually visit Robert Campbell's home," Lew said.

"I thought the cops had yellow tape around the place," Harve said.

"They do. It's about chest high. With enough body flexibility one can actually duck under it."

Harve shook his head. "The people one has to associate with in this business." He sighed. "Okay. Let's hear it."

Lew proceeded to describe his visit to Campbell's house: breaking in through the kitchen window, the magazines and books he'd found, the TV stations, the possibly missing hiking boots, the apparent travel plans on Campbell's computer. He left out the knock on the door and the chat with Peggie Thompson.

"What did you make of all that," Tim asked.

"Still processing it. But I think there are some leads there. I'd like to figure out where he was thinking of going."

He looked around the group. "Anyone else come up with anything?"

"Okay, I'll go," Tim said. He reached into his brief case and pulled out a single sheet of paper, holding it up. "This, folks, is the ransom note. Not a description, not a summary, the actual note."

"Wow. How did you cajole *that* out of them?" Lew asked.

"All in knowing how to massage contacts, boost egos, use the right words."

"Can we see it?" Harve asked.

Tim handed it to him. He studied it for several moments, then handed it to Violet. She did the same and handed it to Lew. It read as follows.

Dear Mr. Hyde: This note is to inform you that we have Robert Campbell in our custody. We are treating him well, feeding him regularly, housing him comfortably. A status that will change in exactly forty-eight hours if you do not meet our terms.

Which are as follows: Place one million dollars in small bills—fives, tens, and twenties—in a suitcase that is not wired or traceable in any way. If we find any evidence it has been, Mr. Campbell will cease to exist.

Place this suitcase next to the giant redwood tree with the big gouge in its trunk five feet above ground level, on the Pembrook Trail of the Tahoe National Forest. The tree is approximately one mile in from the trailhead. The trailhead begins on Pabscomb Road, two miles in from the main highway.

If there is any evidence of an attempt to trace this suitcase, or to observe this location, or to detect the suitcase's removal, Mr. Campbell will cease to exist.

If you meet these terms Mr. Campbell will be released within seventy-two hours. Information will be provided indicating where he may be found. He will not have been harmed. If you fail to meet these terms, information will be provided within seventy-two hours indicating where Mr. Campbell's body can be found.

To repeat, you have forty-eight hours from the time you receive this to follow these instructions.

The Abducters

The four of them looked at each other in silence. Finally, Tim spoke: "Thoughts?"

"They're lousy spellers," Violet said.

They looked at her with blank stares.

"Abductors is spelled with an 'o', not an 'e'."

"Oh, yeah," Tim said. "Hadn't noticed."

"Who is Hyde?" Harve asked.

"Hendrik Hyde," Tim said. "That billionaire who lives in the huge mansion on Sycamore Street. The one who gets mentioned in *Forbes*. Has 'people' who work for him. And several black SUVs."

"Sounds like a Mafia capo. How did he make all his money?" Harve asked.

"He ran one of those subprime loan mortgage houses, and a hedge fund, made cheap loans to people who couldn't afford them, then packaged the debt and sold it to someone else. All of which went south in the great recession of 2008-09."

"So he's a crook?"

"No one was ever convicted in any of that. The government bailed out the banks that were in trouble and the hedge fund managers got off scot free. It was just the people who were below water and lost their houses, and the hedge fund investors, who took a bath."

Harve nodded. "So, as usual, the little people were hurt and people like Hyde got richer. A scoundrel, in other words."

"That would be a nice word for it."

"Whatever the case may be in that regard, this note suggests these kidnappers probably aren't amateurs, their spelling ability aside," Harve said. "They went straight to someone for whom a million dollars would be pocket change."

After a pause, Lew said, "Anybody else got anything?"

"I got some background stuff," Harve said. "Nothing like either of you."

"Like?"

Harve sketched his conversation with Phil Palmer: how he was a close friend who lived near Campbell; they had taught at the high school together for nearly forty years; how hard Campbell worked at being a good teacher and a friend and support for students; the book group they'd formed after retiring; and Campbell's interest in science fiction and crime drama. Also how Campbell loved hiking in the Tahoe National Forest, finding his way into remote areas. And the fact he spent summers off somewhere, apparently a secret place he wouldn't tell even close friends about.

"Sounds like the kind of teacher I wish I had more of in high school," Tim said.

"You have a tough time in high school?" Lew asked.

"It was New York City. The high schools are pretty much all tough. Doesn't help if you're small and Jewish and live in a neighborhood that's mostly Black and Italian.

"You get bullied?"

"I was lucky if I made it to school with my lunch money."

"Is that why you moved to Sienna?" Violet asked gently.

Tim shrugged. "I went to college outside the city, so I'd had some time to recover. Mostly I wanted to see more of the world and thought it would be fun to start with California. A friend in San Francisco mentioned this place to me, said it was kind of a nugget in the foothills."

"You didn't want to live in San Francisco?"

"I tried. The *Chronicle* was laying people off. I decided to drive up here and check it out. It looked kind of idyllic, the western-style storefronts, the old Victorian houses, the mountains and evergreen trees. I saw there was an opening here and decided to apply. You know the rest."

"You miss New York?" Her voice was still soft.

"In some ways, sure. It's endlessly entertaining. But it's also intense. I like the pace here."

"We're glad you decided to stay," she said.

"Thanks." He seemed a little embarrassed.

"Let's get back to the topic at hand," Lew said. He looked at Harve. "That's all good background stuff on Campbell. What should we make of it?"

"Well, it confirms the impressions we have from others that Campbell is a nice man, a good teacher, a friend to students, a prolific reader, and a hiker. Also, his summers seem to be something of a mystery.

"I find it interesting he likes hiking into remote parts of the Tahoe National Forest. I think the trail where the kidnappers want the million dollars left is pretty remote," Tim said. "Sounds like they have something in common."

"You see a connection there?"

"Just something to put in the hopper as we learn more."

Lew turned to Violet. "Your turn?"

"I'm like Harve. Background stuff. Campbell went to the Coffee Roasters every morning after he retired, befriended a waitress there."

"Befriended?" Tim said in an inquiring tone.

"Didn't sound romantic, if that's what you're asking. She's not exactly a great catch, she's older and overweight. He was just nice to her, friendly and cheerful. Left generous tips."

"That it?"

"She mentioned the summer thing also, that he was a regular customer during the year but disappeared over the summer. When she asked him where he'd been she got the same answer Palmer did: no answer."

"Curious," Lew said.

"It seems like he left Sienna," Violet said. "Someplace he could get away from it all."

"Implying?"

"Not implying anything."

"Phil had no idea either," Harve said. "But he did speculate that maybe Campbell had a girlfriend he spent summers with. It does seem a little strange that he seemed to like women and never settled down with one. Maybe that's what he meant by recharging his batteries?"

"This is all interesting background information," Tim said. "How do we get from this to having any actual *evidence*?"

"I have access to Campbell's email," Lew said. "Let me see if I can build on any of this that way."

"You hacked into his email?" Tim said, his tone incredulous.

"No. *I* didn't."

Tim rolled his eyes. "Sweet Jesus. Don't tell me... You know that's illegal." There was an edge in his voice.

Lew nodded, ignored him. "Do you mind if I take a picture of that ransom note?"

"I told Tony I'd keep it confidential. I think we should honor that."

"You've just shared it with three other people."

"Yeah, but you're all responsible adults."

"Thank you, Tim. I'm not always sure you see us that way," Lew said.

"Okay, half-responsible."

Lew smiled. "I think it's fair to say the person I want to show it to is at *least* half-responsible."

Tim sighed, then reluctantly handed Lew the note.

Lew got out his cell phone and took a picture, handed it back.

"We're all going to wind up in jail," Tim said with a note of despair.

"Then it will be a party," Lew said, tucking his phone back in his pocket. "And Tim, since we're out on a limb here anyway, there's something more I wonder if you could cajole out of our friends down there."

Tim scowled. "What?"

"Three things, actually. First, what has their fingerprint analysis showed. Is there evidence other people were in Rob Campbell's house recently? And if so, who?"

Tim sighed. "What are the other things?"

"It could be helpful to know something about Campbell's financial status. Police investigating a crime have legal access to that."

Tim sighed. "What's the third thing?"

"I'd like to see the actual ransom email. Not just the message, the electronic transmission."

"Why?"

"Might be a clue there about where it came from. Like the server it came through."

"Why would they share any of those things with me?"

"That silver tongue of yours you mentioned earlier."

"It'll take a platinum one for all that."

"Okay, here's another motivator." Lew reached into his pocket and pulled out the dark crumpled tissue, held it up for them to see. "This."

"What is it?" Tim said.

"A clue."

"Of?"

"Of the fact that someone lost some blood somewhere in or near Robert Campbell's house."

"Explain."

Lew sketched where he'd found the tissue, largely hidden under the hedge along Campbell's front sidewalk.

"What do you think it's a clue *of*?" Tim asked.

"I have a theory. But why don't we see what the men in blue come up with?"

"You just want me to give this to Christiansen. With no more than that?"

"It will show we're trying to help."

"It will show you've been snooping around Campbell's house."

"Snooping is such a nasty word. I've been trying to assist in their investigation." Lew's tone dripped innocence.

Tim quietly shook his head. "How do I get involved in these things?"

Lew turned to Violet. "Can you find out one more thing from the café waitress?" She waited. "What was the last day Campbell showed up there. Or the first day he didn't. Comes to the same."

"What if she can't remember?"

"Nudge her until she does. You're good at that sort of thing."

She looked at him askance, like there was something she'd really like to say but didn't want to in front of Tim and Harve.

Next Lew looked at Harve, who sat with his hands folded together on the table like he was expecting an assignment. "Yes, boss?"

"This friend of Campbell's, Phil Palmer. He knew Campbell well?"

Harve nodded.

"Can you talk to him again?"

"What for?"

"See if you can ferret out any suggestions Campbell wasn't the perfect citizen everyone describes him as."

"What are you suggesting?"

"Nothing specific. It's just the law of averages. Most people are a mix of good and bad. I get suspicious when I hear someone is all good. I feel like we don't have the full picture of this guy yet."

"You're a suspicious SOB."

"Helps in investigative reporting."

"So, see what mud I can dig up on a guy who by all accounts dedicated his entire career to helping young people."

"Precisely."

Harve shrugged. "Okaay."

Lew looked around the table. "We all clear on our assignments?"

Harve and Violet nodded. Tim just stared at him.

All four got up and left.

The Sienna Police Station

Tony Gonzales rubbed his eyes, leaning back in his desk chair, trying to ease the ever-increasing stress and fatigue. His head ached, his neck hurt, his shoulders felt like he'd been lifting weights for an hour. It was more than anyone could take.

Ros's hair was disheveled, her eye liner was beginning to run, a tic was causing her to squinch up one side of her face. She was responsible for answering the never-ending barrage of calls, explaining that there was nothing new to report and the story on the Internet about the GoFundMe account was accurate. It was quarter to five and she wasn't sure she was going to make it through the last fifteen minutes.

Tony got up and went over to her desk. "Hey, why don't you call it a day. You've already done three day's work today; you need a break."

She looked at him with a tired expression. "You think that would be okay?"

"I'll run interference for you with John. You need to get some rest if you're going to be any good tomorrow."

Her shoulders drooped and she looked at him with a sense of relief. "Is that ever the truth. But, I don't know..." She glanced toward Christiansen's office.

"Go on. Scat. Before anyone notices."

She cocked her head, as if to say, "Really?"

Tony reached for the back of her chair and began gently pulling it out. "Go. Now."

She stood and smiled at him over her shoulder. "Thanks, Tony. You're a godsend."

He made a shooing motion. "See you in the morning."

She grabbed a sweater from the back of the chair and began slipping into it as she walked toward the door. It opened and closed silently, and Tony went back to his desk.

He'd barely sat down again when John appeared. He walked over to Tony's desk and sat down in the chair next to it. In a slouch. Shoulders slumped. Dazed expression.

"Tough day, boss. No question."

"What are we going to do?"

"Well, we've got that GoFundMe thing up and running. Maybe we'll be able to spring Campbell. That should take a lot of the pressure off."

"Any sign of contributions yet?"

"Yeah, actually, they're pouring in."

"How much?" Christiansen asked.

"It was up to a couple hundred thou a little while ago."

"Really? A couple hundred thou? Wow. The people around here. Amazing."

"Apparently Robert Campbell was...is...a well-loved citizen. It's what comes of forty years of teaching, I suppose. You make a lot of friends."

"Did I hear you talking to someone on the phone?"

"That newspaper kid. He's all over me."

"What about?"

"He wants the electronic version of the ransom note," Tony said.

"Why? He's got the content. Isn't that what matters?"

"Seems like it to me."

"Did you agree to give it to him?"

"I said I'd check with you. But he'll just keep asking if we don't give it to him. I was clear it would entail the usual caveats: it can't go anywhere else, and they have to keep running the stuff we need them to."

John sighed. "Yeah. Okay. They got the news flash out fast. I guess we have to give them that. Was there anything else?"

Tony nodded. "What we found out with our fingerprint analyses."

"That's kind of ballsy. That's police information."

"He's not shy, that kid."

"And…?"

"Any financial information we get on Campbell."

"That's confidential."

"What I told him."

"What does he need all this stuff for?"

"He offered to run it past the best minds at the paper, give us any insights they come up with. Pointed out that in a couple days it isn't going to matter anyway, and if it gets out, it will make it look like we were willing to pull out every stop, seek help from any source we could."

"Yeah, okay. Pretty good arguments."

"He's sharp, wears you down, that kid." He paused. "There's one more thing."

"You're kidding?"

"He gave me a bloody tissue."

"*What?*"

"Said it was found on Campbell's front sidewalk."

"When?"

"Yesterday."

"By whom?"

"He wouldn't say. Said he didn't want to implicate a friend."

"What did you do with it?"

"Sent it over to Tom for analysis. See if it matches Campbell's blood type."

Christiansen sat up straighter. "That could be an important piece of evidence if it does."

"Agreed."

"Although I suppose it won't get us any closer to finding him."

"No. It feels like we're still a long way from figuring that out."

John sighed, looking away. "You put any thought into what to do next?"

Gonzales frowned. "You mean what lead to follow?"

"No. What line of work you want to go into when we all get fired."

Two-thirty-seven Chestnut Street

Harve's full name, Walter 'White Cloud' Harvey, included his Nisenan name This was the tribe that lived in and around Sienna before the Gold Rush. This event not only wiped out most of his tribe, it also wiped out much of the local environment. What had been a region with vast forests and abundant salmon in the nearby Yuba River became something of a wasteland.

Hydraulic mining, with huge water cannons washing away hillside after hillside, destroyed not only the land but filled the rivers with silt. This not only reduced the fish population, it also raised the riverbed levels in the Sacramento Valley by as much as seventy feet, leading to widespread flooding during spring snow melts. The steam power needed to drive the pumps that kept water out of the shafts and tunnels in the hard rock mining, which required constant supplies of wood, led over time to the almost complete denuding of trees in and around Sienna. In addition, residents were treated to an endless titanic thunder coming from the stamping machines that crushed the rocks miners brought up, which ran twenty-four seven.

On another front, a culture devoted to communing with nature, living lightly on the land and leaving no lasting imprint, taking only what was needed for survival, was replaced by one that valued gold and whatever it required to obtain it above all else, nature be damned. A culture with sophisticated knowledge of animals and plants was replaced by one having little or no such knowledge or interest, willing to destroy whatever got in its way to satisfy its lust for gold.

Many Indian children were wrested from their homes against the will of their parents and sent to Christian schools, mostly Catholic run, where they were indoctrinated with the dogma of the church, and the endless ways people were bad, their lives focused on overcoming their original sin, as tabulated in the ten commandments. These children were not allowed to speak their own language, even to each other, and knowing no English, lived lonely, isolated existences. Many were abused either physically or psychologically, and the native language was largely extinguished. Harve himself knew only a few words of Nisenan.

But he was focused on another matter at the moment as he sat in his *Sentinel* office, trying to think how to approach Phil Palmer to learn the things Lew wanted to know. He'd talked to Palmer on the phone last time but was thinking a face-to-face visit at his house would be preferable this time. He'd gotten the address, which was less than two blocks from Campbell's.

Harve pulled up in front of Palmer's house in his old pickup and looked out across his yard. It was like most of the others in the neighborhood: the hedges were trimmed, the lawn mowed, the fences upright and sturdy. He sat staring at the front door briefly, then climbed out of the truck and made his way through the gate and up the sidewalk to the front door. He knocked.

It was opened by an older woman, who peered out at him suspiciously. She was dressed in baggy blue jeans and a loose-fitting sweatshirt, and smoking a cigarette. She looked him up and down. "Yeah?"

Harve explained who he was and why he was there, then asked if Phil was around. She sighed, as though this was an imposition, rolled her eyes, and told him to wait. "Haven't been tracking where he is. Might take a minute."

Not having been invited in, Harve waited outside. After a modest delay, Palmer appeared, his expression skeptical. Phil Palmer was a big man, six foot three and heavy-set, with broad rounded shoulders and a few wisps of light hair. He walked with a slight limp.

"Yes?"

"I'm Walter Harvey from the paper. We talked on the phone yesterday."

Palmer nodded. "Oh, right." His tone was decidedly neutral.

"I wondered if I could ask you a few more questions about Robert Campbell. I thought it might be easier if we met and could talk face-to-face."

Palmer sighed. "Like what?"

"Could we talk…inside?" Harve looked past him into the foyer.

Palmer nodded reluctantly and swung the door open wider. Harve stepped into a small foyer which opened into the living room. He found his way to an easy chair, glancing back at Palmer for confirmation this was where he should go. Palmer followed and sat across from him in a matching chair.

"Not sure what more there is to tell you," Palmer said. "I pretty much covered what I know when we talked yesterday."

"I understand. It's just that a few of us at the paper feel a need to try to help if we can. We're not cops, we have no authority in this regard. We're just seeking out Robert's friends and associates to see if we can get any leads."

"So, what do you want to know?"

"You knew him well, between teaching together all those years and being in the book club with him. So I suppose my first question is just whether you have any thoughts on where he might be?"

"You mean where he's being held by the kidnappers?"

"Uh huh."

"I really don't. I mean, it could be anywhere. It's pretty much anyone's guess, isn't it?"

Harve nodded. "Okay, let me ask this. Did he have any enemies?"

"Rob Campbell?"

"I take it that's a 'no'?"

"Everybody liked Rob. Hard to imagine anyone *not* liking him. There wasn't anything not to like. He was just one of those guys who was always friendly and cheerful, even when things got him down. He's a smart, sensitive guy. Avoids arguments. Gets along with everyone. The kind that makes the rest of us feel like we should be better human beings."

"So, no skeletons in the closet? No angry women from his past? No students he flunked who might want to get back at him?"

Palmer shrugged. "None that I know of."

"Was he a good teacher?"

"We already talked about that. He was the best. Worked hard to prepare interesting lessons. Encouraged every student to participate in discussions. Worked to bring out shy kids and rein in ones who talked too much. Graded fairly."

"What about kids who struggled in his classes?"

Palmer leaned back, his eyes narrowed a bit. "They're often ones who don't get much support at home. We have a fair number here. Rob was especially concerned about them. He went the extra mile to try to be helpful."

"How?"

Palmer frowned. "One thing he did that was a little unusual, I suppose, was to invite kids over to his house for help. The ones without a good home life. Or, in some cases, a home. Or kids who just hated school, for whatever reason."

Harve cocked his head, inviting more details.

"I guess he felt they could be more relaxed there. He'd listen to their problems. Let them express their frustrations. He even fed them and gave them a safe place to stay for a night or two sometimes. Helped them find a more permanent place to stay if they needed that. From what I heard he treated them almost as equals."

"Were these kids all from his classes?"

"I suppose those were the ones he knew best, but I'm not sure. I think they were mostly from upper classes, juniors and seniors. In some cases I think it was kids trying to figure out what to do after high school. Whether to go to college or work. How to pick a field to focus on. He'd listen to their interests, try to guide them in appropriate directions."

"Did parents approve of this?"

"I think in many cases the parents weren't involved enough to care."

"Might anything...questionable have gone on?"

Palmer hesitated. "No idea. He didn't talk about it much. I think he knew he was kind of skating on thin ice legally. You'll have to draw your own conclusions."

Harve nodded. "Okay. Well, here's another question. What did he do summers?"

"Didn't we already talk about that?"

"I just thought you might have additional thoughts."

"I don't have a clue."

"Even though you were a close friend?"

"That's a place where Rob drew the line. He said he needed that time for himself. I don't think anyone knew. He'd just disappear every summer. Come back maybe a week before school started in the fall with a great tan."

"Isn't that a little curious?"

"I suppose."

"But you didn't try to press him to find out?"

"I tried. He didn't want to be pressed."

"So he had a private side to his life."

Palmer nodded. "He's a very private guy. You didn't ever really get inside his head. I knew him about as well as anyone, I think. No one knew what all went on in there."

"What about the book group?"

"What about it?"

"Are there any insights that might come from that? Books he chose, comments he made."

"He always chose science fiction or crime dramas."

"Any particular type of crime drama?"

Palmer frowned, thinking. "Who-done-its. Dead body shows up, a sleuth has to figure it out. He didn't like gory stuff, though."

"What about science fiction?"

"He wasn't into space explorations or galactic conflicts, more twists on reality. Like, say, *The Twilight Zone*. Stories that revealed insights into the human psyche. The strangeness of human behavior. Looked at from different perspectives."

"Was retirement hard for him?"

Palmer looked away, thinking. "Actually, I think it was. He loved being around kids. He seemed a little melancholy after he retired. Sometimes in those book group discussions he'd seem to tune out, his mind would be off somewhere else. He never said where, but I had the sense that deep down he was sad."

He paused. "I suppose that makes sense. He was such a popular teacher. They ran an article about the two of us in your paper when we retired. Mostly about him, actually. There was a picture of him teaching a class, holding up a copy of the *Sentinel*, pointing out something in a headline. He'd try anything to get them interested."

"Even resorting to using the *Sentinel* as a prop?"

Palmer smiled. "Didn't mean it that way."

"Okay. One last question. Any idea why he never got married?"

"No, that was curious. It was another thing he didn't like to talk about. If you asked—and I did once—he just passed it off with a casual comment. Said he was like a leaf blowing in the wind, free and unfettered, and he liked it that way."

"Did that seem strange to you?"

"A little. I think he was kind of lonely at times. He would have made a great husband. And dad. I sometimes got the feeling he regretted never getting married and having kids. I really don't know why, although he mentioned a couple times that he was kind of a troubled kid growing up. I'm sure he had the chance; he had a way with women."

"That was obvious?"

Palmer nodded, rolling his eyes. "For whatever reason, he decided to stay single. I guess he just wasn't a conventional kind of guy. He marched to his own drummer, as the saying goes."

"But in spite of that you were good friends?"

"Definitely. He was a bright, interesting guy. Hard not to be a little envious sometimes. But I can't say I knew everything about him. There was stuff inside there I don't think anyone knew."

Harve nodded. "Okay. Well, thanks. I can't think of anything else." Palmer stood and Harve followed suit. "Thanks for your time."

Palmer walked to the front door with that slight limp, opened it for Harve to leave. Harve headed back to his pickup, his expression pensive.

An Old Cedar Bungalow

Lew sat at home that evening contemplating what information he'd been able to assemble. And ruing the fact that it wasn't nearly enough. The time was rapidly evaporating to meet the terms of the kidnappers. He was trying to think what else he could do to speed things up, when the phone rang.

"Hello."

"Yo. Mr. T."

"Zane."

"Got some stuff for you."

"Great. What?"

"I didn't try to get into any of that financial stuff. But I did go back into Campbell's emails. I think there might be some useful stuff there."

"Do tell."

"For one thing, I found a flight reservation."

"I wondered about that."

"He booked a flight on American Airlines to New York City for the morning of September third. There was a confirmation in his email."

"New York? I saw what looked like notes he'd taken for a flight and thought it might be for somewhere on the east coast. So it's New York City. Is that the termination point?"

"Yeah, for the flight he got the confirmation on. I didn't see any continuation flights in his email. But I suppose that's a possibility."

"What time of day was it?"

"Six a.m."

"Arrival time?"

"Six-fifteen p.m."

"So there must have been a layover?"

"Yeah. Three hours. Cleveland."

"Cleveland, Ohio?"

"Do you know of another Cleveland?"

Wiseass kid. "Anything else?"

"I've been looking at the emails from that woman in Ohio, and there was another one of those."

"A recent one?"

"Couple weeks ago. It's the most recent one from her. I guess I missed it last time."

"What did it say?"

"The usual, small talk. She did ask if he'd considered her invitation to pay a visit."

"So apparently he wasn't going to Cleveland to see her, if she had no idea whether he was planning to come, and it was from two weeks ago. That's about when he disappeared."

"Like I said, the reservation was to New York."

"Anything else?"

"I looked back a little further, searched more carefully for the ones that had come from her. There was one about three weeks ago that felt like it had a different tone."

"How so?"

"It was more sober. Not just the superficial this and that stuff. More 'I need to talk to you about something kind of serious'."

"Did she say what?"

"No."

"How did he respond?"

"No idea. Apparently not by email."

"So they must have been talking to each other by phone?"

"That would seem to be a reasonable assumption. Either that or he just didn't respond."

"What was her name again?"

"Donna Livingston."

"Okay. That's helpful."

"One more thing. Since they had this email thing going on I decided to hack into her emails also, see if there was anything there of interest."

"And?"

"She has this habit of sending herself emails, with attachments.

Lot of people do that. It's a way of protecting something from being lost if your computer screws up."

"Okay."

"I found a few attachments that looked kind of like diary entries. Sort of like 'Remembrance of Things Past'. You know, like Marcel Proust."

"Wow. Zane. That's impressive. You read that?"

"You kidding? Of course not. It would take years. But it got mentioned in my English class."

"Okay."

"It's just snippets from her past. Mostly about her husband and son. It seems like the son was adopted. She apparently didn't have any kids with her husband, she mentioned a couple miscarriages, I guess they had problems that way."

"Anything about Campbell?"

"One of them, yeah. Her recollections of their time together in high school."

"Can you forward it?"

"I just did."

"Great. Thanks."

"Okay. Got to go."

"Oh, Zane. I asked Tim to see if he could get the ransom note transmission. He was going to talk to the police this afternoon."

A pause. "I hope you told him not to mention my name."

Lew smiled. Zane was a little sensitive about his computer activities. He did some things where the law wasn't clear. And some where it was.

"I did. I'm sure he was careful."

"Okay. Well, if he gets it, can you forward it to me?"

"I'll have him send it on."

"No, Mr. T. Not him. Please do it yourself. And don't include the email trail. I don't want my email address connected to anything from the cops."

"Got it, Zane. From me. No email trail."

"I'll let you know if I learn anything from it."

"You keeping track of your time?"

"You know that's up to you, Mr. T. I don't want to send an invoice, like a specific amount for 'services rendered'. If anyone saw it, it might raise questions about what services."

"Okay, Zane. Your services are greatly appreciated. You're going to enjoy a nice payday when all this ends."

"Like I said, my girlfriend thanks you."

The line clicked dead. Lew leaned back. Did he have time to look at a diary entry? What the hell.

Alloro, Ohio

Rob Campbell. My god. Long time ago. Don't quite know why I've avoided writing anything about that. About him. But he's never going to leave my consciousness. I guess that's true of most first loves.

We reconnected about a year ago. I didn't think it would ever happen. We hadn't been in touch for forty years. After high school we went our separate ways. I stayed here in Ohio and Rob moved on. He always had that wanderlust, and a fascination with California. Not sure whether it was the weather or the music or the Hollywood glamour.

Back then it was seen as a romantic place. Sunshine and surfing and pretty girls in bikinis. The Beach Boys, The Mamas and the Papas, Jefferson Airplane, Creedence Clearwater. It didn't have all the problems you read about today, the droughts and wildfires and homelessness and drugs. There's a saying out there that California is a bellwether for directions the country is heading. Lately it's become Exhibit A for the country's problems.

I had no idea how to locate him. California is a big place. But I remembered one of my high school friends had married his brother, James. I hadn't kept in touch with her either, but I knew someone who had. I managed to track her down—it was like six degrees of separation—and long story short, I managed to reach Jim. He was sweet, said he thought Rob would love to hear from me, gave me his email address.

So I learned that Rob was living in Sienna, a little town in the foothills of the Sierra Nevada Mountains. Jim explained that he'd been an English teacher at the high school there for nearly forty years but had retired a couple years ago. Doesn't surprise me; he loved to read, and he had a wild imagination. Plus he always liked people, which would have made him good with kids.

The most unusual thing I learned about him was that he never married. That *really* surprised me. He sure liked girls in high school. That year we dated? It was my introduction to love, really. And did I ever love that guy. I was so proud he wanted to be with me. Those were heady times while they lasted. He was the handsome athletic-looking guy who all the girls swooned over.

We had quite a romance, all the stuff you'd imagine: getting pinned, going to drive-in movies, being voted king and queen of our junior prom. Carved our initials in a tree: DL & RC: Donna Livingston and Rob Campbell. I would have done almost anything to keep him. In fact, I guess I did. But he just wasn't ready to settle down. Broke my heart. Took a long time before I could get past it. To the degree you ever can. I am dumbfounded he didn't find someone to marry.

I couldn't have made it without a husband; life is just too hard to go through alone. I got lucky in college, met Cole, not exactly a dreamboat, a little geeky, but he was solid and caring and loved me. The thoughtful, sensitive type. Those two miscarriages: he just kept telling me we'd have more chances. And when it didn't happen, well, we got used to it.

It was tragic when Cole got colon cancer three years ago. He lasted just six months. He was stoic about it, said he'd had the best life he could have imagined because of me. I couldn't think about anything else for a long time.

But eventually I got curious about Rob. When I wrote that email to him the first time I kept the tone casual, just said I thought it might be fun to compare our paths through life after all these years. Didn't know if he'd even respond, want anything to do with me. It took him a while, but eventually he wrote back. He seemed friendly enough, although I couldn't tell if he was just being polite.

Anyway, we struck up an exchange, even traded pictures. He's a lot older of course, but you can still see the young man he was. He's still fit and trim, has most of his hair. I hope he thought the same of me. I've worked at it; I don't think I look too bad for an old broad. At least I still get glances when I walk into restaurants or bars. I admit I sent a picture that was a few years old, wearing a skimpy summer dress, low cut with spaghetti straps. Nature was kind to me that way.

Anyway, we've been 'talking' to each other now for about a year. He's still the thoughtful generous guy I remember. I don't bring up the part about him dumping me, and he doesn't either. I've thought of suggesting we try to see each other. Maybe pretend I had some reason to visit the west coast and would be in his neck of the woods. But I don't want to risk scaring him off again.

He talks about Sienna some. Makes it sound kind of idyllic. Says it's still small, only a few thousand people, but that it's growing. People from more urban places who are looking for a quieter lifestyle. Retirees escaping crowded conditions in LA or the Bay Area. They can sell their houses there, buy something nicer in Sienna for far less, and pocket the difference.

It also sounds like a recreational mecca, near the edge of the Tahoe National Forest. He talks about the hiking trails, says he goes up there often, there are some of the most scenic landscapes anywhere. He likes to get off the beaten track, bushwhack into remote lakes, spend time feeling the breeze blowing through his hair and listening to the birds calling to each other and just generally communing with nature.

All this is interesting enough, but for me I must admit there's a little more than just learning about Sienna and his current life. That first love never quite leaves you. I got bold once and asked him why he never got married, tried to make it sound like a casual question. He didn't respond for a while. I was afraid he was going to stop communicating with me. When he finally did, he just said he didn't want to talk about that, it was a difficult topic for him.

He always was kind of a private guy. I could never tell exactly what was going on in his head, even when we were together. Maybe he got hurt by someone? If you're serious about someone and they dump you, it's beyond painful. Believe me, I know.

Anyway, enough reminiscing about that. It's frankly kind of sad. Thinking about what might have been.

Offices of the Sienna Sentinel

There was a small urn of coffee and a box of cinnamon donuts sitting in the middle of the table as Lew entered the conference room of the *Sentinel*. The other three were already there, munching on a donut and glancing at their watches as he walked in.

"Glad you could make it, Lew," Harve said. "Rough night?"

Lew didn't wear a watch. "What time is it?"

"Five minutes *after* nine," Harve said. "I thought we were meeting at nine."

"What, you're going to make a federal case out of five minutes?"

"Are you suggesting five after nine is the same as nine?" Violet said.

"It's close."

"You mean like stopping at the edge of a cliff and five feet past the edge are close?" she said.

He frowned. "So I'm not a morning guy. You knew that."

"Have a donut," Tim said, pushing the box toward him. "Does cinnamon meet with your approval?"

"Love cinnamon."

"I thought you loved powdered sugar."

Lew frowned. "I'm a broad-minded person, Tim. And now that I *am* here…"

"Precisely our thought," Violet said. "Given the fact we have about…what…twelve hours before the deadline."

"So…who wants to go first?" Lew poured himself a cup of black coffee and took a bite of the donut.

"I can," Tim said. "I talked with Chief Christiansen yesterday afternoon."

"Was he as cheery and forthcoming as usual?"

"He's a little stressed."

"He didn't throw any epithets my way, did he?" Lew said.

"You're not his favorite person. You do get under his skin. Not quite sure how you're so good at it."

"Practice."

Tim rolled his eyes. "They had the Campbell house fingerprint analyses back."

"And?"

"They found several different sets. Lots of Robert Campbell's, of course. And those of another person who they thought was about the same age."

"You can determine a person's age from fingerprints?" Harve said.

"Not with complete certainty. But apparently skin loses elasticity with age, causing the patterns to become less prominent. Compared with young people, where they are quite precise."

"Have they identified who that was?"

"They're working on it, but since we already know he was there some, I'm guessing it was probably his friend Phil Palmer. Or maybe one of the other book club members."

"Can they tell *gender* from fingerprints?" Violet asked.

"Again, not perfectly, but it seems there's a test that works pretty well. It seems women have about twice the level of a certain amino acid in their sweat as men."

"I had no idea," she said. "I'll have to be more careful where I leave mine." She glanced at Lew surreptitiously.

"He told me they can even tell if someone has been using drugs," Tim said. "Cocaine, heroin, morphine."

"*Our* police department can do all that?" Harve said.

"*No.* Of course not. They send them out to some lab that specializes in this."

"So what did they find?" Lew asked.

"In addition to the older man, there were several other sets of prints. All what appeared to be young people."

"Probably from his work with students," Harve said. "Palmer told me Campbell invited students over who were having problems. Went the extra mile to help them."

"Male or female?" Violet asked pointedly.

"Both."

"*Where* did they find these prints?"

"All over."

"Like?"

"Doorknobs, sink faucets, lamps, cupboards."

"Jeez, these kids went everywhere then."

"Yeah. Including upstairs."

"Where his *bedroom* is?"

"There were two different prints found in the upstairs bathroom."

"Boys or girls?"

"Both female."

They stared at him. "Suggesting Robert Campbell might not have been so perfect after all?" Harve said.

"Well, they didn't want to jump to conclusions," Tim said. "There could be innocent reasons. For example, they didn't find any on the bed stand or lamp, just in the bathroom."

"Meaning…?"

"Who knows? Maybe he had boys use one bathroom and girls the other? Or if someone was using the downstairs one, he let the girls use the upstairs one. There *are* innocent explanations."

"Still," Violet said.

"Yeah, it raises questions," Tim said.

"You learn anything else," Lew asked.

"I managed to get the ransom note transmission. Tony forwarded it to me last evening. He was reluctant, but I think they're so desperate at this point they'll do almost anything for a break in the case."

"Can you forward it to me?" Lew said.

"Tony was quite clear that it should go no further. What do you plan to do with it?"

"Have an expert examine it for clues."

Tim scowled. "Please tell me…"

Lew shrugged.

"Jesus, we're all going to jail."

"Where is your confidence in young people, Tim? Zane is a reliable kid. And since he's a teenager and we're not, he's going to be much better at this than we are."

Tim shook his head, continued. "One more thing. I gave that

tissue to John, explaining where it was found. I didn't tell him how I'd come by it." He looked pointedly at Lew.

"What did he say?"

"That they'd pass it on to Tom for analysis. Apparently he *can* do blood types."

"Good," Lew said. He looked at Harve and Violet. "Next?"

"I can go," Harve said. "I decided to go over to Phil Palmer's house to talk to him. Seemed like it might make it easier if we could look each other in the eye."

"And?"

"He didn't add much new. You already know about Campbell inviting kids over to his house for help when they needed it. I also asked about Campbell's summers, which seem to be a complete mystery. He said he didn't have a clue, that it wasn't something Campbell would talk about."

"Isn't that a little strange?" Tim said.

"Yeah. He's a strange guy in some respects."

"Anything else?"

"What books he picked for their book group."

"And?"

"Crime drama and science fiction."

"Crime drama. That's a little creepy," Violet said.

"Yeah. And the kind of science fiction is also interesting. Not *Star Wars*, more *The Twilight Zone*. Tweaks of reality. Different ways of seeing things, hidden motivations, unusual explanations for a person's behavior."

"Also a little creepy," Tim said.

Harve nodded. "Like I said, he's a little strange."

"Well, yes and no," Lew said. "A lot of people like science fiction and crime drama. That doesn't really tell us much. And there's no crime in viewing things from different perspectives. That's how we have breakthroughs in science. Seeing things no one else did."

"So you still think he's the perfect person?" Tim said, his tone skeptical.

"That's not what I said. I just think his taste in reading doesn't tell us much."

"But there *are* reasons to be suspicious," Harve said.

"There are reasons to be suspicious of a lot of possibilities. We're a long way from figuring this thing out."

"Oh. There's one more thing," Harve said. "I almost forgot." They waited. "Since you asked Violet to find out what the last day he came to the café was, I thought it would be useful to know what the first issue of the paper was that Palmer found on Campbell's porch, not picked up."

"Good thought, Harve. And?"

"Monday. He remembered because the Monday edition is usually thin, and he'd almost missed seeing it."

"Making it what day of the month?"

"September second."

Lew nodded. "Could be helpful. Nice thinking, Harve."

"Is that an actual compliment?"

"Research shows positive reinforcement works better than negative. Just trying to reward you for a good effort, so you'll try harder next time."

Harve shot him a nasty look.

Lew turned to Violet. "Your turn?"

She nodded. "I got up *early* this morning and went to the café about *seven*." The sarcasm dripped.

"Yess."

"I talked with Crystal. It was busy, so I didn't get a lot of time with her. But I did manage to ask her what the last day was that Rob showed up."

"And?"

"She didn't remember at first. It *had* been two weeks. But after serving some customers she came back and said she thought she'd figured it out." They waited. "It was a Sunday. She remembered he was looking at the Sunday funnies when she refilled his coffee."

"Making it…?"

"September first."

"Okay. Good. Anything else?"

"I thought that was my assignment."

"It was. Just thought maybe you'd had a thought like Harve I could compliment you for."

She scowled. "You're kind of skating on thin ice, Lew."

"Sorry. Sometimes my tongue gets a mind of its own." He

sounded genuinely apologetic.

"Could we get past these snits and talk about substance here," Tim said. "The clock is ticking."

"Okay. I think we now have a sequence of evidence we can tie together," Lew said. "Namely, what happened on the three last days we know anything about Campbell's whereabouts."

They waited.

"Campbell's last day at the café was Sunday, September first. The first paper Palmer found was Monday's, September second. Which makes sense. He was apparently gone on Monday."

"You said three days," Violet said.

"There's another fact I need to share with you. I talked with my *quite* reliable source last night." He glanced at Tim. "Who has been doing a little sleuthing for me. And has found—I won't bore you with how—evidence of an airplane reservation Campbell made to New York City." He paused. "For Tuesday, September *third*."

They stared at him. "So, putting all this together, it seems he showed up at the café Sunday, September first. Failed to pick up his paper Monday, September second. And flew off to New York City on Tuesday, September third."

"And that's significant, why?" Harve asked.

"It's always helpful to know the whereabouts of someone who vanishes," Lew said. "If we can tie down exactly *when* he disappeared, it may help us to figure out *why*."

"He disappeared when the plane took off."

"On Tuesday. But he was gone Monday morning. It's a morning paper."

"And that's significant?"

"Possibly."

"So to be clear, you have no idea?"

Lew scowled at him.

Port Le Claire, Florida

This is driving me crazy. They still have learned absolutely nothing about Rob, don't even have any leads, and it's been two weeks. Sure, we weren't that close, but we're brothers, and I need him there. I can't face the thought of a world where I can't be in touch with him. He's always been ridiculously healthy and strong; he's done a way better job of keeping himself fit than me. I've always thought of him as my ace in the hole if Gloria's health goes south and I need to turn to someone for help.

I've thought of flying out there, seeing what I could do, but what would I do if I went? I don't know anyone there. I wouldn't know my way around. Without even a clue about where he is, how could I help look for him?

I've talked to that cop three times now. He keeps asking the same questions, over and over. He's clearly grasping at straws. I've told him pretty much everything I can think of.

He's an idealist, always has been, wants the world to be a better place. He's poured his whole adulthood into trying to help kids, steer them in the right direction, provide the help many of them don't get at home. He's the perfect person for that, always giving, never taking. I must admit I've wondered how he does it. I mean, he is human, he must need support himself sometimes.

Which I suppose relates to those summers when he disappears. He always says those are his times to recharge, let the frustrations of the past year dissipate and new energy emerge. R & R. It's what nature demands. After a long hard day we need a good night's sleep. So I suppose it makes sense, after a long hard year teachers need a summer to recover. Maybe that's why school schedules are organized the way they are.

I'll admit that last email doesn't help. He sounded so troubled.

But he was so vague. Hints about some new problem he had to deal with, something that couldn't wait. Something he had no choice about, it had to be dealt with. It was serious, that much was clear. And while he never said what it was, there was that bit that he'd be out of touch for a while. And it somehow involved travel, there was 'a little trip in my near future'.

Also that question about whether he might hole up here for a while. He never defined 'while'. I don't know whether he meant a few days, weeks, months? And I have no idea why he'd want to come here in the first place. Or, maybe, *need* to? Maybe something he's done on the shady side? Or that's too private to talk about in an email? I suppose the fact he would confide in me is good, but why was he so damn mysterious about it? I'm family, for god's sake.

I didn't mention that to the cop. Maybe because I don't really know what it means. Or maybe because there are sometimes things too close to you to tell strangers. Especially strangers who might not have your best interests at heart. If he is in some kind of trouble, I need to know what's going on before I tell a cop anything. The law can be your friend. But it can also be your enemy.

My theories are all over the board. He has some kid who has a big problem he's got to help with. Like he's being threatened with violence at home. An asshole dad who's beating him. Or a girl who's being molested by her father, or more likely, a stepfather. A mom so gone on drugs she can't function, and he has to find a place for the kid to live, maybe somewhere she can't find him. Maybe a friend who's got some terrible disease, cancer or drug addiction or something, and he needs treatment immediately, something Sienna can't provide? So Rob is taking him somewhere that specializes in that. Whatever it is, he's probably helping someone else.

I'm trying not to think about the most obvious explanation. I can't bear the thought of him being taken by kidnappers. Suffering who knows what? Or worse, killed. That just can't be. At least the cops are trying to do something about that one. If they manage to come up with the money, when they deliver it, he should be released. Gonzales said they were getting close, and it looked like they'd just make the deadline.

I think the best thing I can do is just sit tight. Wait to hear more. Maybe the silence will be short. That's what I'm hoping. That any day he'll be released, I'll hear from him, hear he's okay. Or that whatever he had to take care of has been done and his life is back on track.

An Old Cedar Bungalow

Lew sat contemplating as he munched on his sandwich, Earl snugging against his leg. He reached down unconsciously and rubbed behind his ears; a loud purr began. Earl was an independent spirit. He'd pretty much ignored Lew's attempts to teach him not to jump up on things, like couches and tables. He went pretty much wherever he wanted. Which included some unlikely spots, like the dryer when the door was open, the top of the refrigerator, the mantle over the fireplace, and of course Lew's bed. Not that he minded that; sometimes it was nice to have a warm fuzzy creature there at night.

At the moment he was contemplating the growing assortment of facts and possibilities he'd assembled in two days. But there were too many, and they went off in too many directions. In particular he was trying to figure out what might have happened on that day when Robert Campbell hadn't picked up his paper but before he was scheduled to fly to New York. It was a curious gap in the timeline that seemed to have no obvious explanation. He'd apparently disappeared sometime between brunch on Sunday and Monday morning, when his paper arrived. But hadn't flown to New York City until Tuesday morning. What had happened in between?

As he pondered this his cell phone rang. He fumbled in his pocket and managed to punch the little green circle just before it was about to cut out. Didn't have time to glance at it to see if he recognized the number.

"Hello."

"Mr. Travis?" Obviously, someone he didn't know. No one called him Mr. Travis.

"Yes?"

"This is Peggie." Peggie? Did he know any Peggies?

"Hi, Peggie." Spoken apparently with a slight question mark in his tone.

"The one who lives across the street from Rob Campbell's house. We met a couple days ago?"

"Oh. Of course. What can I do for you?"

There was a brief pause in which he heard a deep breath being let out. "I wanted to share another thing with you."

"Okay."

"It's about my husband." The wheels turned. The OCD guy who mowed the lawn every day. "Don?"

"Yes. I'm really worried about him. And I thought I should maybe explain something more."

"Okay."

"But…you have to promise me you won't tell anyone else. It would make him mad."

Lew detected a touch of fear in her voice. He spoke softly. "Okay, Peggie. I can keep it just between us."

"You know, like I explained, he's a little…different. Since the accident. He refuses to see a shrink. Says they're the crazy ones. But he can be a little strange sometimes. Like the lawn mowing thing."

"Okay."

"Anyway, what I wanted to tell you was that I think he went into Rob Campbell's yard early one morning a couple weeks ago."

"Are we talking about the time Mr. Campbell disappeared?"

"Yes."

"What makes you think that, Peggie?"

"Like I said, I was still sleeping. It was early. Before sunrise. So I didn't actually see anything."

Lew waited.

"But what I forgot to mention was that when I did get up, I noticed he had a bandage on his hand. Not a big one, but bigger than just a band-aid. A piece of gauze with adhesive tape."

"Okay."

"So he obviously did something to hurt himself. I asked him how it had happened. I was worried he'd fallen or something. And he was evasive. Just said it was nothing. Brushed it off. I tried to be gentle, nudge it out of him. I didn't want to push him over the edge. But he wouldn't tell me. Still hasn't."

"What makes you think he went into Mr. Campbell's yard?"

"I noticed him glancing over there when he wouldn't answer my questions. And another time later that day. So I'm worried…"

"That he did something to Mr. Campbell?"

A sigh. "Yeah. I'm pretty sure it was the night before he stopped picking up his papers."

"You noticed that?"

"Yeah."

"Do you remember what night that was?"

"A Sunday?"

"Have you tried to get him to tell you about it since then?"

"No. I stopped trying after that morning. He gets antsy if I push too hard."

"Let me ask you again, Peggie. Are you completely safe?"

"He's a good man. I don't think he'd do anything crazy. He's just… he gets so focused on certain things."

"Okay." He waited for her to end the conversation. For several seconds.

"And…there's one more thing."

Lew waited.

"Mr. Campbell is a devoted teacher. Everyone says that. And he sometimes invites students over to his house after school for help. Which is really nice of him."

"I'd heard that."

"Sometimes even in the evening."

"Right."

"I think Don thinks there might be something…not right about that."

"Like?"

"Well, some of them are girls. He just doesn't think a single man should be inviting high school girls to his house after dark."

"I see."

"Don's pretty religious. Actually, he's really religious. He was raised that way. Baptist parents. So he draws a firm line between what he sees as right and wrong."

"And he thought that was wrong."

There was a catch in her voice. "Well…"

"So let me make sure I've got this right, Peggie. You think he came into Campbell's yard early on the day Mr. Campbell disappeared. Which *was* a Monday. We've figured that out. And that he did something that caused his hand to get cut. Which he won't talk about. And you're worried about what that might have been. Is that it?"

"Exactly. I'm not certain of anything. I didn't see anything. I'm pretty sure Don wouldn't do anything crazy. But it has me worried. I just needed to share it with someone."

"Okay. Thanks for telling me. I promise it will stay between us. And I don't think we can draw any firm conclusions from what you've said. But it might be helpful. I appreciate it."

"Thanks, Mr. Travis. It's been torture, not being sure if I should say anything. And I know Don would be upset…really upset…if he knew I'd talked to you."

"Mum's the word."

"He really is just a big old teddy bear. It's just that sometimes…."

"Understood." He started to hang up when a thought occurred.

"Peggie?"

"Yeah?"

"Could I ask you a kind of obscure question?"

"Okay."

"Do you happen to know Don's blood type?"

"His blood type?"

"Uh huh."

There was a moment's silence. "Jeez, I can't remember. But I think I can find out. Why?"

"Just curious. It might be helpful."

"Okay. I'll see if I can dig it out. I'll give you a call if I find it."

"Great."

"Thanks, Mr. Travis. I hope you figure this thing out."

"You take care, eh?"

The line clicked.

The Sienna Sentinel

On the afternoon of Tuesday, September 17[th,] the following News Bulletin appeared in the electronic version of the *Sienna Sentinel*:

Early this morning police recovered the body of a young woman found near a trail in the Tahoe National Forest, about ten miles east of Sienna. A police spokesperson said the body had been there for some time, as much as two weeks. Her remains are currently being examined by forensic experts at the county coroner's office.

While the spokesperson was reluctant to say more, when pressed she did admit it's possible foul play was involved. She quickly added that it's too early to be sure. But she noted that the body was only partially clothed and there were signs of a struggle. She said that an investigation is underway.

The Sienna Police Station

John Christiansen stood next to Tony Gonzales's desk, pointing to the bulletin Gonzales still had up on his computer. His shirt was only half tucked in, his hair askew, his face unshaven.

"This is batshit crazy, Tony. *Two* major crimes to solve at the same time? We're still looking for leads on the *first* one. Robert Campbell is still missing. We have absolutely no clue where he is or what's happened to him. And now we've got an apparent *murder* on our hands?"

Tony nodded, his expression grim.

Christiansen continued, his voice full of exasperation. "A young woman's decaying body turns up in some godforsaken part of the forest. We don't know who she is, where she's from, whether she was hiking up there and ran into a killer or was killed elsewhere and her body dumped there. Tony, we don't know *shit*!"

"I know, boss, I know. It's beyond crazy."

"What made you think to have someone go up there and look?"

"I wasn't thinking about finding a young woman's body, that's for sure. I was thinking about Campbell. I'd learned from that friend of his, Phil Palmer, that he loved to hike up there. And I happened to do some research on missing persons and learned that a surprising number of such disappearances involve people who get lost in national forests. So I sent Alex up there to see if he could find any sign of him. It was total happenstance."

"What the hell are we going to do?"

Gonzales looked at him, his disheveled appearance, his obvious stress. "Why don't you have a seat." He pointed to the chair next to his desk. "Let's think about it. Figure out what we *can* do."

Christiansen reluctantly sat down. He looked away, sighing and shaking his head.

"We need more information," Tony said.

"Oh, good. Shrewd."

"Well, let's think about what would help." He paused contemptively. "Knowing who she is would help. We should be able to get that before too long. The body is at the county coroner's office and the forensic guy there is examining it. Might take a while, but they're pretty good over there; hopefully we'll get an identity soon."

"Which will tell us what?"

"If we know who she is we can start looking into her background. Talk to relatives, maybe her parents, boyfriend, husband, friends. Piece together how this might have happened. Also, there may be other clues about what happened. Like how she was killed. Maybe she was knifed. Hit on the head with something. There are a lot of ways to kill someone. Might even be fingerprints if she was wearing something that they can get a read from."

"That would help. But apparently she wasn't wearing much."

"Maybe she was raped. Then they could maybe get a DNA sample from the semen."

Christiansen nodded morosely.

"It's also possible her clothes are somewhere nearby. Or even a backpack. We don't actually know yet if she was killed. Maybe she was just up there hiking, had a heart attack or something. Maybe this isn't even a crime, just an unfortunate accident."

"Not many people hike naked."

"Regardless, let's see what we get from the coroner's office and from the search up there. Take it from there. Keep in mind, this just happened. The public can't be on us too hard for not solving it yet. Might even create some sympathy for what we're having to deal with."

"They're sure on us about Campbell."

"All we can do is keep pursuing the clues we have, boss."

"We don't have any clues."

"Well, there's that bloody tissue Royce dropped off. The one found outside Campbell's house. Maybe that's from whoever kidnapped him. They had a scuffle out there on the front sidewalk and Campbell scratched him or something. Maybe the guy used that tissue to stanch the blood and kicked it under the hedge. Or maybe it's Campbell's blood. Maybe he was bludgeoned and bleeding, and the kidnappers used the tissue to stanch *his* blood."

"That still won't tell us who it was."

"No, but it might lead to a suspect."

Christiansen glowered. "In the few hours we have left before they kill him."

Gonzales sighed.

"Where are we on that blood analysis?"

"Tom should have it soon. That's an easy one."

"Have you checked on the GoFundMe thing?" John asked.

"Little while ago. It's getting close. Looks like we'll just make the deadline."

"Well, I suppose that's good news."

"What do you mean, suppose?"

"They're kidnappers. Who knows how much respect they have for rules? Even ones they define."

"Let's not assume the worst. He should be released, and when he is it will take a lot of pressure off. We'll still have a crime to solve, but at least we won't be under the Sword of Damocles."

"The sword of what?"

"It's a literary reference. Just means with a threat hanging over our heads."

"Oh."

Valentino's

The lighting was low and warm, the tablecloths checkered red and white, the candles in the old chianti wine bottles lit. Violet and Lew sat at a table in the back sipping on glasses of red wine, waiting for their order to arrive.

The restaurant wasn't crowded; just one or two other tables were occupied. The fear that had gripped Sienna had not eased. In fact, with the discovery of the young woman's body it had grown. It was one thing to have a kidnapping, quite another to have a murderer on the loose.

Lew and Violet had been trying to keep the conversation away from that, but it wasn't easy. He'd asked her about the vegetables she could still harvest from her small garden, part of a larger one that she shared with the other residents of her condo. She'd asked him what Earl was up to lately.

She was as fond of Earl as he was, and wondered about his daily excursions to who knew where. They speculated he had a honey out there somewhere but was keeping it a secret. At least there was no other cat that paid Lew's house visits. Earl apparently hadn't reached the point that Violet and Lew had, where they shared occasional nights together, although neither was ready for a full-time housemate. Violet had lost a husband a few years earlier, a long slow death from cancer. Like Lew, she was still working through the stages of grief that inevitably followed.

Despite their best efforts, however, the topic inevitably turned to the latest news. The landscape had shifted with the knowledge that there were now two crimes visited upon the peaceful town. They were a tad nervous themselves, especially Violet, who Lew was doing his best to reassure.

"Murders—which we don't even know for sure this was—are

almost always the result of an individual situation. The vast majority involve people who knew each other. And serial murderers are rare. This almost certainly is the result of something going on in that young woman's life."

"Easy for you to say. You're not a woman. Do you know the ratio of men killed by women to women killed by men?"

"I have no doubt it's lopsided."

"Men commit ten times the number of murders as women. And most of the murdered women are women they knew. Men murdered by women comprise about five percent of total homicides. And many of those are by battered women."

"How do you know all this?"

"I like to do research, remember?"

"Aren't far more men than women the victims of homicide though?"

"Yes, but the vast majority by other men, not by women." She looked away.

Lew sensed her outrage. He tried to think of something to ease it. "You do know, you're in no personal danger?"

She looked back at him. "Oh? How can I be sure of that?"

"What, you think I'm going to choke you to death?" He reached his hands out in jest like he might grab her neck.

At that moment the waiter arrived with their meals. He hesitated, looking askance at Lew. Then he turned to Violet. "Everything okay here, ma'am?"

She smiled. "Yes. It's just my friend here being a little overly dramatic."

"You're sure? I'd be glad to call someone if you need help."

"I'll keep an eye on him, give you a signal if he gets out of hand."

The waiter reluctantly set the plates down, looking suspiciously at Lew. He glanced back as he walked away.

Violet sat there with an innocent, demure expression.

"Are you pleased with yourself?" Lew said.

"Depends on how you behave the rest of the evening."

He shook his head. "Sometimes...."

"It *is* something that women live in far greater fear of than men," she said.

"Well, if you're really worried, I suppose I could come over and protect you tonight."

"That's a sneaky way to invite yourself over."

He raised his hands in a defensive gesture. "It's strictly an offer of support. Male chivalry."

She rolled her eyes. "Men."

He lifted his glass of wine, offering to clink with hers. "Shall we try our entrees?"

***

They were relaxing, with full stomachs, still sipping the last of the bottle of wine. The waiter had carefully removed their empty plates and silverware, and when he'd asked if they wanted dessert, had addressed Violet, not looking at Lew.

Violet had spoken kindly. "I think we'll pass on dessert. And my friend here" …she nodded toward Lew… "has, at least to my knowledge, never killed anyone."

The unsmiling waiter glanced briefly at Lew, nodded, and carried away their dishes.

Lew stared at her. "*At least to your knowledge?*"

"I have no idea what you might have done before I knew you."

He sighed, shaking his head. "Why do I put up with this?"

"Because you like me. Which I appreciate. And you'd like me less if I didn't give you a hard time now and then."

There was a pause. "So, to get back to reality, I wonder if the cops delivered the ransom money to the kidnappers as they demanded. It was due this evening."

"I suspect not," Violet said.

Lew frowned. "Why do you say that?"

"Because they would have had a very hard time doing so."

"What are you talking about?"

"I did a little research."

He stared at her in confusion.

"They asked for a million dollars in small bills, as I recall."

He nodded.

"Fives, tens, and twenties, to be specific."

"Yeah."

"To be delivered in a suitcase."

"Yes." Annoyance crept into his voice.

"A mile up a hiking trail."

"Okay, okay. What are you getting at?"

"Do you know how big a million dollars in that-sized bills would be?"

He frowned. "No."

"If put into one stack, it would be thirty-five feet high."

His eyes widened.

"And it would weigh two hundred and twenty pounds."

"Really?"

She nodded. "I believe I already pointed out the kidnappers were lousy spellers. They're also lousy mathematicians."

"Violet. That's amazing."

"It's just a matter of asking questions. You can learn damn near anything on the Internet these days."

"So what do you think happened?"

"I have no idea. The police must have figured this out when they tried to stuff that much money into a suitcase. Who knows what they did? But I *can* say, we're dealing with idiot kidnappers."

Lew looked at her with a touch of wonder. "Violet, you're amazing."

"Thank you. And invitation accepted."

One-eleven Prestige Place

They were relaxing on the couch, listening to Philip Glass's Tirol Concerto, eyes closed, lost in the intricate interwoven patterns, the left and right hand of the pianist never pausing, the orchestra providing complementary background. It was one of Lew's favorite modern compositions. He hated being interrupted while listening to it. It provided the most complete absorption of consciousness through a pleasurable sensory experience he knew of, short of making love. He was barely sentient when his cell phone rang. Like a harsh alarm.

He opened one eye. Noticed Violet's eyes were still closed.

It rang again.

Reluctantly he pulled the phone out of his pocket to see who it was, fearing a robo call. They were the one thing that might cause him to commit murder. It took a minute for him to focus clearly. It rang a third time.

Damn. Zane. He'd better answer it. He punched the green circle, standing to leave the room so Violet could continue listening.

"Zane."

"Yo. Sorry to call so late. Hope I didn't interrupt anything."

"What's up?"

"It seemed kind of important, Mr. T. I thought you'd want to know."

"Okay."

"It's that ransom note you forwarded."

Lew worked to get his mind back into the here and now. "Right. What about it?"

"First off, it was sent from a server at the high school."

"What? How do you know that?"

"The IP."

"What's the IP?"

"The Internet provider. It's the one the high school uses. I don't know anyone else in the region who uses it. It's only available to educational institutions."

"You're kidding."

"I am not kidding. And there's more."

He waited.

"It's a fake."

"What do you mean?"

"That picture of Mr. Campbell holding up the current issue of the *Sentinel*? The one the kidnappers sent? That picture has been photoshopped."

"How do you know *that*?"

"If you look at the very edge of the newspaper, where he's holding it, his fingers aren't there. You have to wrap your fingers around to the front of the paper, the camera side, to hold it up. You have to blow it up to see this."

"What?"

"They could place the current edition of the paper in the right position, but when they pasted it in, they had to cover up where his fingers were. When you blow it up, you can see there are no fingers there, just the edge of the newspaper. You can't hold up a newspaper that way. Look yourself. You'll see what I mean."

"Jesus."

"Also, if, again, you blow it up, and then look carefully in the lower right corner, you can just make out the corner of a desk. That's Mr. Campbell's desk at school."

"How do you know *that*?"

"It has a scar in the shape of a heart there, with initials inked in. Right where his desk did. I noticed it when I was in his class my freshman year."

"How did you figure all this out?"

"I just kept looking. Most people, when they scan a picture, begin looking in the upper left corner, like you'd read a book, then move down and to the right. But they usually end up just focusing on what's in the middle. I kept going."

"So they found a picture somewhere of Mr. Campbell holding up a newspaper, and pasted the current issue of the paper into it?"

"Exactly. I even know where they got the original picture."

Lew waited.

"Since it was somewhere they *could* find it, I figured it must be out there on the Internet. I didn't see anything in his emails with him holding up a newspaper, but it got me thinking. I remembered he'd sometimes use articles from the *Sentinel* in class to make a point or provoke a discussion. So I looked through old archives of the *Sentinel*, using Mr. Campbell's name to search. Sure enough. It's a picture that ran in the paper about three years ago, when he retired. There was a story about him and Mr. Palmer, who retired at the same time."

"Harve mentioned that. He's talked with Mr. Palmer."

"Well, that's the picture that ran with that article. Mr. Campbell must have been teaching a class, holding up the paper for the class to see."

"Zane. You're a genius!"

"Well…" Modest tone.

Lew's eye caught a movement. He glanced up. Violet was at the door, looking at him questioningly.

"Hey. I should go. But your paycheck just grew some more. This could be a big help."

"The money is nice, Mr. T, but that's not my main motive. I want this solved as much as anyone. I might have known that woman whose body they found up there. I don't want kidnappers or murderers running around here anymore than anyone else."

"Point taken."

"We still need to figure out what this leads to. I think that's your department. Let me know if there's anything else I can do to help."

"Right. And thanks!" He punched the red icon, clicking off.

He looked up at Violet, who was staring at him inquiringly.

Offices of the Sienna Sentinel

Lew walked into the newspaper conference room the next morning carrying a cup of coffee. He looked around at the assembled team, who looked back at him expectantly. The usual box of donuts was sitting in the middle of the table. Tim and Harve were licking their fingers. Lew bent over the box to see what they'd picked.

"Glazed?"

"That work for you, Lew?"

"I'll force myself." He reached in, picked one out, and sat down. "Seems we have some new developments," he said. "Where shall we start?"

"I can tell you what *I've* learned," Tim said.

Lew nodded.

"I talked with Gonzales again late yesterday. They have the blood analysis back from that tissue you found."

"And?"

"A positive. It's common. Over a third of Americans have it."

"Do they know Campbell's blood type."

"Yeah, they got that from school records. A positive. A match."

"They volunteered that?" Violet said.

"They're desperate. They're looking for help anywhere they can get it."

"Anyone heard where the money drop stands?" Harve asked.

Lew nodded toward Violet. "Want to share your thoughts on that?"

Violet sketched her analysis, how it wasn't possible to package a million dollars in small bills in anything like a suitcase.

Tim smiled. "Not exactly genius kidnappers. The cops were starting to prepare it when I talked to Gonzales late yesterday. They must have figured it out by now. I wonder what they did." He paused. "Another question for Tony."

"And that irresponsible character you like to demean also came up with something," Lew said. He sketched his conversation with Zane, the fact that the ransom note email came via the high school's server, and that the picture of Campbell holding up the current issue of the newspaper, the proof the kidnappers offered that they had him, was fake.

"Holy crap," Harve said.

"Yeah. It puts a new slant on things."

"Like maybe he wasn't actually kidnapped?"

"Violet and I talked about this," Lew said, not specifying when or where they'd talked. "Quite possibly. The ransom note came two weeks *after* Campbell's disappearance. Everyone knew about the disappearance by then. Meaning almost anyone could have decided this was a way to make some easy money, claiming to be the kidnappers, whether they were or not. So let's review the timeline again."

They waited.

"Campbell was here September first, when he got coffee at the cafe. He was someplace unknown on the second, but apparently not at home, since he didn't pick up his paper. And he flew to New York City on the third."

"If he wasn't kidnapped?" Tim said.

"Right. We don't actually know whether he was *on* that plane."

"So what are you saying?"

"I've been pondering this," Lew said. "We have a bunch of information we didn't have three days ago. A new theory has occurred to me."

"You have us on the edge of our seats," Tim said, a touch of sarcasm evident.

"It has occurred to me that maybe there's a whole different interpretation of the evidence. Suppose we turn this whole thing around. Suppose we start with the supposition that Campbell isn't the victim of this crime, he's the perpetrator. Doesn't it seem like an odd coincidence that two crimes happened at the same time in this little place, when one is rare?"

They looked at him in confusion.

"How about this: maybe *Campbell* wrote the ransom note."

"What?"

"Let's review the evidence. First, the flight to New York could be a get-away plan. He could go on to anywhere from there. Or just get lost in New York City. Who's going to track him down in a city of eight million people?"

"He knew those trails like the back of his hand," Harve said, seeing where Lew was going. "Palmer said he loved hiking up there, went all over the place. So he'd know a good place to stash a body."

"He'd also know how to use the school's Internet," Violet said, thinking in the same vein. "Now that we know the fake ransom note came via its IP."

"That kid is actually helping," Harve said. "That's amazing. He's good."

Lew looked at Tim. "Want to make a concession in this regard?"

Tim frowned. "Okay, I admit, that's helpful. But I'm still uneasy with the illegal nature of his efforts. That would not be a good thing for the paper if it got out."

"Who's going to tell anyone?"

Tim shook his head. "I don't know. It just makes me nervous."

"Anyway, to get back to the point, Campbell could have planted the whole kidnapping story as a diversion to throw people off the trail. And one other thing. I noticed when I was at his house that he had hiking clothes in the closet, but there were no hiking boots. I wondered why just his boots would be missing. It seems possible to me he needed those to get up that trail, but since he was flying to New York the next day, he didn't want to wear hiking clothes. People don't generally notice a person's shoes like they do other clothes that might look out of place on an airplane. No one would be likely to notice hiking boots."

"Lots of people wear those these days," Harve said.

"Wait a minute," Violet said. "You said you found notes about his flight to New York on his computer, Lew. Why would he leave them there where anyone who opened the computer would see them? If he's that clever, wouldn't he hide them?"

"I've had two thoughts about that," Lew said. "First, maybe it didn't occur to him that anyone would try to look at his computer. Or he simply forgot about it?"

"In which case he's not *so* clever," she said. "Shouldn't he have thought of it?"

"Maybe. But here's another thought. Maybe he left them there deliberately, thinking someone *would* find them."

"Why would he do that? Wouldn't he want to keep the trip secret?"

"Well, let's go through his thinking. He'd know the house would eventually be searched. And that someone would probably look at his computer. So if it looked like he was planning a trip, and wasn't trying to hide it, in effect it could be a kind of red herring. It would suggest he *wasn't* trying to hide anything."

"Jeez, I don't know," Harve said. "That feels like kind of a stretch. And another thing: don't most people take their computers with them on trips?"

"Maybe, I don't know. I'm just thinking out loud here, trying to see what theory best fits the evidence. But the thought I just expressed—the red herring bit—would fit leaving the computer itself here also. Or maybe he has a tablet he takes on trips. There are other possible explanations."

"What about his truck, Lew?" Tim said. "Wouldn't he need that to get to the airport?"

"Maybe. But again, there are possible explanations. Like airport shuttles? Maybe he took a shuttle to Sacramento and spent two nights in a motel near the airport. The truck could be another red herring to make it look like he'd been kidnapped."

There was a moment of silence as they considered all this. Finally, Tim spoke. "Here's another question. If he's the perpetrator of a fake kidnapping, with the motive of collecting half a million dollars, how is he planning to collect that if he's in New York City?"

They all stared at him.

"It's a good point, Tim," Lew said. "Maybe that's a stretch. But one part of this theory could be right, and not all of it."

"What do you mean?" Harve asked.

"Well, he might have killed the girl, for reasons we don't yet understand, and plotted his escape in advance, but not been part of the kidnapping ruse."

Again, they all sat and looked at each other, in obvious confusion.

"So how are we going to resolve this?" Tim said. "Have you thought about what evidence could tip this one way or the other, Lew?"

"I'm working on that," Lew said. "I'm particularly interested in two things. First, was he on that plane? If he was, then he obviously wasn't kidnapped."

"What's the other?"

"The girl's blood type."

At that instant Tim's cell phone rang. He looked at the screen. He mouthed "Gonzales." He clicked it on. "Hello, Tony."

"Uh huh." Pause.

Okay. Thanks. Oh, before you go?" Pained look.

"Damn. He hung up. I wanted to ask him about whether they delivered the ransom."

What's her blood type?" Lew said.

"They don't know."

"Why not?"

"It's almost impossible to get an accurate blood test two weeks after death. The blood has decomposed."

"Oh. Damn."

"They might get it eventually from a DNA analysis, but that's going to take longer."

They stared at each other. No one said anything for several moments. Then Tim spoke, with a tone of concern. "I'm uneasy about something. The cops are now being quite open with us. And we have evidence they don't, which is not only relevant to the case but obviously important. Don't we have an obligation to share what we know with them?" He paused, looking around.

Harve nodded. "Good point. If for no other reason, we could be charged with a crime if we don't."

They all nodded, realizing Tim had a point. And who knew, maybe it *could* speed the investigation. There was always a chance that whoever had killed the young woman was still out there, a serial killer.

The last thing any of them wanted was to slow down solving this thing.

The Sienna Police Station

The six of them sat around the police station's conference table: John, Tony, Tim, Harve, Violet, and Lew. This was not Lew's favorite thing. He viewed the men in blue as impediments, complicating his own efforts with their yellow tape, withholding of information, and rules about what he could and couldn't do. Of course he ignored most of them, but still. After some brief expressions of gratitude on both sides, John said, "So, do you want to go first, or shall we?"

"Either is fine, John," Tim said. "But I'm wondering, before we start, since it may bear on what we know, have you identified the young woman yet?"

John nodded to Tony.

"Just a little while ago. From dental records." Tony paused, sighing. "It's sad. She dropped out of Sienna High School several years ago, was living in a homeless camp in the forest with several other young people. We've now confirmed with them that she disappeared a couple of weeks ago. Apparently it's not unusual for those folks to come and go, so they didn't think anything about it."

"What's her name," Tim asked.

"Trixie Lawson."

"How old was she?"

"Twenty-two."

"Relatives?"

"None alive, at least that we've been able to locate. Apparently her mom died a few years ago of a drug overdose…a couple of her homeless friends knew… and we're looking for her father, who as far as they know disappeared a long time ago. Since the mother kept her maiden name, Lawson, we don't even have a name for him, so we're not holding out a lot of hope of finding him."

"Siblings?"

"Not that her friends knew of. We're trying to get in touch with a couple of her old teachers to see if they know."

"That's a tough story," Tim said. "You probably don't want that in the paper, do you?"

"Actually, we think it might help to put her name out there, see who turns up who knew her and might offer more information."

Tim nodded. "Okay. We can do that."

"Are you conducting an autopsy?" Lew asked.

"*Yeess.*" John's tone suggested he resented being taken for an idiot.

"When do you expect those results?"

"The body had been there for about two weeks. It was about a hundred feet off the trail, partially covered with dirt and leaves. Under the best of circumstances, after two weeks there's a limited amount of information you *can* get. And those aren't the best of circumstances. It's not clear how much we'll learn, maybe something from hair analysis or the cerebrospinal fluid, which typically lasts longer than blood and other tissues. The coroner has a good forensic guy, but it will take a while."

Lew nodded. "Not a pretty picture."

"No dead bodies are, but after two weeks it's more than most people can stomach."

"What trail was it?"

"We're not putting that information out until we finish our investigation."

"Why not?"

"We don't want people going up there and mucking up what little evidence we have. Like footprints."

"I just thought I might see if I could add anything to the picture."

John scowled. "You have to keep it quiet if we tell you."

"Understood."

He sighed, rolling his eyes. "It's the old Pembrook Trail. Doesn't get used a lot."

"Thanks, John. I didn't mean to question your work; I'm just trying to think how we might help to figure this out."

"As are we." His tone remained irritated.

"Any progress locating Campbell?"

Tony shook his head. "We're nowhere on that. He seems to have simply vanished."

Tim nodded to Lew, suggesting he share what they knew.

"Maybe not," Lew said. "We have a possible lead. And a theory."

John and Tony stared at him inquiringly.

Lew sketched the series of clues that had led them to think the two crimes might be linked: the sequence of events from September first to September third; Campbell's after-school and evening activities with high school students, including upper class girls; the flight reservation; his missing hiking boots; his knowledge of the trails in the Tahoe National Forest; and the fake ransom note.

Both officers were gawking at him openly. "How did you learn all *that*?" Christiansen said.

"We talked to a waitress at the coffee shop he visited mornings, who remembered the last morning he was there: September first. According to his neighbor, the first newspaper that *wasn't* picked up at his house was September second's. The neighbor also mentioned there had been rumors related to his inviting students to his house for extra help. The flight reservation came from a web search. His hiking boots were missing from his closet. The ransom note can be seen to be fake under close inspection. The current issue of the paper that Campbell is holding up that accompanied the ransom note was photoshopped in. That picture of Campbell is from three years ago."

They sat there staring at him. Finally Tony spoke: "The ransom note is a fake?"

"Blow it up. Take a close look. There are no fingers holding the paper where they should be."

He looked at Lew in confusion.

"The picture of Campbell came from a story we ran about his retirement three years ago. Apparently he sometimes used stories in the *Sentinel* as props in his teaching. The current issue of the paper was photoshopped in."

"Goddamn."

"There's also the fact you can't package a million dollars in small bills in a suitcase", Violet added. "Which you must have figured out?"

Tony nodded. "Yeah. That's a shitwad of money."

"So what did you do?"

"We got a steamer trunk and crammed it to the gills. It weighed a ton, so we used a motorized dolly to get it up there. Even then it took two of us, and over an hour."

"So you did actually deliver it?"

"We figured the kidnappers just hadn't thought out how much money that would be, but that we didn't really have a choice if we wanted to save Campbell."

"Do you know what's happened to it?" she asked.

"No. The note was clear we couldn't track it without putting Campbell's life in danger, so we haven't."

"So it might still be there?"

Tony frowned. "I suppose."

"Assuming whoever wrote the ransom note hasn't spirited it away by now," Tim said. "You might want to send someone up there to check."

John nodded to Tony. "Let's put someone on that."

"Have you told anyone where you put the money?" Lew asked.

John scowled, looking at Tony.

"No," Tony said. "Well, except for the guy who put up the half million. We figured we owed him that much, since he was being so generous."

"Is it the same trail as where her body was found?"

"Yeah, as a matter of fact. Why?"

"No reason, just trying to assemble all the facts I can. Did the big donor know that?"

Tony scowled. "I think I mentioned it to him. Again, he's an ally."

"But you don't want to tell us who it is?"

"He asked us not to. He's a private kind of guy, said he doesn't want people giving him credit for something anyone should do."

"Stand up guy," Lew said.

John nodded. "Yeah. Which brings up the question, how did you know Campbell's hiking boots were missing?"

Lew sighed. "Okay. Confession time. I searched Campbell's house."

Christiansen's tone became stern "That's illegal. We had yellow tape around the house. It's a possible crime scene."

Lew nodded. "Sorry. I violated your yellow tape. But it was for a good cause: I wanted to help solve this, and I needed to see what I could see there."

"Tony had already searched the house. We knew what was there."

"Except for the missing hiking boots. And the notes on his computer about exploring a flight somewhere. And the bloody tissue."

"Exactly where did you find that?"

"Stuffed under the hedge that runs along the front sidewalk."

"So…Campbell could have murdered her right there," he said.

"Possibly," Lew said.

"She might have threatened to report him, so he killed her to shut her up. Took her body up to the forest to hide it. Then disappeared so we couldn't catch him. And sent the fake ransom note to cover his tracks."

"Seems possible," Lew said.

"One god-damned shrewd son-of-a-bitch."

An Old Cedar Bungalow

In stark contrast to the dinner at Valentino's the previous evening, Lew had fixed himself a sandwich and heated a can of soup for dinner, accompanied by his third gin and tonic. He was sitting in his den, studying his notes and pouring over the latest information, trying to find something he'd overlooked that might provide new leads. Earl was camped out on his lap, a loud purr vibrating down his legs. Having just had dinner, he was at his happiest.

He was studying the considerably lengthened list of questions he had and who might help answer them when his phone rang. He looked at the screen: a number he didn't recognize.

"Hello."

"Mr. Travis."

The voice sounded familiar, but it took him a second to recognize it. Then it came to him. "Hi, Peggie."

"Hi."

"How are you doing?"

"I'm okay. And I think I've found what you were looking for."

"What's that?"

"Don's blood type. It was in an old folder he kept from his time in the army. I guess they type the blood of all recruits in case they might need a transfusion. It's on their dog tags and ID cards. He still has those."

"I didn't know that."

"I didn't either. But I just thought to check, and there it was."

"So?"

"A positive."

"A positive?" Lew struggled to keep the surprise out of his voice.

"Is that...not what you were expecting?"

He worked to keep his tone even. "I didn't know what to expect."

"I guess it's kind of common?"

"A little over a third of Americans have it."

"So does that help you?"

"It may. There are a lot of clues piling up. But it might be very helpful. Thanks for getting it."

"I just want to get this thing cleared up. I tried to ask him again how he got that cut—it was more of a deep scratch. I got a look at it after he took the bandage off—and he still won't tell me. He seems embarrassed by whatever it is."

"A deep scratch?"

"Yeah, it had those uneven edges you get from a scratch, it didn't look like it was from a knife or anything."

"Okay. That might be helpful too."

"I read about that young woman's body they found up there. I just can't believe he'd do anything that crazy. Plus I don't think he had time. Although I don't really know how long he was out that night. Are you getting any closer to figuring this out?"

Lew hesitated. "Not really. There are a lot of possibilities. But every bit of new information helps. I really appreciate you letting me know this."

"I can't tell you how worried I am. He was always such a good man. And he still is." Her voice broke slightly. "It's just that damn accident."

"I understand, Peggie. I'll let you know when we do have an answer. There are still lots of possibilities. Let's not worry too much until we know more."

She sighed. "That's not easy."

"I know. But if you do learn anything more, can you let me know?"

"Yeah. I hope you figure it out soon."

"So do we all."

There was a click. Lew sat there, trying to process this new information. What was the likelihood of two A positive blood tests, Campbell's, and now Thompson's? One-third by one-third: one ninth. Regardless, it left Don Thompson and Rob Campbell as equally likely to be responsible for it. Did the scratch tell him anything? It could have come from a struggle, especially with a woman, whose fingernails could cause that kind of cut. He wondered where the cops were in learning what Trixie Lawson's blood type had been. That would answer one question: whether it *could* be hers. But if it was male, it wouldn't determine whether it was Campbell's or Thompson's. Or for that matter, someone else's.

He tried to picture a struggle going on where he'd found the tissue on Campbell's front sidewalk. Resulting in an attempt to stanch the blood with that tissue. Which, as he thought about it, wasn't very much blood, really. He tried to put this together with the place her body had been found, a mile up a sometimes-steep trail. Which would have required a serious carry. Were either of them capable of that?

As he contemplated this, it all seemed somehow improbable. Both were pretty old men, and carrying a woman up a mile-long trail? Even if she weren't very big, she would probably have weighed one hundred and twenty pounds. It just didn't seem likely.

Which triggered an ah ha moment. He hit his forehead with the palm of his hand. It wasn't going to be Trixie Lawson's blood on that tissue, for a reason he should have long since realized. It was a related fact that he'd failed to relate. He shook his head in disgust— at himself.

The newspaper article reporting the discovery of Trixie Lawson's body had mentioned there was evidence of a struggle where her body had been found. If she was putting up a struggle there, in the forest, she *couldn't* have been killed outside Campbell's house. Meaning whoever's blood it was on that tissue, it couldn't be hers.

He was pondering this thought when the phone rang. This time he recognized the number.

"Zane."

"Hi, Mr. T."

"What's up?"

"Two things I thought you'd want to know. First, I just read the bulletin in the *Sentinel*. About the identity of the girl's body they found up there."

"Right."

"I knew that girl."

"Really?"

"Not well. She was a senior when I was a freshman. She was older."

"She would have been, I guess. Twenty-two. How old are you?"

"Eighteen. I graduate next June."

"That's four years, not three."

A pause. "Is that math you learned in college, Mr. T?"

Wiseass kid. "Kindergarten." He heard a chuckle.

"I think she had to go back for a fourth year. She'd missed a bunch of credits."

"Oh."

"How did you know her?"

"She was hard to miss…a woman among girls, you might say. She was no kid, even then."

"Really."

"She was also a good athlete. She played on the women's basketball team, and she was good. Kind of a roughneck, she was what they sometimes call an enforcer in hockey. You didn't mess with her on the court."

"Didn't know you were a sports fan, Zane."

"I'm not, really. But that team was good. They were fun to watch."

"Okay. Anything else about her you remember?"

"She was attractive, no question, but she seemed kind of tired, worn down. Like someone who even at that age had had a tough life. I felt kind of sorry for her."

"Living in a homeless camp in the forest would seem to confirm that impression."

"Yeah, she was kind of a sad case. But the main thing I wanted to tell you was that I'm pretty sure she was in Mr. Campbell's class."

"Oh?"

"Yeah. I remember seeing her coming out of his classroom once with tears in her eyes. I got the sense she'd talked to him about something difficult."

"Like what?"

"No idea. He was a supportive teacher. I think a lot of kids talked with him about their personal problems."

"You mean confided in him?"

"Yeah."

"Do you know anything else about her?"

"Not really. Like I said, I was just a freshman. But I did wonder about her sometimes. It's a sad thing, her death."

"That it is."

"Did you say there were two things, Zane?"

"Yeah. I got to thinking about the transmission of the ransom note. Those sometimes have clues in them."

"Like?"

"You remember I said this one came from the high school's IP address. Which would seem to implicate someone there, a teacher or student."

"I've been thinking about that."

"Well, it's actually not that simple."

"Why?"

"It came from an email address created by Hotmail. Which is a way of avoiding using a name, keeping an email anonymous. But it often includes the IP address of the sender's computer in the header. And that can give you an approximate geographic location of the sender. To see the sender's IP address, you have to select 'more info' and then 'show original', which has a bunch of numbers separated by periods."

"You're starting to lose me, Zane."

"Sorry. Here's the point. The IP address through which the ransom note came was located at the high school. But that's not where it originated."

"What?"

"As a student, I'm on that network a lot, so I know it well. And there are times when it can be accessed remotely. Meaning someone can log in and use it from afar, making it *look* like an email came via the high school's IP. I don't know why, maybe so teachers can use it evenings. Anyway, studying that ransom note email, I realized that was the case. So I tracked it back to the IP address where it had *actually* originated. I couldn't pinpoint the exact spot, but I could see the approximate location where it came from."

"What do you mean by 'approximate'?"

"Maybe a quarter mile radius. Not the precise building, but near it."

"Which was where?"

"Over on Sycamore Street. You know, that high-rent neighborhood?"

"Sycamore Street? That rings a bell."

"Whoever it was, that's where it came from."

"Interesting, indeed. Good work."

"It just popped into my head to track it. I got lucky."

"Well, you got lucky using skills not many people have."

"You always say that. Anyone who knows what I do could have done it."

"Which isn't very many people."

"Maybe." He paused. When he spoke again his voice had a slightly raspier tone. "Like I said, I want this solved, just like everybody else. This is *not* okay."

"I appreciate that, Zane. And I couldn't agree more. Somehow we need to figure it out. This could really help. Thanks."

"No problem. Hope you figure it out soon. This is wearing."

"I'm doing my best. Hey, take care of that girlfriend of yours, eh?"

"Not letting her go on any hikes up there in the forest, I can tell you that."

Lew pushed the red spot and heard the line click dead. He sat there contemplating this new information. Earl was still purring on his lap. He glanced at the empty glass of gin and tonic, decided he could use one more.

The Sienna Sentinel

The *Sienna Sentinel* ran the following lead story in the top right column of the front page on the morning of Thursday, September nineteenth, under the headline, "Student Accuses Campbell of Having an Affair with Her".

A recent graduate of Sienna High School, Sherry Wingate, today charged that Robert Campbell had an affair with her when she was a student at the high school. She asserted to this newspaper, and through it to the Sienna Police, that they had frequent 'trysts' during her senior year when she was in his English class. She says some of these were on hikes with him on weekends in the Tahoe National Forest, and some at his home evenings when she went there for 'help'.

Wingate asserts that Campbell frequently invited upper class students to his house after school and evenings with the purported excuse of providing help to struggling students. While he did provide such help to some, not all were innocent encounters. She said she can provide proof of these through recordings she made while

with him, unknown to Campbell, and
pictures of Campbell in partially
undressed states while drinking
with her.

This adds a new element to the
disappearance of Robert Campbell.
As does the discovery yesterday of
a young woman's body near a trail in
the Tahoe National Forest east of
Sienna, as reported in yesterday's
edition of this paper. That woman
has been identified as Trixie
Lawson, who apparently had been
living in a homeless camp in the
Tahoe National Forest.

Police are now seeking
information on Lawson's background
and relatives, and are asking anyone
who has any such information to be
in touch with them. They are also
now asking that any other past or
current students who were in
Campbell's class come forward and
share any other examples of
inappropriate behavior on his part.

A picture of Trixie Lawson accompanied the article, taken from
the high school yearbook. She was strikingly beautiful, with strong
features, long dark hair, bold eyes, lean cheeks, and dramatic eye
shadow and lipstick. It conveyed a sense of worldly experience and
maturity beyond her years.

A second article ran in the top left column of the front page under
the headline, "Still No Sign of Robert Campbell".

The kidnappers of Robert Campbell
promised to release him if their
million-dollar ransom demand was
met in forty-eight hours. A wealthy
Sienna resident, to whom the ransom

note was sent, generously put up half this amount, and countless smaller contributions came in from other citizens, allowing police to reach this goal in the nick of time. So just before time ran out members of the Sienna Police Department deposited the full million dollars in the location specified by the kidnappers.

However, as of this morning, now more than thirty hours since that drop was made, there is still no sign of Campbell, even though the ransom note specified that he'd be released within twenty-four hours of receipt of the money. A reporter who talked with the lead investigator in this case, Tony Gonzales, explained that there are three possible explanations for this:

1) The kidnappers still hold Campbell and are planning to demand more money.

3) They killed him despite their promise to release him, to protect themselves from detection.

3) The ransom note was a fake, perhaps sent by someone trying to benefit from Campbell's disappearance, and bears no relation to that disappearance.

Deputy Gonzales said that police are now pursuing investigations in all three directions. They have sent a party into the Tahoe National Forest to search the area where the money was left. They are also following up clues that they say have emerged about Campbell's possible departure from the area. While Sergeant Gonzales would not go into detail, he said that it involved possible evidence that Campbell had taken flight.

This could offer a new theory about Campbell's disappearance: that it was due not to his having been kidnapped, but as a way to escape law enforcement after an altercation with the deceased. Gonzales said they may have evidence that implicates him and are trying to determine whether he did leave the area. He said they will keep the public informed as they pursue these leads.

The Coffee Roasters

It had been another rough morning. Her alarm clock had screwed up again, come on with only a light wash of static instead of the station she'd left it on. She'd awakened just in time to toast a couple Pop-Tarts before rushing out the door, her makeup barely on and her lipstick a little uneven. She looked in the rear-view mirror as she careened down the street, trying to wipe clear the slight smear around her lips.

The place was as busy as usual as she hurried through the back entrance, only to encounter Sam in an obviously foul mood. He was trying to save a pile of home fries from becoming scorched while he dealt with a dozen eggs in various states of readiness. His dark glance propelled her into the front where Velma was hurrying from table to table trying to keep up with new orders and coffee refills.

Crystal grabbed her order pad and plunged into the morass, taking orders from three tables of waiting customers. It was an hour before things settled down enough for her to take a deep breath as she cleared two of the last tables of dirty dishes and refilled the coffee in two others where late customers lingered.

When she finally had a chance to take a break and look at the morning paper, things only got worse. Her expression grew progressively darker as she read first about the accusations of the young woman claiming she had had an affair with Robert Campbell while she was in high school. Then about the fact Campbell's whereabout were still unknown more than a day after the ransom had been delivered. And finally that the police were now viewing Campbell as a possible suspect in the death of Trixie Lawson.

Velma sat down on the stool next to her and sighed. "Wow. That was quite a rush."

Crystal glanced at her, waiting for the comment about arriving late. "I'm sorry, Velma. I know it's starting to sound suspicious, but my damn radio alarm clock screwed up again. It won't stay on a station from when I set it at night until it goes off in the morning. Just static. I'm ready to toss the damn thing in the garbage."

"Why don't you use your cell phone?"

Crystal stared at her. "What do you mean?"

"Cell phones have alarms. They're always dependable."

"Really?"

Velma nodded.

"Jeez. Who can keep up with this stuff. Okay, I'll try that. If Sam doesn't fire me before I get the chance."

"Sam's not going to fire you."

"You didn't see the look on his face when I came in."

"He was under a lot of pressure. I'll talk to him. You'll be okay."

Crystal sighed. "Thanks. You're a pal."

"We old broads have to stick together."

Crystal nodded toward the front page of the paper, lying on the counter in front of them. "Have you read that?"

Velma sighed. "It just makes no sense. None of it."

"I doubt the cops have anything solid on him. I think they're just grasping at straws."

"Sounds like they have a lot of straws. An affair with a high school girl in his class? Evidence that would implicate him. Disappearing at the time Lawson was killed?"

"It said *might* implicate him, not that it did. And they don't know whether he left the area. They have no proof of anything."

"Maybe not, but you have to admit, it doesn't look good."

"There has to be a different explanation."

"Like?"

Crystal lowered her head into her hands, sighing. For several moments. She looked entirely woebegone. Then she slowly raised her head again, with a different look in her eyes.

Velma glanced at her. "What?"

"I bet it's a scam!"

Velma looked at her with skepticism. "What do you mean?"

"I bet someone pretending to be Rob made that airplane reservation. Somebody trying to frame him."

Velma frowned at her. "Why would someone do that?"

"As a way of throwing off the cops! Whoever has him wants them to think he's escaped to cover up *their* crime."

Velma cocked her head. "You really think that's possible?"

"It seems a lot more likely to me than Rob killing someone and flying off to escape."

Velma nodded. "You got a point there."

"I bet the cops would never think of it!" She looked at Velma with wide eyes. "Maybe we should tell them."

Velma frowned. "We don't actually *know* anything."

"Neither do they."

Velma sighed. "You have a point. But I don't know about going to the cops."

"Hey, they don't know Rob Campbell. They don't know what an impossible thing it would be for him to kill someone. *We* know Rob Campbell."

Velma nodded. "True. But I'm not comfortable talking to the cops. What if we're wrong?"

"How could we be wrong?"

"Well, for one thing, you have to present a picture ID to get on an airplane."

"It didn't say anything about getting on a plane, just making a flight reservation."

"Are you saying you think they killed Rob, or still have him kidnapped?"

"I don't know. Could be either. I'm just saying Rob Campbell didn't kill Trixie Lawson."

Velma sighed. "I admit, that doesn't seem likely." She paused, frowning. "Okay, Crystal. Talk to the cops if you want to. I just don't think I want to be involved."

"You chickening out?"

"I'm just not the type to talk to cops. About anything."

"But you think I have a point?"

Velma nodded, spoke hesitantly. "Yeah. I can't make it seem real that Rob Campbell killed someone. But do we really know him all that well?"

"You think I'm jumping to conclusions?"

"I don't know, Crystal. It's a tough one."

"Well, you might be right about going to the cops. But if they find him and arrest him and charge him with murder, I'm going in."

"Okay. If it gets to that, I'll go with you."

There was the tinkle of a bell over the entrance as a new customer walked in. They glanced at each other.

"I'll get it," Crystal said. "Least I can do after getting in late."

The Offices of the Sienna Sentinel

The clock on the wall of the conference room read eight-forty-five. Lew sat there by himself, sipping on a cup of coffee and nibbling on a donut. A cardboard urn of coffee and box of donuts sat in the middle of the table.

The next to arrive was Violet. She stopped in the doorway, a look of shock on her face. "Do my eyes deceive me?"

Lew glanced at his watch, then at her. He cleared his throat. "Have a nice sleep?"

"Excuse me. I think I've entered the wrong reality." She turned and left.

About thirty seconds later she reappeared, this time accompanied by Tim. They both stood in the doorway, staring in at Lew, still sipping on his coffee and nibbling his donut.

"It *looks* like him," Tim said.

He felt his head, then feigned taking his pulse. "I seem to still be conscious and aware."

Harve appeared behind them. "Is there a problem?" he said. Then he glanced into the room. "Oh. My. God."

"Do you think we should try touching it, see if it's a hologram?" Violet said.

Lew looked at them. "Are you all having a good time over there? We do have a serious matter to deal with here."

They walked in cautiously, staring at him, and took places around the table.

"Did your alarm go off early or something?" Tim said.

"As it happens, I've been putting some thought into our situation. I had a little trouble sleeping. Which none of you seem to have experienced."

Harve looked into the box of donuts, took one, examined it.

"Jelly-filled, in case you're curious," Lew said.

"Are there any kinds of donuts you *don't* like, Lew?"

He ignored the question and turned to Tim. "You been in touch with the men in blue?"

"I have. Tony called last evening. He wanted to let me know that they were surveying motels near the Sacramento airport to see whether Campbell had stayed there on the night of either September first or second. They're also checking with American Airlines to see if he was *on* that flight September third."

"Will airlines reveal that?" Violet asked.

"Not to just anyone, no. Passenger lists are considered protected. But if there is a legitimate reason, they'll usually cooperate. Being part of a police investigation qualifies."

"That will obviously be helpful," Lew said. "If he was on that flight, at least it will tell us he wasn't kidnapped."

"I think they're relieved they have an actual lead to work on," Tim said.

Lew turned to Harve. "Anything new on your part?"

"There's one thing. I don't know if it will help, but I've seen that girl who was killed, Trixie Lawson. It took me a while to remember where, but it finally came to me."

"Where?"

"One Mile Down, that bar."

"Hitting the dive bars alone again, Harve?"

"Who said I was alone?"

"Oh. Anything you want to share?"

"No."

Harve had hinted once or twice lately that he kind of wanted to find someone to settle down with, now that he was approaching forty. He had gone out with a lot of women over the years. Lew suspected that, despite his hints, he kind of liked his bachelor status. Or maybe he was just picky.

"To get to the point," Harve said, "Trixie Lawson was there with some older guy who was buying her drinks."

"When was this?"

"Maybe a month ago."

"Do you know who it was?"

"He looked vaguely familiar, but I'm not sure. He certainly

didn't seem to have trouble affording drinks. The young woman was laughing at his jokes, kind of hanging on him, and he seemed to be liking it. They were having a good time."

"Kind of fits with what we know about her," Lew said. "It would be nice to know who the man was."

"I have this sense it was someone who's been in the news," Harve said.

"I have a thought," Violet said. "Give me a minute." She pulled her computer out of a brief case and opened it up, began typing. They watched her, no idea what she was doing.

"Is this related to what we're discussing, or are you buying some perfume on Amazon?" Lew said.

She looked up with an annoyed expression. "I'm doing a little search. It's a long shot, but give me a minute." She looked back down and typed some more. Waited a moment. Hit the enter key. Waited another moment. Then smiled and turned the computer around so Harve could see it. "The man buying drinks for Trixie Lawson wasn't by any chance this guy, was he?"

Harve stared at the computer screen, his face blank at first, then his eyes widened, he leaned in closer and studied it. "My god."

"Who is it?" Tim asked.

Violet nodded to Harve. "Tell them."

He looked up, his expression dumbfounded. "Hendrik Hyde."

She smiled. "I couldn't think of who else from this little place might have been in the news."

"He's the guy who received the ransom note," Tim said. "What a coincidence."

"Maybe," Lew said, his tone thoughtful.

"What does that mean?"

Lew was frowning. "Hyde is having drinks with a woman who a couple weeks later is killed. Someone living in a homeless camp and hanging on him, guzzling drinks, laughing at his jokes. Does that feel like a complete coincidence?"

Tim looked at him inquiringly. "Isn't it kind of a stretch to go from that to…." He let the thought linger.

"Maybe," he mused, "he got tired of her hanging around his neck? Someone he picked up in a bar who then wouldn't leave him alone. He has a reputation as a heartless bastard."

"You're suggesting Hendrik Hyde *killed* Trixie Lawson?" Tim said. His voice was tinged with skepticism.

"It's probably a stretch. It just seems like an unlikely coincidence."

"Where does Hyde live?" Harve asked.

"What's that got to do with anything?" Tim asked.

"Just curious. I have a vague sense…"

"Let's find out," Violet said. She began typing away on her computer again. Waited. Looked up. "One Sycamore Street."

Harve nodded. "I thought so. That upscale neighborhood with all the mansions."

"Makes sense," Tim said.

Lew spoke, nodding slowly. "Okay, guys. I need to share something else with you."

They looked at him, waiting.

"I learned something interesting about the ransom note," he said. "Where it actually came from."

"What?" Tim said. "I thought it came from the high school Internet Provider."

"It came *via* that IP. But it originated somewhere on or near Sycamore Street."

"How do you know *that*?"

Lew sketched his conversation with Zane, explaining the line of logic Zane had used to track the ransom note's origin.

"Hyde is the guy who *received* the ransom note," Violet said.

Lew nodded.

"Are you suggesting he sent it to himself?"

Lew shrugged. "I don't know. But it seems possible, doesn't it?"

"Why would he do that?" Harve said. "I don't follow the logic. Didn't he put up half the money to *pay* the ransom. Why would he cost himself half a million dollars?"

"A good question," Lew said.

The Tahoe National Forest

Lew stopped to get his breath. He was in good shape for a seventy-two-year-old man, but the hike up the trail was taxing. It curved left and right around granite outcroppings, followed grades that were sometimes steep, all the while winding through stands of firs, pines, and aspens. The aspens were just beginning to turn a soft yellow.

Aspens are interesting trees. They're related to poplars, part of the same genus, along with cottonwoods. People often confuse them with birch trees, which are not of the same genus. A distinguishing difference is that birch tree bark peels back like paper, whereas aspen bark doesn't. Often called quaking aspens because of the way their leaves rustle in the wind, they're the most widely distributed trees in North America, growing from Alaska to Mexico. But perhaps their most interesting feature is the fact that any given stand all grows from the same root system, meaning they're all genetically identical. Large stands of aspens are among the largest living things on the planet.

Lew had taken his cell phone with him, which tracked distances. He pulled it out to see how far he'd come. It read nine-tenths of a mile; he must be close to the money drop spot. He resumed his trek, looking ahead for the redwood tree with the large gouge in the trunk. As he came around a bend, there it was.

He slowed his pace as he approached and began looking down at the trail for signs of boot prints. In the rocky sections there was nothing discernable. The ground was dry from not being rained on for months. But that meant there were patches where the dirt was loose, almost sandy. There it was possible to detect boot prints.

Lew reached the scarred tree and stood studying the ground around it. There were lots of boot tracks, of several varieties. Most were partial or smudged. But the most obvious tracks were those from a set of tires off to one side of the tree. Not from a full-sized car or truck, which would be impossible to get in there, but from something the size of an ATV. In fact, there were two different types of such tracks, one an aggressive style that would be useful for off-track recreational purposes, and a second made of simple parallel lines. These followed in the tracks of the first, suggesting a trailer being pulled by an ATV.

As Lew tried to imagine what they were doing there, it suddenly dawned on him. Tony had said the steamer trunk was heavy, Violet's calculations suggesting over two hundred pounds. It would have been too much for even two men to carry very far. But an ATV with a trailer would work perfectly. It was an obvious way to carry away a trunk containing a million dollars in small bills.

With this ah-hah insight Lew turned his attention to the boot prints. He knew the cops had been there, which would account for some of them, including the two officers that had dropped off the trunk using the motorized dolly. Plus whoever had picked it up. Plus it was possible there were prints from ordinary hikers, even though it was not a heavily-used trail. As he tried to sort out the mass of treads, it became apparent it was going to be nearly impossible to come up with a clear picture.

As he was ready to give up, a thought came to him. He pulled out his cell phone and began taking pictures of the better-defined prints. He could spend as much time as he wanted studying them at home to see if he could discern any clearer patterns.

After getting as many shots as seemed practical, he tried to think what more he could do. Might there be boot prints further away from the tree that could provide a clue? How could he look in a systematic way? Just going off in any random direction wouldn't help; the forest spread out in every direction endlessly.

He decided the only way to do this systematically was to walk in concentric circles, just a few feet apart, gradually moving away from the tree. It took a while—he walked slowly so he could search carefully. This went on for half an hour, after which time his legs and neck were tired from walking and looking down. And, unfortunately, he hadn't found anything that provided any actual clues; there was just a morass of boot prints near the tree that thinned as you got further away.

He sat down on a stump and considered whether there were other things he should do while up here. An obvious one came to mind: where did the ATV tracks lead? He had no idea how far he'd have to track them to find out, but what the hell, it wasn't like he had a lot of other things on his schedule.

He started off through the woods, following the tracks this way and that as they wove through the stands of trees. They weren't hard to track, having left imprints where there was soft earth and sometimes over twigs that had been crushed.

He'd been walking for about ten minutes when he noticed a clearing ahead. He approached it slowly, looking around to be sure he was alone. Soon it became obvious what it was: a forest service road. They ran through many parts of the forest, a way for forest rangers and others to clear deadwood and have access if there was a fire.

Lew reached the road and studied the pattern of tracks there. Again there were several types of boot treads, some probably from the cops who must have done what he was doing, plus whomever had made off with the trunk. The ATV tracks came to a stop a little way into the road, at which point larger tracks began. Probably the point where the ATV and its trailer had been loaded onto a larger trailer, pulled by a full-sized vehicle.

He walked along the road a little way, following these wider tracks, which again revealed a more aggressive set, presumably the vehicle pulling the trailer, and the parallel lines of the trailer tires. There were no footprints beyond where the larger tracks began.

Having satisfied himself he'd figured out how the trunk had been removed, Lew headed back to the redwood tree. Once again, he stopped to consider his options. He remembered that the notice in the paper had mentioned that the place where Trixie Lawson's body had been found was not very far from here. He didn't know exactly what 'not very far' meant—a hundred yards or several miles—but decided to head further up the trail to see if he could find it.

He'd been hiking another ten minutes when he saw some yellow tape marking off an area a little way to one side of the trail. He walked to the edge of it and studied the ground. Once again there were several varieties of boot treads. Lew got out his camera and took pictures. In doing so, he noticed that there was one set smaller than the others, presumably those of Trixie Lawson.

He walked around the periphery of the taped area, studying the ground inside and outside the tape. There were several spots where the ground had been dug up or twigs and branches were broken and scattered. These seemed to confirm that there had indeed been a struggle here.

He decided to repeat the broader search he'd done below, using the concentric circle system. Again he spent a half an hour at this, and again noticed nothing unusual. He was about to give up when his eye caught something tiny poking out from under a log. He leaned down for a closer look: a burnt matchstick. Apparently someone had stopped to light a match.

He studied the dirt around the matchstick and noticed some lighter dust-like substance: ashes. He squatted and looked under the log. Sure enough, a cigarette stub. Someone had stopped here to have a smoke, far enough from the body no one would be likely to notice. He poked the stub out with a stick, then, being careful not to touch it, flipped it into a small plastic bag he'd brought. He put it in his jacket pocket, noticing the stub had no filter.

Realizing this might be a useful clue, Lew studied the ground around the log for footprints. If he could find clear ones here it would link the cigarette smoker to his boots. While this might not be definitive—anyone could have come here for a rest and a smoke—it might be useful. Most of the ground was covered with layers of soft needles, making it hard to find clear imprints, but as he looked carefully, he could just make out two well-defined partial prints. He got out his camera and snapped pictures of them. Then he started back for the taped area.

Tired now from what had been two hours of walking and searching, Lew decided to head back down the trail. Forty minutes later he reached the trailhead. There was Old Blue waiting for him. He climbed in, leaned back, and took a deep breath.

A thought came to him: he had not seen one other person the whole time he'd been there. It was a Thursday, and he knew from his own hikes that things were usually busier on weekends when working people could get out. But it was still a little unusual to see no one for that long. Apparently it was indeed a little-used trail.

Then a second thought occurred: he needed to make another foray. Not into the forest, but to the house of Hendrik Hyde. Might he find a trailer there with an ATV and small trailer on it? This admittedly felt risky. Because of the huge fortune he'd amassed, Hyde was in the news from time to time, stories which often touched on how ruthless he'd been in building his fortune. He would have to conduct such a search carefully, and surreptiously. And it would help to have someone else along who could keep a lookout for danger while he conducted the search.

He turned the key and pulled out from the trailhead, starting back to town with renewed energy. Some of this came from the sense he was doing what he could, gathering information that might help solve this thing. He felt fully engaged, with a strong need to bring the perpetrators to justice. Some also came from his concern for the people of Sienna, worried about their children—and themselves. Kidnappings, murders—these were serious issues wherever they occurred. But in this little burg they represented a shocking departure from the norm. Plus there was a third element: the challenge, the sense of the chase, the drive to win. It was a grim kind of competition, but it was still a test, a trial of his ability to outsmart whoever had done this.

An Old Cedar Bungalow

Lew parked Old Blue in his one-car garage, leaving the door up. It was an old-style door that swung up and in on a pivot system, as opposed to running on electricity on little wheels set in rails. It was hand powered, and it took most of his strength to move it—it needed oil, one of the many items on his to-do list—and wouldn't close quite all the way when he did pull it down. So mostly he didn't try to close it. He figured no one was going to steal a twenty-year-old car anyway. And if they did, they needed it more than he did.

Earl greeted him at the back door with a vociferous meow. Lew pulled open the screen door and held it while Earl eased his girth through, anxious to get inside.

"You been on one of your neighborhood haunts?" Lew said.

Earl looked back at him, eyes narrowed, as he headed for his food bowl.

"Earl, you had breakfast three hours ago."

Earl sat down in front of his food dish and stared up at Lew. Then he glanced at the cupboard above, an obvious hint.

"You're already overweight. Don't you know you're risking heart disease?" Lew said.

Another sharp meow.

He sighed, reached up for the bag of kibble, and sprinkled a bit into Earl's bowl, who launched into it with the usual enthusiasm.

Lew poured another cup of coffee from his old Mr. Coffee coffee maker, zapped it for half a minute in the microwave, carried it into the den, and sat down in front of his laptop. He glanced at the time: almost noon. As he tried to think how to go about a search of Hyde's place the phone rang. He glanced at the screen: Tim.

"Hi, boss."

"Boss? Wouldn't that imply I had some influence over you?

Like the ability to require an occasional story?"

"No, no. It's strictly a pro forma greeting, a superficial recognition of your titular position at the paper."

"Titular?"

"You just admitted you had no influence over your employees."

"I admitted I had no influence over *you*."

"Doesn't that mean that from my perspective 'titular' fits."

"You know, my morning was going along okay until about thirty seconds ago. I'm going to hang up."

"Wait. You may be titular, but you have my total admiration."

A moment of silence. "Keep going."

"You're the best boss a person could ask. Thoughtful, understanding, supportive."

An audible sigh.

"So, what's up?"

"I just talked with John Christiansen," Tim said.

"Oh. Great."

"They found the motel Campbell stayed in in Sacramento. Both nights. And they've confirmed he was on that flight to New York."

"Wow. So he *wasn't* kidnapped."

"No. The ransom note was clearly bogus."

"We suspected that."

"Well, now we know it."

"Do they have any idea where he went?"

"You mean other than New York City? How could they?"

"So what are they doing?"

"They want us to run an article letting the community know he wasn't kidnapped."

"Wouldn't that also add to the evidence he's the one who killed Trixie Lawson?"

"It does kind of look that way, doesn't it?"

"Yeah, I suppose it does." Lew paused. "Although I haven't eliminated Hyde as a suspect."

"Isn't that kind of a long shot? We have nothing but speculation it was him."

"So far."

"What does that mean?"

Lew hesitated. "Nothing, really. Are the cops doing anything to try to track down Campbell?"

"They've been in touch with the police in Port Le Claire, Florida."

"And what are *they* doing?"

"Staking out James's house."

"Have they talked to James?"

"Yes. He says he doesn't know anything, except that Rob alluded in a recent email that he might be paying him a visit at some unspecified time before too long."

"Sounds like as good an idea as any."

"If nothing else, it makes it look like they're actually doing something."

"So John must be feeling better?"

"He is. They have a credible theory about what happened, and at least some strategy to catch the perp. They want us to get a story out on all this."

"What did you tell him?"

"I can't see any reason not to. Can you?"

Lew thought for a moment. "Not really."

"So what are *you* up to?"

"I've got a lead I'm going to try to follow up on."

"What kind of lead?"

"Let me see if I get anywhere with it. If I do, you'll be the first to know."

"Goddamn it, Lew."

The line clicked dead.

***

Lew picked up his phone and dialed. He waited while it rang four times. He was getting ready to leave a message when a voice answered.

"What do you want?"

"Jeez, Harve. That's not a very friendly greeting."

"I was in the middle of something."

"A nap?"

"I'm working on an article. Something you wouldn't be familiar with."

"No, I'm only trying to solve a murder case."

"Are you making any progress?"

"Maybe."

"What's that mean?"

"You want to help me get a little closer?"

"How?" His tone was guarded.

"Going on a little sleuthing operation."

"What kind of sleuthing operation?"

"Casing out Hendrik Hyde's place."

"You have to be kidding."

"Why would I be kidding?"

"He's the richest SOB this side of the Mississippi. He probably has guards with AK-47s at the ready stationed all over that spread of his."

"You going to let a little AK-47 scare you?" Lew said.

"Yes."

"Well, I doubt that's true. He may be rich, but I don't think he's stupid. And he'd have to be to station guards with military-style weapons around his house. It would damage his image."

"When did Hendrik Hyde ever demonstrate any concern about his image," Harve said.

"When he ponied up half a million dollars for Rob Campbell's ransom? Which he might have gotten back."

"What does that mean?"

Lew described his experience in the forest, finding the place where the million dollars had been picked up and the ATV tracks from there to the forest road.

"What are you suggesting?"

"I think it would be interesting if we found an ATV with a trailer sitting around Hendrik Hyde's place."

"Why don't you just drop by and accuse him of killing Trixie Lawson? That sounds about as safe."

"Harve. You're not up for a little adventure?"

"That guy has more thugs in his employ than the Godfather."

"Come on. It'd be fun. You could pretend you're Eliot Ness."

"Or Jimmy Hoffa. I'd feel about as secure."

"Okay. I'll have to do it on my own, I guess. See you." He started to hang up.

"Wait."

Lew put the phone back up to his ear. "Yes?"

"You're not really going to do that are you?"

"That's the plan, yes."

"You're nuts."

"Sometimes seeking justice requires taking a little risk."

"Sweet Jesus, Lew. You've gone around the bend."

"Lot of people have told me that."

A deep sigh. "Well, you can't do it by yourself. That's beyond crazy."

"That's why I called you."

"So let me get this straight. Exactly what are you hoping to get?"

"To see if he has an ATV with a trailer there. And if he does, get a close-up view of their treads."

"And how do you see me helping?"

"Your charming personality and wonderful company?"

"It's my *company* you're requesting."

"And...someone to watch my back."

"So you admit you're scared."

"It's probably not one hundred percent safe. I can envision a scenario in which there could be trouble."

"So you want me there to get into trouble with you."

"You're being overly dramatic, Harve."

Another pause. "How do you dream up these idiotic schemes?"

"It's not idiotic. If we find an ATV and trailer over there with matching treads, we've got a prime suspect identified."

There was an audible sigh. "How do I let myself be talked into these things?"

"See you in half an hour?"

"God dammit. I was looking forward to a nice quiet afternoon."

"I'll be in a blue Accord."

"I *know* what you'll be in. You've been driving that junkheap for as long as I've known you."

"Then you won't have any trouble spotting me when I get there."

There was a click on the line.

One Sycamore Street

Lew parked on a small unpaved street—more alley than street—that ran along the side of Hyde's three-acre compound. The compound was surrounded by a six-foot redwood fence. This was ringed on the inside with a series of cedar trees, dozens of them, blocking out the view from the outside.

"Well, here we are," Harve said. "How do you plan to get in there?"

Lew nodded toward the back seat. "That's what the rope is for."

Harve looked around. "You brought a rope?"

"It's called anticipation. Like when you picture something you're going to do and figure out it's going to require a certain kind of equipment."

"You planning to hang him?"

"I'm planning to throw that rope over one of the branches overhanging the fence so we can climb up and over it."

Harve stared at him with lowered eyebrows. "You think you can make it that high, old man? You're not exactly a kid."

"I'm not a cripple either."

"What do you plan to do if you actually manage to make it in?"

"See if there's an ATV with a trailer in there."

"What if it's a guy standing there with an AK-47?"

"That's why you're going first."

Harve smiled. "At least your sense of humor is still intact."

"You're going to let me tell people you made a seventy-two-year-old man test this rope before you to enter the lair of a dangerous criminal?"

"I'd be glad to tell them if you'd prefer."

Lew rolled his eyes. "Where's your spirit of adventure?"

"It's been overruled by my spirit of staying alive."

"Oh, come on. This could be fun."

"You have a strange sense of what's fun, old man. And you still haven't answered my question about meeting a guy with an AK-47."

Lew nodded toward the back seat. "See that little tubey thing next to the rope?"

Harve glanced into the back seat. "You into kaleidoscopes?"

"Not a kaleidoscope. It's a periscope. Like they have on submarines."

"We going for a submarine ride too?"

"It's how we're going to get a peek at what's inside before we go there. Come on. This will be fun."

Lew got out, opened the back door, and got out the periscope. He pulled out its several telescoped sections until it was about four feet long, then slowly raised it until it reached just over the top of the fence.

Harve got out and walked over next to him. He spoke in a whisper. "What do you see?"

"Twenty guys, all with AK-47s pointed right at us."

Harve grabbed for the periscope. "Gimme that thing."

Lew let him have it and Harve peered into it.

"Well?"

"I only count fifteen."

"What did I tell you? Piece of cake."

"Did you happen to notice the camera on the inside of the tree, pointing toward the house?"

"Yeah, that's part of your job."

"My *job*?"

"Yeah. It's why I brought this electric tape." Lew pulled a small roll of black tape out of his pocket and held it out to Harve. "You need to cover it while you're up there on the fence."

"Is that right?"

"Unless you'd like one of those thugs to actually show up with an AK-47."

"Any other jobs you have in mind for me?"

"Yeah, but let's stick with the here and now for the moment."

There was a deep sigh. "I'll get the rope."

After several attempts Harve managed to get one end of the rope looped over a large cedar branch above the fence. He reached up and pulled it down. "There you go."

"Thanks. I'll hang onto it to anchor you while you climb over."

Harve cast him a scornful glare, then reluctantly took the rope, pulling himself up hand over hand with his feet against the fence until he'd cleared it. When he got to the top, he grabbed a low branch with one hand and fished out the roll of electric tape with the other. He struggled to stay balanced while he tore off a piece, reached up, and placed it over the lens of the camera. He put the tape back in his pocket and let himself down in reverse fashion on the inside.

Harve whispered through the fence, "It looks all clear from here. Your turn."

Lew copied the process while Harve held on to the end of the rope now inside, struggling to make it to the top of the fence, but finally getting there. He let himself down slowly inside and stood next to Harve.

"See, nothing to it."

Harve rolled his eyes.

They turned and looked around. They were in a large, wooded back yard with a mix of cedars, pines, and sycamore trees. They could barely see the house through the trees, a couple hundred feet away. It loomed up three stories high with gables on all sides, a classic old Victorian. There were two cars parked next to it, both black SUVs. The house was quiet and seemed deserted.

"Let's see what we can see," Lew said. He began to walk quietly toward the house.

Harve shook his head and followed along.

As they neared Lew stopped, studying the back of the house and the driveway along the side. He noticed another security camera on a six-foot post looking toward the back of the house and signaled to Harve to hand him the tape. He approached quietly, reached up, and taped over that lens also.

The SUVs in the driveway on the side they could see looked huge; they reminded Lew of those the Secret Service used when traveling with the President. But there was no sign of an ATV there. However, they couldn't see the other side of the house. Lew signaled Harve to follow him that direction.

"You're going to get us killed," Harve whispered.

They made their way quietly through the trees until they had a view of the other side. Sure enough, he could just make out something shiny parked there. Lew crept slowly toward it, glancing back to make sure Harve was following him.

As he grew near, he got a clear view: a flatbed trailer with an ATV and small trailer on it. Then he noticed a third security camera, pointing toward that side of the house, on another six-foot post. He pulled the tape out of his pocket and repeated the process he'd used with the second camera. He crept past it to get closer to the ATV and trailer. He quietly got out his phone and snapped a picture.

"Okay, you got your picture," Harve hissed. "Let's get the hell out of here."

Lew ignored him and crept closer. It occurred to him that there were probably lots of ATVs in the vicinity; he wanted to get something that would identify this one specifically. Like a picture of the tire treads. Which, he realized, was probably not going to happen, since it was on the larger trailer. He'd have to settle for pictures of the tires themselves.

He was nearly to the front corner of the house when he heard a noise. He stopped dead in his tracks, listening and watching. It sounded like a door opening. He crept behind a tree and got down on one knee, continuing to listen, Harve doing the same a few trees behind him.

A voice became audible. "...ought to be good for a couple mil, boss. I'll get back to you."

"Make it snappy, Luis. Time's money."

"Right."

A car door opened and closed on the other side of the house, an engine started up, and a black SUV backed out. But there was no sound of a door closing in the house.

Lew peeked around the edge of the tree. There was Hyde, standing on this end of his porch, looking out over his side yard in their direction. Lew edged back behind the tree, holding his breath. His knee was beginning to ache.

Finally there was the sound of footsteps, gradually growing softer. Lew gritted his teeth to help withstand the pain. When he could hear the footsteps no more, he stood up. There was the sharp snap of a branch breaking.

"Shit!" he mouthed silently. He glanced at Harve, who was

shaking his head in disbelief. The footsteps grew louder again. He breathed as shallowly as he could, leaning his back against the tree, eyes closed, waiting. For what seemed a very long time.

At last the footsteps started again, and gradually grew fainter. Then there was the soft click of a door closing. He forced himself to wait several more minutes.

When it seemed clear that Hyde was not coming back out, Lew glanced at the trailer and ATV. They were about thirty feet away, and not at an angle that let him get a clear shot of the tires. He took a tentative step toward it, glancing at Harve, who rolled his eyes in disbelief. There was no point in having gone through this if he didn't get that shot. He took another step. And another.

After perhaps fifteen steps he managed to get a clear view of the ATV's tires. He quietly pulled out his phone and snapped three pictures of them. Then two of the small trailer's tires. He pushed a button on the camera and looked at them. Perfect.

About to head back he noticed the trailer was backed up to the edge of the pavement, with a dirt area behind it. Where, he realized, there might be footprints. He stood unmoving for a moment, trying to decide, then glanced toward Harve, who was madly waving for him to get out of there.

He took a few steps closer to the trailer, and sure enough, there were several clearly embedded footprints in the dust at the edge of the pavement. He tiptoed closer, glancing at the house to be sure he was still unobserved. He pulled out his phone again, pointed it at the nearest footprints, and clicked the camera twice. Looked at the result. Perfect.

He reversed course, edging back to the tree he'd hidden behind, and nodded for Harve to head toward the back yard. They took the same course they'd followed on their way in, quietly making their way back to the fence. They reversed the system, using the rope to climb back out. Pulled the rope down, coiled it up, and put it back in the back seat next to the periscope. Climbed back into Old Blue. And took deep breaths, letting them out slowly.

He looked at Harve. "You okay?"

"No thanks to you, you damn fool."

"You didn't think that was fun?"

"You're crazier than I thought. If that's even possible. You could have gotten us killed, stepping on that branch. Not to mention the camera idiocy." His voice dripped scorn.

"That was the whole point." Lew pulled out his phone and handed it to Harve. "Have a look."

"When we get the hell out of here. Start the damn car."

Lew shrugged. "Okaay." He started Old Blue and pulled away, heading back to Harve's house.

An Old Cedar Bungalow

It had been quite a day. The meeting at the newspaper offices with Tim, Harve, and Violet. Two hours in the Tahoe National Forest searching the ransom site, the ATV and trailer pick-up site, and the murder site. The discussion with Tim. Sneaking into Hendrik Hyde's compound, getting the pictures, barely escaping detection. Lew was tired.

He'd fixed himself a ham and cheese sandwich for dinner, which he'd eaten slowly, washed down by a generous slug of gin, with just a splash of tonic to let him pretend it was a gin and tonic. Now he sat at his desk in the den, pouring over all the pictures he'd taken.

He had transferred them to his computer so he could see them more clearly and broken them into four groups: those from the ransom drop; from the forest road where the ATV and trailer had been picked up; from where Lawson's body had been found; and from Hyde's property. He'd also separated out the ATV and trailer tire tracks from the forest and grouped them with the pictures of the actual tires he'd taken at Hyde's place.

The boot treads had proven to be complex and confusing. There were many kinds of treads at both the ransom and murder sites. These could have come from a lot of sources, including those who had left the trunk, picked it up, murdered Lawson, Lawson herself, and the police. The only place he could logically conclude there were only treads from suspicious boots was at Hyde's house. Meaning the only thing he could really determine was where else those had been.

Even that was difficult, as in most cases there were only partial treads, leaving a largely indecipherable mishmash. After studying them for some time, the only thing Lew was sure matched were those from where the ATV and trailer had been loaded onto the larger trailer in the forest, and those at Hyde's place.

The better news was that the tire treads were more revealing. While he didn't have a picture of tire imprint on the ground at Hyde's place, he was able to match those from the forest with the tires themselves. Which made it clear: Hyde, or someone he'd hired, had picked up the trunk with the million dollars and brought it to his compound. The trunk itself had not still been on the trailer, but he had little doubt it was somewhere inside.

This led to an inescapable conclusion: Hyde had actually *made* half a million dollars from the ransom scheme. He'd put up the half million to make himself look good, all of which he'd gotten back, along with the half million the many others who'd been concerned about Campbell had contributed. All in small denominations that would be difficult to trace.

But he still didn't have a good handle on Hyde's motives with respect Trixie Lawson. She was a young woman—he was not a young man—who, according to Harve's description, seemed quite happy to be hanging out with Hyde. If he had a beautiful young woman who liked being with him, why would he kill her? Even if she was acting, just pretending she liked him to milk him for money. He had a virtually endless supply of that. Was he so desperate for more that he'd kill someone to hang on to just a bit of it?

He'd read that wealth became an addiction if you had enough of it. You'd do almost anything to get more. But still. Could it be she'd just gotten on his nerves, that he was a private man who after a while wanted his privacy back? Or maybe the theft and murder weren't even related? There seemed like too many possibilities, without enough information to sort them out.

He leaned back in his chair and looked up at the ceiling, when an idea struck him. He leaned forward, picked up of the phone, and dialed.

A sleepy voice answered. "Hello."

"Did I wake you up *again*?"

"Oh, hi, Mr. T."

"It's only nine-fifteen, Zane. You go to bed that early?"

There was an audible yawn. "Just tired today for some reason. What's up?"

Lew explained the analysis he'd just gone through.

"Okay."

"So here's my question: assuming Hyde murdered Trixie, what was his motive? I suppose it's possible with this guy it doesn't take much. He was quite willing to rip off a half million dollars from unsuspecting citizens who don't have a zillionth of his wealth. So maybe after having his ego boosted by the attentions of an attractive young woman, something about her got on his nerves. I'm just wondering if there could be something more, something we might uncover from clues in his email."

There was a moment of silence. "Like what?"

"I don't know. I just thought maybe you could spot something."

"That's a little vague. Maybe…" His voice trailed off.

"Why don't you put a little thought into it when you're more awake."

"Okay. I'll get back to you."

The Sienna Sentinel

On the morning of Friday, September twentieth, the following article ran on page one of the Sienna *Sentinel*:

There has been a new development in the disappearance of Robert Campbell, now missing for nearly three weeks. Police Chief John Christensen shared with the *Sentinel* that they now have evidence that Campbell booked a flight on September third to New York City.

Further, they also have evidence Campbell spent the nights of September first and second in a motel near the Sacramento airport and was in fact on that flight on the third.

This, combined with the fact Campbell has not reappeared more than two days after the ransom was paid as demanded by his "kidnappers", has led police to conclude that the ransom note was a fake. It was apparently sent by someone trying to benefit from Campbell's disappearance.

Police have conducted a search of the place where the ransom funds were left. They are pursuing possible leads to track down that money. If recovered, all funds will be returned to those who contributed them.

Police continue to suspect Campbell's disappearance may be related to the death of Trixie Lawson. Investigators have determined that her time of death was close to the time Campbell disappeared.

The recent charges made by Sherry Wingate, that she had an affair with Campbell while a student in his class, add to this suspicion. Police believe this could mean Campbell had reason to stop Lawson from going public with a similar charge.

The article went on to describe a timeline and other details of the kidnapping, ransom, and Lawson's death.

The Offices of the Sienna Sentinel

The three of them had been there since eight forty-five, anticipating Lew's possible early arrival for a second time. Which had not occurred. It was now nine-fifteen and he still hadn't shown up. Tim and Harve were each working on their second cream-filled donut when he walked in.

"Nice to see you," Violet said, glancing at a pretend watch.

"Morning," Lew said, looking like he was still trying to fully wake up. He poured himself a mug of coffee, blew on it, took a sip.

Tim nodded at the box of donuts. Lew glanced at it. "Maybe later."

"You look a little bedraggled," Violet said.

He ignored her, looked around at the three of them. "So where are we?"

"Waiting for you."

"Sorry. I was up late again."

"Doing what?"

He ignored the question. "Did you get a chance to talk with our public safety defenders?" he asked Tim.

Tim nodded. "Late yesterday. Tony called to say they had the tissue blood analysis back from the lab."

"And?"

"They couldn't determine the age—apparently it doesn't always work. Could have been any age."

"That's it?"

"No. They're pretty sure about the gender."

"Let me guess," Lew said. "Male."

Tim stared at him. "How did you know that?"

"Am I right?"

"*Yes.*"

Lew nodded, not answering.

"*Well?*"

Lew explained his reasoning, which he was still annoyed had taken so long to come to him. "The article about finding Trixie Lawson's body mentioned that there were signs of a struggle there."

"So?"

"So if she was attacked and struggling up there in the forest, it seems unlikely she was killed at Robert Campbell's house. At least she was still quite capable of putting up a fight. Plus the amount of blood on that tissue was minor, not the kind that would be associated with a serious wound."

Tim nodded. "Good point, Lew. Score one for logic."

"Meaning the blood on the tissue probably came from someone else. You'll recall Campbell's blood type is also A positive."

"So you think it was Campbell's blood? Even though we now know he flew off to New York shortly thereafter?"

"I don't know whose it was. It might be Campbell's. He could have accidentally nicked himself somehow. It could be someone else's." He didn't mention that it also matched Don Thompson's blood type, keeping his pledge to Peggie.

He looked at Tim. "Where are they on capturing Campbell?"

"Nowhere. They've got his brother's house staked out. That's about it. What else can they do when he took a plane to New York City? He could be anywhere. But they're at least feeling better they have *some* lead. Tony said the phone calls from angry residents have mostly stopped."

Lew turned to Harve. "You want to catch us up on your efforts?"

Harve scowled at him. "Why don't *you* tell them about your attempts to get us killed."

Tim and Violet looked at him inquiringly.

"Oh, go ahead, Harve. You'll give it more color."

Harve proceeded to describe the invasion of Hendrik Hyde's compound, and in his words, their near escape from the claws of death at the hands of an AK-47.

They looked at Lew. "Jeez, old man, that sounds crazy," Tim said.

"Harve likes to exaggerate. We had fun sneaking around in there. Felt like we were characters in a TV show."

"You should be a character in a show about deranged mental patients," Harve said.

"Did you look at the pictures you took?" Violet asked.

"I did."

"You planning on telling us what you found?"

Lew described finding the ATV and trailer tracks in the forest and tracking them to where they were apparently loaded onto a trailer. And how the tracks from the forest were a match with the tires themselves. Also how the boot treads for the two locations matched.

"So Hyde must have taken that million dollars?"

"Looks that way."

"That man is pond scum," Violet said. She scowled at them. "He pretends he's doing a good deed by putting up half a million dollars, all of which he plans to get back, along with half a million from people who can't afford it. He deserves a special place in hell."

She looked at Lew. "Are you going to tell the police about this?"

Lew nodded to Tim. "You're our contact there. What do you think?"

"I think we have to. We've already connected him to Trixie Lawson. The fact he was both seen with her at a bar *and* tried to benefit from her death is pretty damning. I'll say this for him, if he is the culprit: he may be a sociopath, but he's a damn clever one."

"They usually are," Lew said.

"I'm not sure the boys in blue will like it though."

"Why not?"

"They think they have an open and shut case against Robert Campbell. The matching blood type on the tissue adds to that. This brings it into question."

"They may be right," Lew said. "Bilking the public out of half a million dollars and committing murder may both be the acts of a sociopath, but they're a little different. He's shown he's a sociopath for a long time. That's exactly what the subprime lenders and hedge fund managers were. But that's different than committing murder. Up to now his motives all seem to have been financial."

"So your money is on Campbell?"

Lew shook his head. "My money isn't anywhere yet. I don't think we can dismiss either one at this point."

"I'm having a little trouble understanding why he'd kill an attractive young woman who laughs at his jokes and seems to like his company," Tim said. "Even if it's costing him a little money."

"Maybe his wife?" Violet said.

"Is he married?"

"No idea."

Lew looked at her. "Another opportunity for your research skills?"

"I'd be more than happy. If he is married, I'll personally tell her what he's been doing with a woman half his age."

"I'll get back in touch with Tony," Tim said. "We can't withhold this, however it turns out. They don't even have Hyde on their radar screen. Maybe another face-to-face meeting?"

They nodded in agreement.

Lew looked at Violet. "While you're looking into Hyde's marital status, could you find out if he's a smoker?"

"Why?"

Lew reached into his pocket and pulled out the plastic bag with the burnt match and cigarette butt he'd found in the forest. He laid them on the table.

"What's that?"

He described his search and how he'd discovered them.

"So you think whoever killed her is a smoker?"

"I don't know. But it wouldn't hurt to find out whether Hyde is."

"How do you propose I do that?"

"No idea. That's your department."

"Thanks a lot. I suppose you want me to find out if he is, whether it's filtered cigarettes or not also?"

Lew nodded. "That would be helpful. You'll notice that one isn't."

She rolled her eyes.

He handed the bag to Tim. "Why don't we see if the boys can find any fingerprints on the stub."

"Is that possible?"

"No idea. Let's find out."

He turned back to Violet. "While you're at it, there's one more thing."

She scowled at him.

"See if he rented an ATV and trailer from some local outfit recently."

"Is that *it*?"

"For the time being."

The Sienna Police Station

They were again gathered around what was becoming a familiar table, all six of them: John, Tony, Tim, Harve, Violet, and Lew. John still looked tired, but not as discouraged as last time. He spoke first.

"Okay, why are we here?"

"It's in the spirit of cooperation," Tim said. "It seemed like it was time to brief each other on developments. We know you've made some progress, and we have something new ourselves we wanted to share with you."

"Fire away."

"Can we make sure we're clear on developments here first," Lew said. "It might help to put what we've learned in context."

"Like what?"

"The autopsy. Any progress there?"

John glanced at Tony.

"Like we said before, we're probably not going to learn a lot. But there are a couple of things. One comes from Lawson's cerebrospinal fluid. They found high levels of cortisol, which indicates a high level of stress at the time of death."

"That's not really a surprise, is it?" Lew said.

"No. They're now analyzing her hair. That's one thing that doesn't decompose quickly. It can show the presence of drugs...or poison. We're hoping to learn whether either were present at the time of her death."

"When will you have those results?"

"Soon, we hope."

"Okay. Thanks. Anything else?"

"Not from the autopsy. But we have a theory about Campbell."

"Okay."

"You know he skipped town," Tony said.

"That's one interpretation," Lew said.

Tony scowled. "Did Tim share the fact that the blood on the tissue on his front sidewalk matched Campbell's blood type?"

They all nodded.

"And the fact that another young woman has charged that she had an affair with Campbell while in his class. With what appears to be solid evidence to support her claim."

Another nod.

"And about the 'support sessions' he had with students evenings and weekends?" He made air quotation marks around 'support sessions'.

This time they frowned.

"You don't agree?" Tony said.

"There are different possible interpretations of those get-togethers," Violet said. "Phil Palmer says they were his attempts to go the extra mile to help needy students."

"Including attractive young women. Hosted by a charming English teacher they all seemed to adore. With female fingerprints found all over his house, including upstairs, where the only bedroom is located."

"There were boys' fingerprints everywhere also."

"Except upstairs. And we don't know that boys and girls were there at the same time."

"We also don't know they weren't."

"Fair enough. But look at all the other pieces of evidence. Trixie Lawson, like Sherry Wingate, was in his class and quite possibly involved with him sexually. And perhaps threatening to expose him, just like Wingate. At the exact time of Lawson's death he skipped town and disappeared into the wild blue yonder. It all adds up to a damning picture." Tony leaned back, glancing around at the four of them, waiting for responses.

When no one spoke, he continued, "Of course we can't confirm all this until we can capture and question Campbell. But at least we have a viable theory to go on. On the chance he turns up at his brother's place in Florida, we've been in touch with our counterparts there. They have his place staked out." Again he looked around the group for reactions.

"It *is* a good theory," Lew said. "I hope you do catch him. I'd like a chance to talk to him myself."

"But?"

"It's not quite watertight, is it?"

"You got any other explanation for his disappearance at the precise time Trixie Lawson was killed?"

Lew shook his head. "No."

"You said you had something new for *us*?" John said pointedly, looking at Tim.

Tim nodded to Lew. He sketched how they had tracked the ransom note back to Hendrik Hyde, omitting certain details like Zane's name, but making it clear it required some computer savvy.

John frowned. "That makes no sense. Hyde is the one who *received* the ransom note. And the one who put up half a million dollars to pay the ransom."

Lew nodded.

"So you're saying he sent it to *himself*?" His tone was beyond skeptical.

"Yes."

"Why would he do that?"

Lew described his visit to the Tahoe National Forest and his examination of the boot prints and tire tracks there.

"We saw those," Tony said. "There were a ton of boot tracks."

"And ATV tracks, followed by trailer tracks."

"We saw those too. There are tons of ATVs around. How can you know where those particular tracks came from?"

Lew nodded to Harve. "Why don't you handle this one?"

Harve shot a nasty look back at Lew, then sketched their visit to Hyde's compound.

"That's illegal," John said sternly. "That's trespassing on private property. If he caught you, he could press charges."

Harve nodded. "He didn't."

"Are you suggesting you found something relevant there?"

Harve glanced at Lew, who was holding out his cell phone with the pictures he'd taken of the ATV and trailer tires. John took the phone and studied them, then handed it to Tony, who did the same.

"What about them?" John said.

"Those tires are a match with the tracks in the woods," Lew said. "I can show you those too if you'd like."

Tony scowled. "So you're saying that Hyde put up half a million dollars, and not only got that back but wound up with the half million that others contributed also?"

"Looks that way."

Tony leaned back. "Sweet Jesus."

John sighed. "Is it that you enjoy making life difficult for us, Travis? Hendrik Hyde is the fattest cat in Sienna. He has more thugs working for him than we have officers. He's not going to just roll over if we try to talk to him."

Lew nodded, not unsympathetically.

"Even if we somehow get an admission from him, it's not really going to help. It's a different case. It has nothing to do with the murder of Trixie Lawson. He may be a lowlife who ginned up a kidnap story and stole half a million dollars. But that's a different matter from killing a young woman."

"Maybe," Lew said.

"What do you mean, *maybe*?" John said, the irritation in his voice clear.

Lew again nodded to Harve, who explained how he'd seen Hendrik Hyde and Trixie Lawson together at a bar, with Hyde buying her drinks and she laughing and draped all over him.

"When was *this*?" John said.

"Maybe a month ago."

John sighed. "God dammit."

"We have no evidence that he was involved in her murder," Lew said. "It just seems like kind of a suspicious coincidence."

John rubbed his face. "I guess we have to investigate it. Which will be one huge pain in the ass with that guy."

No one said anything for several moments. Finally Tony spoke. "Is that it. You got anything else?"

"A request," Lew said.

Tony sighed, clearly nearing the end of his patience. "What?"

"I'd like to see the evidence Sherry Wingate gave you regarding her trysts with Campbell."

"Why?"

"They're one of the key reasons you suspect him of this murder. I'd just like a chance to examine it."

"You don't think *we're* capable of doing that?"

"I have no doubt you are. But the more eyes you can put on something the better. Sometimes different people have different perspectives on what to look for."

Tony grumbled something incoherent.

"I won't do anything suspect with it, just give it a look. If I find anything there of interest you aren't already aware of you'll be the first to know."

John scowled at him. "What makes you think you'll find anything we're not already aware of?"

"I didn't say I would. It's just a matter of trying to be thorough."

John shook his head slowly in exasperation. "What the hell are we coming to here?" Rolling his eyes, he nodded reluctantly to Tony.

"You sure, boss?"

"He's not going to leave us alone until we do it. I know this son-of-a-bitch."

"*John*," Lew said. "I thought we were friends."

"Well, disabuse yourself of that notion."

"Think of us as partners. If we do learn more, it will enhance your efforts."

John was again rubbing his face. "Will somebody wake me up when this is over."

An Old Cedar Bungalow

Lew was worried. It was dinner time and there was no Earl in evidence. He'd gone outside and called once, but no cat had appeared. This was not like him. He never missed meals.

All kinds of thoughts had passed through Lew's brain, from a cat flattened in the middle of the street, to one chewed up by a mean dog, to one stuck high in a tree somewhere, plaintively meowing. He considered that last one and dismissed it. Earl would never climb high in a tree. He wasn't sure Earl *could* climb a tree.

He'd fixed himself another elaborate dinner: a tuna sandwich and a gin and tonic. With a dill pickle on the side. He'd looked for chips to go with it but discovered he was out. He knew chips were bad for him, but when he was under pressure it was hard to worry about his diet. And he was feeling a lot of pressure. This thing had become way too complicated.

How was he going to sort this out? He just wanted to see justice done. Not getting it right would inflict an injustice. If Hyde was innocent, as much as the scumbag needed a come-uppance, it still wouldn't be fair to convict him of a murder he hadn't committed. If Campbell was innocent, it would be just as unfair, with the cops trying him using circumstantial evidence, however convincing it might appear.

He nibbled on the sandwich, swallowing slugs of what was mostly gin between bites. He'd been studying the evidence Tony had agreed to send over: Wingate's pictures of a partially-naked Campbell and the tape of his voice apparently talking to a woman. Tony had been adamant these should go no further. But while they seemed convincing, and certainly damning about Campbell, he couldn't help wondering if there was something bogus about them. So after weighing the options, he'd reluctantly forwarded both on to

Zane. He was hoping to hear back from him before too long.

He carried the empty plate and glass out to the kitchen and added the former to the growing pile in the sink. Then he fixed himself another gin and tonic. As he walked back into the den, the phone rang. He picked it up hopefully.

"Mr. Travis?"

Not the 'Mr. T' he'd been hoping for. He tried to place the voice. It was familiar. But he was tired, not at his best.

"It's Peggie."

"Oh. Hi, Peggie. Sorry, I was kind of lost in thought there."

"I can call back later?"

"No. It's fine. What's up?"

There was a sigh. "I'm worried."

"About Don?"

"Yeah. He's gotten stranger."

"How so?"

"I decided I really needed to draw him out about what happened that night. The night he went for that walk. You know, when Mr. Campbell disappeared? And around when that girl's body was found?"

"Okay."

"You remember, I was worried he did something to Mr. Campbell. But then the news about that girl's body...." She hesitated.

He heard her catch her breath. "Take your time, Peggie."

There were a couple deep breaths. "Sorry. This has gotten crazy."

He waited.

"Well, I kept looking at Don's scratch, and all I could think about was a girl's fingernails. It looked exactly like the kind of scratch they'd cause."

"Did you ask him about it?"

"Yes. Gently. I knew he wouldn't like it."

"And?"

"He wouldn't say a thing. Just completely clammed up. And now he's avoiding me. Every time I go into a room he leaves. He doesn't say a thing at dinner. I know he's hiding something that he can't tell me."

"Is he angry?"

"He gives me these stares, like I'm accusing him of something. Which I'm not. I just want him to tell me what happened."

"That does sound troubling."

She paused. "So I was wondering…I know it's a big favor to ask…if you'd talk to him?"

"You want *me* to talk to him?"

"I know that's a lot to ask. But I'm desperate."

"Why would he talk to me if he won't talk to you, Peggie?"

"He probably won't. But I thought if he knew someone more official was looking into this, it would maybe jar him into opening up. And maybe talking to a man would be easier for him."

"I'm not exactly official. I'm just an investigative reporter for a newspaper."

"Well, that's more official than I am. And I think he sees me as a nag."

"Aren't you worried about him thinking anyone else knows about this?"

"Yes. You haven't told anyone have you?"

"No. I gave you my word."

"What I'm hoping is, if I explain to him that you are the only other person who knows, and you're not a policeman, just someone trying to help, that you can't arrest him or anything, if that might make it easier for him to talk."

"Are you going to ask him if that's okay, first?"

She hesitated. "I don't know. That might make him even more defensive."

"I think you should do that first, Peggie. I don't want him to get mad at you if I show up unexpectedly."

A sigh. "Okay. But I know he won't like it."

"If he says okay, I don't mind trying. I wouldn't hold out a lot of hope, though."

"I just don't know what else to do. I know he wouldn't talk to the police. And it's killing him. It's killing me. We have to find some way to get him to open up."

"Okay, Peggie. You ask him. Carefully. Make clear it's up to him. And if he says okay, just let me know."

"Thanks, Mr. Travis."

"Lew. And good luck. I'll look for your call."

"Okay."

A click.

There was a noise at the back door. He got up and looked out. There he was, sitting proudly outside the door, with something in his mouth. Lew opened the door and he trotted in, carrying whatever it was.

Lew closed the door and followed him into the living room, onto the couch, where Earl set it on the cushion next to him. Where, to his chagrin, Lew noticed a movement. Whatever it was, it was alive. He stared at it as he approached. As he drew near, it became clear.

A slug. A large, slime-covered slug. He looked at Earl, who seemed quite pleased with himself, glancing at Lew, then back at the slug. An ordinary garden slug, squirming now on the dry couch, beginning to leave a trail of slime.

"Did you catch that all by yourself, Earl?"

Earl looked at him.

"And you're kind of proud of yourself?"

Earl began to lick a paw. Then he lay down next to the slug, poking it with a paw.

"How long did it take you? That looks like a speedy slug."

Earl poked it again. Gently. Like it was a plaything. Or maybe a new friend.

"So, am I going to hurt your feelings if I put it back out in the yard, where it belongs?"

Earl looked up at him.

Lew reached for the slug, gently picked it up, felt the sticky goo of its slime. He held it up for Earl to check out. "Want to come with me?"

Earl licked his other paw, rolling to one side in a gesture that looked like someone relaxing after a hard day.

"Okay. I'll be back."

He walked out to the back yard, found an untrimmed shrub, and gently tossed the slug under it. Then he went back in and spent the next thirty seconds washing his hands in the kitchen sink, trying to get the gooey slime off. Followed by two minutes with a sponge in the living room trying to get the slime off the couch. While Earl rested his chin on his paws, purring.

***

Lew returned to his contemplations. The complexities were only getting worse. He felt blocked at every turn, like every possible lead was out of his hands. All he could do was wait, hoping Campbell might show up at his brother's, or the cops would learn more from Hyde, or Don would talk to him. None seemed likely. It felt like dead ends everywhere.

He took another slug of gin and tonic, glancing at Earl, lying next to him on the couch. Why couldn't he have been a cat, whose greatest concern was catching a slug? Or pursuing some attractive female cat he had a thing for that lived down the street. Or sneaking a meal from some unsuspecting neighbor's cat food dish left outside. These were the kind of concerns he could deal with.

Lost in this thought he swallowed the last of the gin and tonic. Sighed. When the phone rang.

He pulled it out of his pocket and looked at the screen. Violet. Jeez, he hadn't talked to Violet in days, other than in meetings. What kind of boyfriend was he?

He punched the green circle. "Where you been?"

"Where have *I* been?"

"Sorry. I'm feeling a little overwhelmed with this thing. It's kind of time consuming. Mea culpa. How are you?"

"Alone."

"That's good to hear."

"Thanks, Lew." The sarcasm dripped.

"I worried you'd resorted to one of your other boyfriends."

"It's crossed my mind."

"How close are you?"

"What time is it?"

"Want to come over?"

"Not especially."

"I thought you were lonely."

"You do any dishes lately?"

"What's that got to do with it?"

"The smell."

"You're going to let a little thing like the smell of dirty dishes keep you away?"

"Yes. How long has it been?"

There was a pause.

"Well?"

"I'm *thinking*."

"That bad?"

"Want me to come over there?"

"Well, I don't have any week-old dirty dishes in the sink."

"Who said anything about week-old?"

"My powers of deduction."

Lew sighed. "I may be lousy company."

"So my choices are lousy company or no company? I've had better offers from derelicts on the street."

"You talk to derelicts on the street?"

"When it's been days since I've heard from my boyfriend."

He sighed. "You got any gin over there?"

"Sounds like you've already had a fair amount."

"Which is relevant how?"

She chuckled. "You're a reprobate, Lew."

"Yeah, but I'm your reprobate."

A pause. "Okay. I'll try to forget how far I've fallen."

"Is that a yes?"

"If you hurry up. Before I change my mind."

"On my way."

One-Eleven Preston Place

Lew was sipping on his second cup of coffee while Violet took her last bite of the scrambled eggs he'd made. She wiped her mouth and leaned back. "Not bad for an old reprobate."

"Reprobates have good qualities too, you know."

"You feeling better?"

"A couple more cups of coffee and I will be."

"How much of that stuff do you drink?"

"How much you got?"

"Your diet seems to be degenerating into gin at night and coffee in the morning."

"You know of a better formula? The research findings keep getting better: turns out both booze and coffee are good for you."

"In sensible amounts."

"That's a relative term."

She shook her head. "You know, a man your age needs to start taking some precautions."

"I do take precautions. I only hang out with beautiful women."

She leaned over and gave him a peck on the cheek. "You old flatterer."

"Is that better than reprobate?"

"Marginally."

"Where's your paper this morning?" he asked.

"What paper?"

"The one you *work* at. *The Sentinel*."

"I don't subscribe to that rag," she said.

"You're kidding. Why not?"

"Because I have to read it every evening before it goes to press. In addition to being the chief gofer for every Tom, Dick, and Harry at the paper, I'm also the proofreader. I already know everything that's in it."

"What if something happens overnight?"

"Rarely happens. If it's big, there's a way to slip it onto the front page. They save a slot, some secondary story, that can be popped out."

"How did I not know that?"

"From barely ever submitting anything?"

He scowled at her, swallowing another slug of coffee, and reached for her plate.

"What are you doing?"

"I thought maybe I'd do some dishes. I'm starting to detect some unpleasant odors around here."

She whacked him—gently—on the side of the head. Just as his phone rang. He glanced at the screen. Pushed the icon.

"Zane. Isn't this a little early for you?"

"Couldn't sleep."

"Shouldn't you be on your way to school?"

"I have first period off."

"How did you arrange that?"

"I hacked into the school's scheduling program."

"You're kidding."

"Nope. But let me get to the point. It's about Sherry Wingate. Turns out I knew *her* also."

"Are there any older women at the high school you *didn't* know?"

"Okay, I didn't exactly *know* her. But I knew who she was."

"How?"

"By her reputation."

"Which was?"

"Same kind as most reputations."

"I see."

"And the rumor was she liked to use her…reputation…to get favors from teachers."

"What kind of favors?"

"Grades. Word was she didn't do much actual schoolwork."

"So you're suggesting she traded…*favors*…to pass classes?"

"I have no personal knowledge of this. But I *can* say she had the…equipment?…to pull this off."

"So you did know her?"

"No, but I had friends who did. And I knew what they thought."

"And you're suggesting this might have been the case with Mr. Campbell?"

"I don't have any specific information about that."

"So it's just something to look into."

"Exactly."

"Okay, Zane. That could be helpful."

"Just thought you'd want to know."

"What about the evidence she gave police? Her involvement with Mr. Campbell."

"I can't explain the pictures. So far the only thing I'll say is that he looks quite relaxed in them. Not like he's, shall we say, in pursuit of anything."

"So maybe he was just lounging around his house or something, and someone got pictures of him?"

"Yeah. But I really have no idea."

"What about the drunken speech?"

"You know, I'm not sure, but it somehow sounds suspicious to me."

"How?"

"What he says. It does sound like he's talking to a woman, and there is a woman's voice responding, but there's something not right about it."

"Like?"

"I don't know, Mr. T. I need to think about it some more."

"Okay, Zane. Anything else?"

"Nothing solid. But when I couldn't sleep last night, I got to looking through Campbell's emails again. There haven't been any since he disappeared. I'm talking about the old ones."

"Okay."

"You know that exchange he had going with that woman in Ohio? His old high school friend."

"Yeah."

"When I tracked them back further, I noticed they were exchanging emails more than once a week. But there weren't any that last week."

"Before he disappeared?"

169

"Yeah."

"And you're suggesting…?"

"It just seemed like an anomaly."

"An *anomaly*? Zane. Good word."

"Well, I *am* in my fourth year of English."

"It seems to be working."

"Thanks. Anyway, I want to think about it some more. I'll let you know if I come up with anything."

"Okay, great. So, off to school now?"

A pause. "I have second period off too."

Lew chuckled. "Zane, you're a reprobate."

"What's a reprobate?"

"Ask your English teacher." He clicked off.

Violet was looking at him. "Breakthrough?"

He shook his head. "Just more stuff to try to figure out."

"Can I help?"

"Any luck figuring out if Hyde is married or was a smoker?"

"He's not married. Used to be. Got divorced about seven years ago."

"Surprise, surprise."

"Yeah, who would want to be married to that turd."

"What about the smoking?"

"I'm stuck on that one. I don't know how to even get started. But…" Her tone was enticing.

"Yes?"

"He did rent an ATV recently. With a small trailer it could pull."

"Wow. How did you learn that?"

"I thought you didn't care about the how. You said that was my department."

"Well…I just meant that I knew, left to your own devices, you'd figure out a way." He hesitated. "Because you're so smart."

She cuffed him on the side of the head again.

"What was that for?" Wounded tone.

"Wanton flattery."

He frowned. "Well, how *did* you learn that?"

"There are three places that rent ATVs locally. So I went to all three and told them I was interested in renting an ATV with a trailer."

"And?"

"One of them didn't rent trailers, just ATVs. Another had just one and it had been out for a while. But the third one said they'd just had one returned. I got to joking around with the guy, said something like 'You mean there's someone else as nuts as I am?' And he said, 'Looked like a thug. Brought it back behind this huge black SUV. I thought the damn President was going to step out of the back seat." Her eyebrows were raised. "Sound familiar?"

He leaned over the table and kissed her on the mouth. "You're not just smart, you're a god-damned genius."

She frowned at him. "Didn't I warn you about wanton flattery?"

"Is it working?"

For a third time she cuffed him on the side of the head.

The Sienna Sentinel

A front-page story ran in the *Sentinel* on the morning of Saturday, September twenty-first, as follows:

Police shared with this newspaper early this morning that there has been a break in the disappearance of Robert Campbell. At first thought to be the victim of a kidnapping, Mr. Campbell is now considered a person of interest in Trixie Lawson's apparent murder.

Campbell was picked up late yesterday outside the house of his brother, James Campbell, in Port Le Claire, Florida. Police there had been alerted to the possibility he might visit from an email James had received from his brother. Accordingly, they had staked out his house.

Robert Campbell was apprehended as he left his rental car and was approaching James's house. He was charged as a refuge fleeing from custody.

Mr. Campbell put up no resistance as the police arrested him. He has been taken to the city jail in Port Le Claire for questioning. Once finished with their questioning, the Port Le Claire Police Department has agreed to return Campbell to Sienna, under armed guard.

Sienna Police Chief John Christiansen, in a statement early this morning, said he was looking forward to an opportunity to question Campbell. He reiterated that Campbell is a 'person of interest' in the death of Trixie Lawson.

Chief Christiansen said that while more evidence needs to be collected, hopefully some from Campbell's own statements, the police feel they are making good progress in solving the case.

Campbell's disappearance and Lawson's death have garnered a great deal of interest locally, partly because Campbell was so well known in the community from his long teaching career at the high school, and partly because of the fear it has caused that there might be a killer on the loose.

More details on this matter will be shared with readers as they become available.

Port Le Claire, Florida

That was shocking. I'd received a call from Rob twenty minutes earlier to let me know he was on his way here from the airport. No advance notice he might be paying me a visit other than that email a couple weeks ago. I don't know what prompted the visit, nor what could possibly have happened to cause the police to arrest him.

As I've said before, Rob is a very private guy. It always seemed like there was a lot going on inside his head that he didn't talk about. I think the teaching helped because he had a daily job, all that prep work and those kids to relate to, which took a lot of energy and focus. He was really devoted to that job, it filled up his days, and sometimes his evenings and weekends. He's seemed more distant the last three years since he retired. I think he's been going through a difficult time.

I can only speculate on what might have happened. He does have a dark side; I've mentioned that before also. There was that dead cat incident when we were kids. He always denied it, but I don't know how else to explain it. And there were the mental problems, the times he wouldn't come out of his room or talk to anyone. The attempted suicide. Someone depressed enough to try to kill themselves? Who knows what they might do?

I don't think he ever sought help for that either. He didn't have much respect for therapists. Told me he thought they were just paid friends. They mostly listened to you, asked probing questions without offering much meaningful insight, and ultimately blamed your parents for whatever problems you had.

To be fair, parents probably are to some degree responsible; they're the ones who guide you through your formative years. But there are other influences also. Genetic ones, for instance. Not to mention teachers and friends as you grow up. None of us escape without some scars to deal with. That's life. Just seems to me that at some point you accept the fact you are who you are, use whatever tools you have to deal with your problems, and get on with your life.

Not that our parents were perfect. They had their own problems to deal with, and they didn't always know how to help us with ours. But they tried, however imperfect they might have been. If there's one thing that I'd criticize them for now it's that I think they pushed us a little too hard to always be responsible, do the right thing. They lacked the cavalier side you see in some parents, thumbing their noses at this rule or that. I guess I had thicker skin than Rob, resisted some of that idealistic moralizing, especially when I saw what it was doing to him.

He took that guidance seriously. It caused him to push himself hard, go the extra mile, which came out in his teaching. But we all have our limits, and the tensions those efforts cause have to be released some way. I'm not saying Rob did anything wrong. But who knows? Maybe a lifetime of forcing himself to do everything right finally got to him? Maybe a dam broke and he rebelled against the standards he'd always forced on himself? When that happens, who knows what you're capable of?

After the police grabbed him, one of them came to the door and asked if he could speak with me. He took a statement, mostly about Rob's background and what little I knew about his current life. I told them as little as I could.

One thing he didn't ask me about was why Rob never got married. Which is a good thing, I suppose, since I don't really know. But I have sensed, especially since he retired, that he regretted it, not having a family of his own to share his life with now that his connection to students was gone.

They also didn't ask about his summers. No clue there either. It's kind of amazing how many things you don't know about someone you grew up with and feel close to. I guess we all have our private inner lives.

Three-Forty-Three Chestnut Street

The call had come to Lew after he got home that morning. He was still reluctant to talk with Don Thompson, but Peggie had pleaded with him, and he couldn't think of a good excuse not to. Plus he was genuinely curious. Not that he thought it was likely the man would open up to him. But what the hell, it was worth a try.

He pulled up in front of the house, glanced across the street at the still cordoned-off house of Robert Campbell, then at the Thompsons' house. It was ranch style, with brick trim up about two feet, vinyl horizontal siding above that, painted white. The roofline ran parallel to the street, the length of the house. There was a big picture window to the right of the entry. The grass was as short as ever.

He took a deep breath and climbed out of Old Blue. The picket fence gate clicked shut behind him as he started toward the front door. As he neared, Peggie opened the door and stepped out. Her expression was grim.

Lew nodded to her. "Morning."

"Good morning, Mr. Travis."

"Lew."

She nodded. "Lew."

"How is he?"

"More or less comatose. I'm not optimistic. He's mad at me. But I had to do *something*."

"Okay. Let's give it a shot. From what you've told me I don't hold out much hope either, but it can't hurt to try."

She ushered him in. They entered directly into the living room. Don was sitting in a chair on the far end, his expression impassive. He didn't look at them as they entered, just stared ahead.

Peggie led Lew toward a chair facing Don. "This is Mr. Travis, honey. He's not a policeman, he has no authority to do anything. He just wants to hear whatever you have to say. Okay?"

Don glanced at her, then back ahead, not looking at Lew. He didn't speak.

She nodded to the chair across from Don's. Lew shrugged and sat down.

"I'm going to leave you two alone," she said. She turned and left.

Lew's first impression was of the size of Donald Thompson. He was huge. He must have stood six feet four inches tall and weighed two hundred fifty pounds. His shoulders were massive, his chest deep, his arms looked almost comical they were so thick. His head must have required a hat size off the charts. A lantern jaw. Hair cut in a short buzzcut. He looked like he could be a professional wrestler or a lineman for an NFL football team.

His expression was not friendly; jaw set and eyebrows furrowed, like he was ready to attack the first person who challenged him. Lew couldn't help feeling a little intimidated.

He said nothing, just sat there waiting to see if Don would even look at him. Which he finally did. One glance, then away again. Lew continued waiting. Eventually another glance, this one longer. Finally he looked at Lew steadily.

"So?"

Lew nodded. "Hello."

Don frowned. "I don't have anything to say to you." His voice was low, almost a growl.

Lew shrugged. "Okay. You don't have to say a thing. Peggie just wanted me to meet you."

"There's no reason."

"I think she's worried about you. She does really love you."

He frowned, not responding.

Lew glanced out the window. "The yard looks great. You must take good care of it."

He shrugged.

"I guess your neighbors aren't all so conscientious?" He nodded toward Campbell's house.

"That guy should be jailed."

"Because of his yard?"

He nodded.

"It doesn't fit with the rest of the neighborhood, does it?"

Don cocked his head, scowling at him. "Did you come here to talk about yards?"

"I came here to listen. But only if you feel like saying anything."

"Who are you?"

"Nobody, really. I'm half retired. I work for the newspaper the other half."

"So you're looking for a story?"

"No. This is not about getting a story."

"So why *are* you here?"

"Like I said, your wife invited me. She's worried about you and thought it might be easier for you to talk to someone other than her. About whatever's bothering you."

"What are you, a counselor or something?" He said 'counselor' like it was the equivalent of felon.

"No. I am definitely not a counselor. Just someone trying to help."

"How do you know Peggie?"

"She saw me looking around Campbell's house the other day and came over to say hello. That's it. I don't really know her."

"Why were you looking around Campbell's house?"

"You know he disappeared a couple weeks ago?"

He nodded.

"Friends of his are worried about him. One of them asked me if I'd see if I could find any clues about what happened to him."

"So you're an investigator?"

"Not in any official sense. But I do work with people at the paper who want to help try to figure this out. It's something that's causing a lot of concern in the town."

"So you are going to write a story about it?"

"This is a completely private conversation, Don. You have my word; it's just between you and me. Nothing you say will go any further than you want it to. Peggie made me promise that."

"How do I know I can trust you?"

Lew hesitated. "Well, like I said, I made the promise to your wife. And now I've made it to you. I guess you'll just have to trust that. I don't lie."

Don looked out the picture window, then back at Lew. "What do you expect me to say?"

"Whatever you want to. Like I said, Peggie is worried about you. She senses there's something you can't say to her, but that is causing you to withdraw from her. She wants you back. It's that simple."

He nodded. "Do you have a specific question?"

"Just what's bothering you."

He stared at Lew for some time. "She thinks I did something bad."

Lew nodded. "And I take it you didn't?"

"That's what I can't talk about."

"Okay." He paused. "Do you know what she thinks you did?"

"Not really. But I can tell she thinks it's bad."

"So there isn't something she suspects?"

His eyebrows were furrowed. He shook his head. "I don't know."

Lew nodded. "So if it's something you can't talk about, I guess there's just no way out of this?"

Don closed his eyes, sighed. Shook his head again.

Lew decided, since he'd taken the trouble to be here and it didn't look like he was going to learn anything meaningful, he might as well try a gambit. "I can tell you one thing, Don. I found a tissue near Mr. Campbell's front sidewalk with blood stains on it. The police have analyzed those blood stains and determined they were from a male." He waited for Don's reaction.

"They think it's mine?"

"They don't know whose it is, only that it's from a male."

After a pause, he said, "Aren't you going to ask me if it's mine?"

"Like I said, I'm not here to ask you questions. You can tell me whatever you want to, and not tell me whatever you don't want to."

Don stared at him, apparently considering this. After a bit he just shook his head.

When it seemed clear Don wasn't going to say anything more, Lew began to stand. To his astonishment, Don's eyes closed and tears began to run down his cheeks. His shoulders shook and small sobs became audible. This lasted just a few moments, then he rubbed his eyes with his fists.

"Whatever you tell me is just between us, Don. No one else. I won't even tell Peggie if you don't want me to."

His expression deeply pained, he said, "I did something bad. But I can't tell you what."

Lew waited. The tears had stopped. Don spoke in a tortured tone. "I just can't tell you."

"That's okay." He stood to leave. Don stared at his feet, said nothing more. Lew started for the door. As he neared it, he spoke in a loud clear voice, "Peggie, I'm leaving,"

She emerged from the back of the house, looking at him inquiringly.

"You'll have to ask Don. I told him whatever he told me was just between him and me."

She nodded. "Okay. Thanks, Lew."

Lew nodded, opened the front door, and headed back out to Old Blue.

An Old Cedar Bungalow

Lew felt restless when he got back. There had to be something more he could do to figure this thing out. He sat down in front of his computer, his fingers drumming randomly on the keys. A thought came to him.

He opened the pictures he'd taken in the forest, and at Hyde's compound. While he'd figured out the link between Hyde and the ATV, he was still nowhere with the boot prints. There were just too many different kinds, and most were too fragmented to permit any clear picture. But maybe if he tried again. It was at least something to do.

He studied the boot prints from Hyde's compound. They weren't perfect, but they were clearer than those from the forest. Then he studied those from the drop spot where the trunk with the money had been left. There were only fragments among these, probably from the police officers who had carried the trunk up there, or who had searched the area after it disappeared, or from Hyde's thugs.

Next he looked at the ones from the forest road where the ATV and trailer had been loaded onto the larger trailer. Here there were several with a clear enough tread to be matched with those from Hyde's compound. There were none of the other types here. He put these next to the other two sets. Looking across the three sets he realized that all they did was confirm what he already knew: Hyde's crew had taken the money.

He sighed. One more set to go. He brought up the pictures he'd taken where Trixie Lawson's body had been found. Here there was a mishmash of confusing partial prints, few of them clear enough to distinguish from each other. He had taken more than two dozen shots here. As far as he could tell none matched those of Hyde's thugs. Suggesting they were either from police officers, or Trixie

Lawson, or…the killer. But that didn't really help either.

Finally he gave up in frustration. He leaned back and rubbed his eyes, tired from staring at the screen. Two indisputable facts seemed clear: Hyde's men had been the ones who found the trunk with the million dollars, loaded it onto the ATV's trailer, and then loaded the ATV and its trailer onto the larger trailer and taken it to his house. Hyde was clearly implicated in the theft.

But when it came to the place where Trixie Lawson's body had been found, he just couldn't draw any clear conclusions. Except, from what he *could* identify, it didn't look likely that Hyde's men had been there.

He got up and wandered into the kitchen, noticing the time: just after noon. He'd started fixing himself a tuna sandwich when the phone rang. He looked at the screen. Did the boy go to *any* classes?

"Hi, Zane. Another period off?"

"I'm supposed to be in trig."

"You're cutting class?"

"I don't like trig. In what future will I need to know sines, cosines, and tangents? Do you ever use trigonometry?"

Lew hesitated. "Now that you mention it, not that I can think of. So what's up?"

"I've been studying those pictures you sent me. The ones of Mr. Campbell without much on."

"Okay."

"I think they've been photoshopped. If you look closely, there are some clues there."

"Really?"

"To begin with, he's always alone. There are no pictures of him *with* Sherry Wingate. Which alone seems a little suspicious to me."

"Good point."

"But the clearest one is of him lying on his 'couch' in his boxer shorts. If you blow this one up and really study it, there's a tiny corner that looks to me like the edge of a rope hammock. I think someone took a shot of him in his hammock in a bathing suit or his shorts and doctored it to look like he was on his couch."

"Wow."

"There's more. I think the tape could be doctored also."

"What? How?"

"Unlike the pictures, it does have two voices, Mr. Campbell's and that of a young woman."

"Okay."

"But you remember how it rang kind of a bell for me?"

"Yes."

"I think I've figured it out. Mr. Campbell would sometimes read a scene from a play in class to bring it alive. He'd apparently had some acting lessons and was good at this. He did sound a little drunk, but I think he was acting."

"Really?"

"He's talking with a young woman, that much is clear. But somehow the lines felt wrong. They didn't sound like the kind of language one would actually use in that situation. So I did a little digging. One of the plays he taught was *Romeo and Juliet*, which seemed like a likely source. I went through that whole damn play and nothing there fit what he said."

"So…how does that help?"

"Let me finish. I remembered Mr. Campbell used a modern version of the play to teach it, because he thought it would make it easier for students to relate to. So I looked at that version."

Lew waited.

"Let me read you a couple examples. 'Come sit here with me.' Okay, that's not all that strange. And he does sound like he's trying to lure the woman to sit next to him. It's followed by a young woman's voice saying, 'Well, if you insist, Mr. Campbell', in a very friendly tone."

"Okay."

"But here's another. Tell me if this sounds real to you. 'Back in the day I whispered sweet nothings in a beautiful girl's ear, but never realized what true beauty was before tonight.'"

Zane paused. "Does *that* sound like anything anyone would say today? Even if you were trying to lure a young woman into bed? It's followed by the same young woman's voice saying seductively 'Mr. Campbell, you old flatterer. You're not trying to seduce me, are you?'"

"Interesting."

"And here's the thing. Both of those lines that Mr. Campbell supposedly spoke are direct quotes from a scene between Romeo and Juliet in the modern version of the play."

"So you think Sherry Wingate recorded them in class and dubbed in her voice?"

"That's what I'm thinking."

"Meaning there's no clear evidence Robert Campbell had an affair with her."

"Exactly. I'm not saying he didn't. But I don't think Sherry Wingate's so-called proof holds up."

"Any idea why she would do that?"

"I wondered that myself. On a hunch I hacked into the high school's archives, where they keep records of students' grades. Mr Campbell gave her a D minus in English her senior year."

"So you think she might be holding a grudge?"

"Seems possible, doesn't it?"

"Indeed. And you, my friend, are a genius."

Zane hesitated. "You wouldn't want to talk to my trig teacher, would you? I don't think he shares that view."

Lew chuckled. "A lot of geniuses hated school, Zane. Neither Bill Gates nor Steve Jobs graduated from college. There are many kinds of intelligence."

"Well, before you take my word for it you should listen to the tape yourself to see what you think."

"I will."

"Okay. I should go."

"Back to trig?"

A brief pause. "I think it might be over."

Lew chuckled again. "Thanks, Zane."

Offices of the Sienna Sentinel

It was an unusual time for the meeting of the crew, but Lew knew the other three would probably be at the paper's offices and decided to go in and see if he could free them up. Becky, a young woman who worked the reception desk in the afternoon, greeted him.

This was Becky's first job. She'd only been there a few months. But Lew already liked her. She had short dark hair, a tattoo of a butterfly on her forearm, a tiny diamond nose pin, and despite her age, didn't take guff from anyone.

"Hi, Mr. Travis. Haven't seen you around here for a while."

"Because I've been here first thing in the morning lately."

Becky frowned. "You're kidding."

"I know, it's not my favorite time of day. I'm working on a story and needed to consult with my staff."

"Your staff?"

He nodded.

"Who's that?"

"One of them is that kid who works here. Tim Royce."

She hesitated, then smiled knowingly. "Shall I give your underling a ring?"

"Please."

She dialed a number and listened. Lew could hear the phone ringing, once, twice, a third time. Finally someone answered.

"Hi, Mr. Royce. This is Becky. A man who says he's your boss is here to see you." She glanced at Lew.

There was a moment's hesitation. "Tell him I'm busy."

She looked at Lew, who spoke in a stage voice, projecting loudly. "Actually, tell him I'd rather see Harve and Violet. Tell him to forget it."

She frowned, not sure what to do. Tim's voice came through again. "Ask him how the story is coming."

She looked at Lew inquiringly. He shrugged. "Slowly. Hard to get good help these days."

She waited for Tim.

"Tell me about it. What does he want?"

She looked at Lew.

He shook his head. "Can you just let Harve and Violet know I've made a breakthrough and need to see them in the conference room?"

She waited for Tim to respond. There was just the sound of quiet swearing.

Lew nodded his thanks and headed for the conference room.

***

Lew, Harve, and Violet were just sitting down when Tim entered.

"Things free up?" Lew said.

Tim flashed him the bird and sat down.

"Tim. Isn't that a little unbecoming for an editor?"

"Not one who has to deal with a certain investigative reporter. What's the breakthrough?"

Harve and Violet looked at him. "There's a breakthrough?" Harve said.

"Of sorts. But first I think we need to get an update from our esteemed editor regarding developments in the police department." He looked at Tim.

"Nothing new there," Tim said.

"When will Campbell arrive?"

"His plane arrives late this afternoon."

"Have they talked with our friend Hendrik yet?"

"They tried. He wasn't home when they went over there."

"Okay. Harve?"

"Nothing, boss."

Lew frowned. "You talk with Phil Palmer lately?"

"No. Why should I?"

"I don't know. Except that he was Campbell's best friend. And there have been some developments since the last talk you had with him. Like finding Trixie Lawson's body. Maybe he knew her? And Sherry Wingate's claims. Maybe he knew *her*? Might be worth another visit. Just in case he has any insights into either one?"

"Okay. I can do that."

He looked at Violet. "Why don't you update us on your findings."

Tim and Harve glanced inquiringly at her, then at Lew. "She's quite good at this sort of thing," Lew said.

Violet explained her visits to the ATV rental agencies and what she'd learned about the ATV and trailer that had just been returned.

Harve said, "Wow. That pretty much ties that one up in a nice little bow."

Lew glanced at Tim. "A reason to be in touch with our men in blue again?"

Tim grudgingly nodded back. "Is that the 'breakthrough'?" he said sarcastically.

"No. I spent some time studying the pictures of prints where Trixie Lawson's body was found."

"And?"

"I couldn't find any clear prints that matched those of Hyde's thugs."

Tim frowned. "In other words, you learned nothing?"

"Well, I suppose you could argue that the absence of such prints could lead you to conclude they weren't involved in her murder."

"But you couldn't really tell?"

"Not conclusively, no."

"In other words, there *isn't* any breakthrough," Tim said sarcastically.

"Not on that front. But there's another. It has to do with the evidence Sherry Wingate provided that she'd had an affair with Robert Campbell."

"The tape and pictures."

Lew nodded. Without mentioning Zane, he sketched what he had discovered about both the pictures and tape, detailing especially what was on the tape.

They looked at him with open mouths. Harve was the first to speak. "Goddam it, Lew. That practically clears Campbell."

"It certainly brings into doubt his affair with Sherry Wingate."

"That's the *only* evidence he had affairs with high school girls."

"Yes. But disproving one allegation in this respect doesn't necessarily mean he wasn't involved with other young women. And Trixie Lawson was also in his class."

"Still."

"That's not bad, Lew. You figure that out by yourself?" Violet said.

"I had a little help from one of my other assistants."

Tim scowled at him. "The usual one?"

Lew nodded. "I think he deserves serious recognition. He's done more on this than anyone else."

Tim sighed. "I just have one request. Don't let our men in blue know some high school kid is better at this than they are."

"Finding pictures that are photoshopped? Recognizing passages from *Romeo and Juliet*? Aren't *most* high school kids better at this than middle-aged men?"

"Probably. But I still don't think they'd appreciate it."

"Well, it's not a problem, Tim. He doesn't want his name mentioned there any more than you do."

Two-Thirty-Seven Chestnut Street

Phil Palmer had not sounded thrilled about another visit from Harve. It took some work on Harve's part to elicit even a half-hearted agreement for him to come. So when he pulled up in front of Palmer's house he was feeling a little trepidatious. Harve was not a confrontational person. He liked getting along with his fellow travelers through life. But he felt a compunction to see if he could extract any additional help, however minor.

Palmer's wife greeted him at the door. "*You* again?"

"Is Mr. Palmer around?"

"Doubtless. Somewhere."

"Could I talk to him?"

"Why would you want to?"

"I just thought he might have some new insight into Robert Campbell's disappearance."

"Well, he doesn't."

"You know that?"

"He doesn't have new insights into anything. He's an idiot."

Harve leaned back, eyebrows raised. Not knowing how to respond, he just stood there.

"But if you insist, I'll get the scumbag."

Harve waited while she went to find her husband. He heard her berating him as Palmer approached the door. He arrived and looked at Harve. "Yeah?"

"Like I explained on the phone, I'd like to ask you a couple more questions?"

Palmer rolled his eyes and nodded for Harve to come in and sit down, following him to the chair opposite Harve's. Palmer sat down slowly, easing himself into the chair. Harve noticed the rolls of fat around his belly.

"Bad leg?" Harve asked sympathetically.

"Arthritis. Acts up sometimes."

"Sorry."

"Getting old is a pain in the ass. Diabetes, arthritis, insomnia. It doesn't end."

"And now you've got an old friend who's in trouble."

Palmer sighed, nodding. "Yeah. Which is doubtless why you're here. What can I do for you?"

"Probably nothing. I just hadn't touched base with you for a while, and as you doubtless know, there have been some developments."

"Such as?"

"The discovery of Trixie Lawson's body?"

Palmer nodded.

"Did you know her?"

"Yeah. She was in my class one year."

"Do you know whether Mr. Campbell did?"

"He did. She was one of those students he invited to his house for extra help."

"How do you know that?"

"I'd see her going past here on her way over there."

"Do you know how often that happened?"

Palmer shook his head. "No."

"Do you know anything about how close they were?"

Palmer looked away, like he was thinking, then back. "I think she was one of the students he got pretty close to." He hesitated. "I'm not suggesting there was anything amiss there."

"Understood. What about Sherry Wingate?"

"Again, I knew who she was."

"You had her in your class?"

"No. For other reasons."

Harve cocked his head in an inquiring gesture.

"She was one of those girls who...let's say was more woman that girl. Well endowed. And flirtatious."

"Did she flirt with Mr. Campbell?"

"I don't know but it wouldn't surprise me. It was kind of her MO, if you know what I mean."

"Flirting with teachers."

"Flirting. I don't think she restricted herself to teachers."

"Did any of them flirt back?"

"A little, sure. We're not made of stone. She had a way of presenting herself, dressing and walking and leaning over in front of you to expose her cleavage. She was a little hard to ignore."

"So she flirted with you?"

"Once or twice."

"And...?"

He frowned. "Teachers have to be careful about that kind of thing these days. It's easy to get in trouble."

"How about Mr. Campbell?"

"I don't know how he resisted sometimes."

"Except for maybe when he had students over to his house?"

"You'll have to draw your own conclusions there."

"Students never talked about it?"

"Not much. They knew we were friends."

"But a little?"

"Yeah. A little."

"What did they say?"

"Nothing particularly revealing." He hesitated. "You could tell they liked it."

"Because of the help he gave them?"

"No comment."

"Mr. Campbell never said anything to you about that?"

"No. Rob didn't talk about that."

"Did students call him Rob?"

"I heard one or two do that. He didn't seem to mind. He wasn't a formal person. And he always seemed to have students' respect."

"Which would suggest this was still in place when students visited him at home?"

Palmer scowled. "Look, we've talked about that. I've told you what I know. Can we get off that topic?" There was an edge in his tone.

"Sorry."

"Any other questions?"

Sensing the tension, Harve spoke carefully. "You mentioned when we talked last time that he liked to hike in the Tahoe National Forest."

"Yeah."

"And that you sometimes went with him."

"Yeah."

"Did he ever go near where Trixie Lawson's body was found?"

"As a matter of fact, it was one of his favorite trails. They found the body just off that trail."

"Have you been up there recently?"

"You mean since they found her?"

Harve nodded.

"No."

"Do you happen to know what kind of shoes Mr. Campbell wore?"

Palmer leaned back, scowling. "What kind of *shoes* he wore?"

Harve nodded.

"I have no idea. Hiking boots, I suppose. Isn't that what people wear when they hike? Why?"

"It's just something we've been looking at, and I thought if we knew what kind of boots he wore it might help us sort that out."

"Sort *what* out?"

"Who wore the boots that left prints there."

Palmer nodded slowly. "Okay, I see your drift. No, I have no idea what kind of boots he had." There was a pause. "So, is that *it*?"

It seemed clear it was. "Sure. Thanks for your cooperation."

Palmer nodded. Harve stood. Palmer stayed in his chair.

"I can find my way out," Harve said as he started for the door. "Thanks."

"Yeah. Good luck."

Harve let himself out and headed for his old pickup.

One-eleven Preston Place

Lew was sitting in front of his computer, lost in thought, when his phone rang. He picked it up, punched the green dot without looking at who it was coming from, and said hello.

"You busy?"

"If you count getting a headache from looking at the same pictures over and over."

"Pictures of what?"

"Boot prints."

"You a foot fetishist."

"Just a frustrated old man, apparently out of his depth."

"Would you like some company?"

"Are you a frustrated old woman out of your depth?"

"I'm a thoughtful and insightful woman offering you a life raft."

"So this is pity?"

"You above that?"

"No. Are you suggesting coming here?"

"You do any dishes?"

"No."

"I think we've established my position on that."

"So you're inviting me over there? Two nights in a row?"

"I have something I think you'll find interesting."

"That's been established for quite some time."

"Relating to this investigation."

"That's disappointing."

"Yes or no?"

"What time?"

"Whenever you think you can break away from whatever you're doing."

"Can you give me thirty seconds?"

"What for?"

"I need to take a pee."

"You're such a silver-tongued devil, Lew."

"Flattery will get you everywhere."

"I'll see you when you get here."

***

He arrived a few minutes later. He knocked lightly, then let himself in, knowing the door would be open. He glanced at a small repast on the coffee table as he entered. Violet had set out some cheese and crackers, with bread and butter pickles, and a gin and tonic with a twist of lime. She knew it was a combination Lew liked.

"You know you're going to have trouble getting rid of me when you treat me like this."

"I have other ways of getting rid of you."

He looked at her askance. "That sounds ominous."

"You don't have to worry as long as you behave."

"Yes, ma'am." He sat down and took a slice of cheese, speared a pickle, and placed them between two crackers. "What was it you thought I'd find interesting?"

"I've done some more sleuthing."

"Regarding?"

"Cigarettes."

"Cigarettes?"

"Your hearing going along with your bladder?"

"You talking about the butt I found?"

"I'm talking about who might have smoked the butt you found."

Lew's eyes widened. "You're kidding. I thought you had no idea how to even start on that."

"I got an idea."

"Don't keep me in suspense."

"Archives."

"Archives?"

She sighed. "Have you been to an audiologist? They've made a lot of advances with hearing aids these days."

"Give. What did you turn up?"

"An old picture of Hendrik Hyde, at a benefit he gave."

194

"Hyde gives benefits?"

"He does worry about his image a bit, apparently. It was for some other billionaire who was starting a foundation. He was standing at the dais, apparently speaking to a small gathering, the mic in one hand."

"And?"

"A cigarette in the other."

"You! Are! A! Genius!"

"Thank you."

"Did it have a filter?"

"It was hard to tell. I blew it up as big as I could and still have any focus, but I don't think so."

"An *extraordinary* genius!"

"I thought you'd like it."

"Did you know not many people smoke non-filtered cigarettes anymore? I looked it up. It's less than ten percent. Of the roughly twelve percent of Americans who still smoke cigarettes at all. Which makes this a genuinely high-value find. Barely one in a hundred people smoke non-filtered cigarettes."

"Not good news for our boy Hyde."

"That is a great discovery, Violet. Have I told you how much I admire you?"

"I remember something from a couple years ago."

"That recently?"

She cuffed him on the side of the head.

"Ouch. You've got to stop doing that."

"So did you make any actual progress in *your* analysis of boot footprints."

"Not much. They're a mishmash, frankly."

"I think we knew that."

"They're just too smudged up to be sure of anything. Except for one pattern. Maybe."

"Yes?"

He hesitated. "I couldn't make out anything from near where her body was found. But there's one style that's a little clearer, in a different place."

"What place?"

"Near where I found the cigarette butt."

"Bingo."

"Maybe. But we have no way to identify them."

"We would if we had Hyde's hiking boots."

"What are the chances of that?"

***

They had just finished dinner: salmon cooked in lemon and butter, a butter lettuce salad, and fresh sourdough bread. Lew was wiping his lips with his napkin, looking appreciatively at Violet, when his phone rang. He looked at the screen. Punched the icon.

"Mr. Harvey. To what do I owe this pleasure?"

"I'll give you three guesses: Your charming personality. Your good looks. A report on my meeting with Phil Palmer."

"Wow, that's a tough one." He drummed his fingers on the table, holding the phone nearby so Harve could hear. "We can eliminate option three right off the top. But the other two…"

"You want this or not?"

"Fire away."

"I came away with three main impressions."

"Is this another joke?"

"No. First, I don't think he's a happily-married man."

"How is that relevant?"

"It's probably not."

"Are the other two?"

"You decide. Number two: He was a little careful about what he said about those visits students made to Campbell's house. I tried to nudge him to say more, but he was closed mouth. Still, reading between the lines."

"I think we kind of already suspected that, didn't we?"

"I suppose."

"And number three?"

"In spite of hiking with Campbell a number of times, he doesn't know what kind of boots he wears."

"You thought he would? Who notices that kind of thing?"

"It was a long shot."

"That's it?"

"Well, maybe one more."

Lew waited.

"I don't think he'll talk to me again."

"Not exactly the mother lode of information there, Harve."

There was a click.

The Coffee Roaster's Cafe

It was a typical morning at the Coffee Roaster's Café, with the usual wave of customers coming in for their morning hit of caffeine. Crystal and Velma were scrambling to keep up. It wasn't until after nine o'clock that it slowed and they had a chance to sit down and talk. With a focus on the usual topic.

"You still think Rob is innocent?" Velma said between sips of coffee.

"Absolutely," Crystal said. "The idiot police in this town have no idea what they're doing."

"Even with all the evidence against him? His history with Trixie Lawson? That young woman claiming she had an affair with him? His going on the lam at the same time Lawson was killed? And now his arrest in Florida, where he apparently fled to escape arrest?"

Crystal looked at her. "What do you mean, 'going on the lam'? Or 'fleeing to escape arrest'. You sound like the damn cops."

"Just telling you what I read."

"In the *Sentinel*? I thought you were above that."

"How else can you keep up with things in this town. It may be a rag, but it's our rag."

"Point taken. But those stories have it all wrong."

Velma looked at her with an inquiring expression. "How so?"

"First off, it could be a false identification. Maybe they arrested the wrong person."

"What? How?"

"They made a mistake. Cops are human. They make mistakes."

"In identifying who someone *is*?"

Crystal shrugged. "It happens."

"You don't think the cops are capable of identifying who someone *is*?"

"They're just people. People make mistakes."

"Come on."

"Okay, even if it was him—and I'm not admitting it was—it doesn't mean he's guilty."

Velma frowned.

"You've met him. You know what he's like."

"Yeah, when he's here having breakfast. I don't know anything about his personal life. Men can be animals. They're made different. Especially when it comes to sex."

"Not all men."

"Look, I have no idea what he did or didn't do. But still."

"Well you must agree our cops are idiots. Don't get me wrong, I like Tony. He's a nice guy. And they're okay when it comes to small-town crime. But they're in way over their heads here. They have no idea what they're doing."

"Still, you have to admit, it doesn't look good."

"I don't know what information they think they have. And frankly it doesn't matter. I just know they're wrong."

"How?"

There was a long pause. Velma looked at Crystal, waiting.

Finally Crystal spoke. "Because I have information they don't."

Velma leaned back, looking at Crystal skeptically. "What are you talking about?"

Crystal hunched her shoulders in a defensive posture, not responding.

Velma frowned. "Talk to me. What do you mean?"

"I can't talk about it."

Velma frowned. "*Crystal.*"

She hesitated. "We have an information channel no one knows about."

"What?"

"That's all I can say."

"Forgive me, but that sounds a little…strange."

"Think whatever you want to. I probably shouldn't have said anything. But it's true."

"That you have an 'information channel' with Rob Campbell? I don't even know what that means."

"There are a lot of forms of communication."

"What are you talking about? ESP or something?"

"No. Not ESP. That stuff is nonsense."

"Well then?"

"I shouldn't have mentioned it. Forget it."

"Crystal. Come on." She looked away, frowning, then back at Crystal. "Are you going to let the police know about this?"

"Of course not. They're idiots."

"What if they bring it to trial and he gets convicted?"

"They'll figure it out. Eventually."

"How?"

"I don't know."

"I just don't understand how you can be so sure."

"You'll just have to trust me. I know."

Velma shrugged. "Okaay. You want some more coffee?"

"No thanks."

The Sienna Police Station

Tim had called Tony to learn what he could about Robert Campbell. Which was little. He had arrived the previous afternoon and been questioned, but had refused to say anything. He wouldn't even answer yes or no questions put to him. So he'd been locked up for the time being. However, there had been some developments regarding Hendrik Hyde.

The upshot was that another meeting had been arranged for this morning. The six of them sat around the usual conference table at the police station. The tenor of the exchanges had changed little. To try to soften the tone Tim had brought a container of coffee and a dozen bear claws. All five men were munching on a bear claw, and all six participants were sipping on coffee.

"Not bad," Tony said, holding up the remains of his bear claw.

"Seemed like the least we could do."

"Let's get things underway," Christiansen said, his tone stern.

"Right. I suppose you want to know about Campbell?" Tony looked at the four newspaper people.

All four nodded.

"Well, he's here. Not much more than that to say. He refuses to talk. At all. Won't answer any questions, won't volunteer anything, won't even give us nods about whether he wants something. Like dinner or breakfast. He's eaten nothing. Frankly, he seems depressed. Really depressed."

"I suppose that makes sense," Tim said. "He's been captured with a likely charge of murder facing him."

"What are the new developments with Hyde?" Lew asked.

Tony sighed. "We went over there with a search warrant, given the evidence you shared. Three of us, in case we had trouble. He wasn't home. A housekeeper let us in and there were a couple of his crew hanging around, but they didn't interfere with our search."

"What did you find?"

"The biggest find was the trunk in which the money had been stuffed. They hadn't even bothered to take the bills out. We had a few dusted for fingerprints, which seems a little superfluous. It's obvious who took it. We have it in our evidence locker in case this goes to trial."

"Did the trunk have the whole million still in it?" Lew asked.

"Not sure. We've got people counting it now," Tony said.

"That would seem to wrap up that part of the case."

"Yeah. We owe you one there."

Lew nodded in acknowledgment. "Did you learn anything else?"

"We questioned the housekeeper about where Hyde was. She pleaded ignorance, said he goes on trips all the time, has business meetings all over the country. Neither of his men would talk to us, just said they did what they were told and didn't ask questions."

"Did you ask them about taking the trunk?" Tim said.

"Yes. They said they couldn't comment, that we'd have to ask Mr. Hyde. My sense is they were scared."

"Did you ask them whether they'd gone up to where Lawson's body was found?"

Tony nodded. "Yeah. Same response."

"Can't you bring them in on a charge of withholding evidence?"

"We could, but there seemed little point. They were no more likely to talk here than there. It's clear Hyde pulls the strings." Tony shrugged.

"Are you looking for him?"

John cut in, glowering at Lew. "*Yes*. Of course. There's a warrant out for his arrest for grand theft."

Lew turned back to Tony. "Did you find anything else of relevance there?"

Tony glanced at John, as though seeking guidance. John rolled his eyes, nodded slightly.

"One thing. A pair of men's hiking boots that neither of the men said they recognized and clearly wouldn't fit the housekeeper."

"So they must be Hyde's?"

Tony nodded.

"That could be important. What have you done with them?" Lew asked.

"They're in the evidence locker along with the trunk."

"Any chance we could have a look at them?"

Again Tony glanced at John for guidance, who growled, "We could let you take pictures of them. They can't be removed from police hands, for obvious reasons."

Lew didn't see any point in arguing. "Okay, we'll get some pictures before we leave if that's okay. Thanks."

John nodded grudgingly.

"One more question. Anything more from the autopsy?" Lew said.

"Yeah, we got the hair analysis back," Tony said.

"And?"

"No evidence of poison. There *was* evidence of drugs, however, meth and cocaine."

"Ah. So she was using drugs."

"That's not surprising. It's widespread among the homeless. They'll do almost anything to escape the depressing effects of being homeless."

"And that was at the time of death?"

"Hard to say. With hair analysis it's possible to track back over time and get a retrospective picture of past drug use, by gradually looking at hair that's grown further out. But it's not precise enough to determine whether drugs were taken the day of death or the day before."

"Anything else?"

"No. Her body was so far decomposed they just couldn't get any other clear readings."

"Not even whether she was she raped?"

"Determining even that is difficult after two weeks. Evidence of semen in the vagina only lasts for a week or so, sometimes less. But since we were particularly interested in that question, the examiner agreed to check her cervix, where semen can sometimes be detected for up to two weeks. There was evidence of it there."

"So she *was* raped?"

"In all likelihood."

"If you found evidence in her cervix, why is there any doubt?"

"We know nothing about her sex life. If she'd had intercourse the day before, it could have been from that."

"Can you determine who it came from?"

"They're attempting to conduct DNA analyses now. We won't have those results back for a while."

"Okay. Thanks."

"Your turn?" John said pointedly.

"We have some new information on Sherry Wingate's alleged evidence of an affair with Robert Campbell."

"Alleged?"

"We conducted an analysis of both the picture and the tape."

"Which, together, provide pretty damn *clear* evidence."

"Unless you happen to have read the modern version of *Romeo and Juliet*."

"*What*?"

"The recordings of his voice are direct quotes from that play."

"No way!"

"Sherry's voice is interspersed with his, but that's from dubbing hers into what he was saying to make it sound like he was flirting with her."

"How…?"

"Mr. Campbell sometimes read scenes from the play he was teaching to his class to bring it alive, make it seem real to students. She must have recorded this when she was in his class."

"What about the pictures? Those are pretty damn revealing."

"They are. Of Mr. Campbell lying in his hammock in his back yard, by himself."

"He's on his damn couch!"

"Photoshopped to look like that. But there are tiny bits of a rope hammock visible in the bottom corner of the picture."

"In his *underwear*?"

"Possibly. Or a bathing suit. Or maybe a pair of shorts. Nowhere are there pictures of Sherry Wingate with him. He's by himself."

"How would she get pictures of him practically naked if she weren't involved with him?"

"Presumably someone went to his house while he was outside napping in his hammock and took them. Maybe over his fence? I don't know, but he's by himself in a hammock."

"Goddam it. Is that it or do you have other things to screw this up?"

Lew nodded to Violet.

John's tone softened. "Yes?"

"You remember the cigarette butt we gave you a couple days ago. The one found near the spot where Trixie Lawson's body was found."

"Yes. We couldn't get any prints off it."

"We found in our archives a picture of Hendrik Hyde smoking a cigarette. While it's hard to see clearly, it appears to be an unfiltered cigarette, like the one found up there."

"Interesting. But a lot of people smoke cigarettes."

"We did a little research on that and learned that only about ten percent of the cigarettes sold in America today are unfiltered, and only about twelve percent of Americans still smoke cigarettes, which puts the likelihood it's Hyde's butt somewhere close to ninety-nine percent."

Christiansen frowned. "Did you guys major in statistics or something?"

"Just trying to help," Violet said sweetly.

"Well, if we ever catch the son-of-a-bitch we can ask him about that, too," Tony said. "Is that it?"

"We'd like to take those pictures of Hyde's boots," Lew said.

"Right."

"And one other request."

Tony frowned, waiting.

"Any chance I could talk with Campbell while I'm here?" Lew said.

"You think he's going to talk to you when he won't talk to us?" John growled, his irritation back.

"Probably not. But I'd like to give it a shot."

Tony and John exchanged glances. "What are you trying to pull, Travis? This man is a suspect in a murder investigation. The last thing we need is to have some amateur interfere in a way that prevents him from talking with us."

"You mean like he is now?" Lew said innocently.

John glared at him.

"How about you have someone with me when I talk to him," Lew said. "That way you'll know exactly what gets said."

Tony and John again exchanged glances. John took a deep breath, let it out slowly. He looked to one side, frowning and shaking his head.

Tony didn't speak, waiting for directions.

Finally, John said, "Okay, but anything he says—if he says anything, which is doubtful—belongs strictly in police records. No *Sentinel* stories about it. Is that understood?"

"Perfectly," Lew said.

Looking at Tony, John said, "You go with him. Don't let one word pass between them without you hearing it. And take a recorder. We need to have anything said recorded."

Tony nodded, then looked at Lew. "That work for you?"

Lew nodded.

"Okay. Follow me." Tony pushed back his chair and stood.

Violet spoke quietly to Lew as he stood. "I'll get the pictures of the boots, Lew. You just deal with Campbell."

***

Campbell's cell was of the classic variety: three concrete walls, with the fourth comprised of vertical bars facing the hallway. There was a single built-in cot along one side, a sink and toilet along the back wall. Nothing more.

Campbell was lying on the cot on his side, facing the wall, his knees pulled up in a fetal position. He wasn't moving and didn't appear to be awake.

"You have a visitor, Mr. Campbell," Tony said, in a loud clear voice.

Campbell rolled half onto his back and opened his eyes, looking at the two of them.

"Mr. Lew Travis is helping us with the investigation into the murder of Trixie Lawson. He's asked, and been granted, a chance to speak with you."

Campbell acknowledged this in no way.

"I'm going to let him into your cell for a few minutes to ask you some questions. You have no legal obligation to speak with him. I will be here listening to anything that passes between you."

Still no acknowledgement on Campbell's part.

Tony unlocked the cell door and Lew stepped through. Tony handed him a folding chair and Lew opened it and sat down, facing Campbell's cot. Crossed his leg. And said nothing.

Campbell watched him, still making no acknowledgement of his presence.

Lew remained like that for several moments. Then he spoke one word: "Hello."

Campbell eyed him suspiciously.

Lew said nothing more, just waited.

After several more moments, Campbell leaned up into a half-sitting position. He stared at Lew.

Lew waited. He looked relaxed and calm. He said nothing.

Campbell sat up a bit straighter. A frown appeared on his face.

Lew waited.

Campbell sat fully upright, leaned his back against the wall, facing Lew straight on.

Lew waited.

Campbell glanced at Tony, standing outside the cell, holding a small recording device, then back at Lew.

Lew waited.

Finally, Campbell said, "Who are you?"

"My name is Lew Travis. I work part-time for the *Sentinel*, the newspaper."

Campbell bent his head down slightly, looked at Lew through the upper part of his vision. "Have we met?"

"I don't think so."

"And you're here, why?"

"To listen."

Campbell stared at him. "Listen?"

Lew nodded.

"You don't have any questions?"

Lew shook his head. "I only want to hear what you want to tell me. Nothing more."

Campbell glanced again at Tony, then back at Lew. "What's the point? I've already been tried and convicted." His tone was bleak, not angry. He glanced at Tony.

"Not by me," Lew said.

"What, you think I'm innocent?"

"I have no idea."

"Are you a lawyer?"

"No. Just what I already explained."

"So what business do you have being here?"

"None, officially."

Campbell frowned. "I don't understand."

"It's nothing more than what I've already said. I'm here to listen. Only to what you want to say. I have no specific questions."

"What if I don't want to say anything."

"That's up to you."

"Well, I don't."

"Okay."

Campbell stared at him. "So, that's it?"

"If that's what you want."

"It is."

Lew nodded. "Okay." He stood and Tony pulled open the door and stepped in to retrieve the chair. Lew nodded to Campbell and turned to leave.

Campbell said nothing.

Lew stepped out of the cell. Tony followed, carrying the chair, swung the door shut behind him, and relocked it. They headed for the front of the station.

As they did so, there was a ruckus audible coming from the front. It sounded like the receptionist speaking loudly to someone, and a man's voice just as loud, demanding something.

Tony opened the door to the reception area and they stepped in.

A middle-aged man wearing a suit and tie was saying, "Everyone is entitled to legal representation. As a practicing attorney, I insist on the right to speak to Robert Campbell."

"Mr. Campbell has not requested a lawyer, Mr. Livingston."

"Has anyone asked him?"

Ros, the receptionist, looked at Tony with an inquiring glance.

"It's presumed," Tony said. "Who are you?"

"Presumed does not meet the legal standard. He must be asked directly if he wishes legal representation."

"Who are you again?" Irritation had entered Tony's voice.

"My name is David Livingston. I'm a fully-credentialed practicing attorney. With a legal right to speak to your prisoner.

Every prisoner has a right to legal representation, and you have an obligation to make sure that right is fulfilled. You can either grant me a meeting with Mr. Campbell or I will file a complaint with your legal office."

Tony's voice took on an edge. "File away."

The man's face turned red. "You *are* breaking the law, Mr...?"

"Gonzales. Police Sergeant Gonzales to you."

"It will be in your legal office before it closes today."

Tony nodded. "Look forward to seeing it."

An Old Cedar Bungalow

Violet was waiting for Lew outside the police station when he emerged. He looked at her inquiringly.

"Just following orders, boss."

"About?"

"The pictures."

"Ah. Of course. Sorry. I was distracted."

"Ros *is* kind of cute."

"By meeting Campbell."

"What about it?"

"I'm not sure. He wouldn't talk. I didn't really expect he would."

"So?"

"It was his demeanor. He seemed depressed."

"He was just arrested for murder. Wouldn't you be depressed?"

"I suppose. But it felt like something more than that."

She shook her head. "Men are so perceptive sometimes."

"Where are the pictures?"

"On my phone."

"Can you forward them to me?"

"I could, but I thought an airdrop might be better. That way they're not out there on the Internet somewhere."

"What's an airdrop?"

Violet sighed. "Give me your phone."

Lew pulled it out of his pocket and handed it to her. She hit a few keys, held it against her cell phone, hit a couple keys on that, waited a moment, handed it back."

"Really?"

She nodded, rolling her eyes.

"How do you know all this stuff?"

"It's called keeping up."

"I feel stupider every day."

She smiled. "No comment."

He had turned to leave when she said, "There's one other thing."

He stopped and turned back, waiting.

"There was still some stuff in the treads of his shoes. Bits of dirt and needles, a little piece of a pinecone."

"Meaning?"

"Seems like evidence to me he'd been hiking somewhere in the woods recently."

Lew nodded. "Well, I suppose that's what you often do with hiking boots. Do you see some particular significance in that?"

"Did you note the word 'recently'?"

Lew nodded, his head cocked in an inquiring gesture.

"It just seemed to me that maybe the fact he'd been up there fairly recently might be a useful bit of information?"

Lew nodded. "Good point. Have I mentioned how smart you are recently?"

"You have, but I like to keep it fresh in your mind."

***

When he got home Lew transferred the pictures from his phone to his computer and studied them. There were shots from several angles. Top down. Both sides. And two of the treads, the only ones he cared about.

He searched through his own collection of pictures for those he'd taken where Trixie Lawson's body had been found, in particular the ones near the log where he'd found the cigarette butt. These weren't a full boot print, but enough to identify. He put them next to the pictures of the boot treads Violet had given him. Studied them, looking back and forth. Blew them up and leaned in, as much as he could and still have a good focus. It seemed too good to be true: they were almost certainly a match.

He leaned back in his chair, reflecting. The conclusion was inescapable: Hyde had been at the scene of the murder. The cigarette butt. Now his boot prints. Was the evidence finally coming together?

Lew tried to fit this new information with what he knew about Robert Campbell. Lawson's body was found near a trail Campbell often hiked. He disappeared at the same time she was killed. Now that he was captured, he wouldn't talk. These all seemed to jibe with the likelihood he was guilty of the murder.

But Hyde had apparently gone on the lam himself. Did that suggest guilt on his part? There *was* the stealing of half a million dollars that might explain that, except that stealing money from innocent people was something he did to pass the time. He didn't have what most people would consider a conscience. Nevertheless, committing murder could certainly be something that had motivated him to skip town. In short, the evidence was building into a case for both being guilty. Was it Campbell or Hyde? And how was he going to figure it out?

Lost in this maze of conflicting clues, Lew decided to focus on one that seemed clearer. He knew it was the wrong time of day, but maybe he'd get lucky. He picked up his phone and typed in a brief text, hit the send button.

He waited to see if there would be a quick response. There wasn't. He set the phone down and leaned back in his chair, rubbing his eyes. When the phone rang.

"Hello."

"Mr. T?" Spoken in a whisper.

"Zane?"

"Yeah. Give me a minute. I need to get somewhere."

Lew waited. In a few moments Zane's voice returned, louder and clearer.

"Where are you?"

"The bathroom."

"At school?"

"*Yes*. I just couldn't speak freely where I was."

"Which was?"

"Trig class."

"So you just got up and walked out?"

"It was as boring as usual. The only reason I'm not dropping the damn course is I need the credits to graduate. What's up?"

"Do you have any idea how to get in touch with Sherry Wingate?"

"Sherry Wingate? Why?"

"I'd like to talk to her."

"About what?"

"Why she made up the story about the affair with Campbell."

"I already explained that. The D minus."

"Yes. But I'd like to talk to her, see what was going through her head. And maybe even see if she'll own up to it."

"Ah. Okay. Let me think. I don't have it in my phone; that's where I mostly keep contact information. As I explained, I didn't really know her; she was four years ahead of me. But…it might be in a school file. Let me see what I can find."

"Will the school show you those?"

There was a pause. "Did you really ask me that?"

"Oh. Duh."

"I'll get back to you if I have any luck."

The line clicked dead.

Molly's Cafe

To his surprise, Zane texted Sherry Wingate's cell phone number within an hour. Which Lew made immediate use of, sending her an invitation to have lunch, on him. He explained he was a reporter for the *Sentinel* doing a story on recent graduates and someone had suggested she would be a good person to talk with. Because of her recent revelations about one of the teachers. And more broadly, about the problems young women face in the world today.

She texted back almost immediately, asking for more details but seeming to show interest. He sensed it was going to be one of his lucky days. He texted back that there wasn't much more to explain, he just wanted to interview her for a possible article. Which had apparently been sufficient, along with the offer of a free lunch, to garner her interest. She agreed to meet him at Molly's at noon.

Molly's was a little hole-in-the-wall on a side street in Sienna, run by a buxom woman with a knack for good cooking. It only had six tables, and Lew decided to arrive a bit early so he could watch for Sherry's arrival. He scanned around the room as he entered, glancing at his phone—eleven-forty-five. There were only two free tables, one in each of the back corners. He picked the one on the left and sat down facing the front door.

At precisely twelve the door opened and an attractive young woman walked in. She was wearing skin-tight blue jeans, a woven top with a bare midriff and plunging neckline, dangly earrings partially hidden by her long dark hair, lots of mascara, several prominent silver rings on the fingers of both hands, a lip ring, a nose pin, and heavily applied purple lipstick. She glanced around the room as he waved.

She approached his table with what might be described a

lascivious walk, her hips doing the talking, her expansive bust bouncing along for the ride. She smiled at him as she approached.

"Mr. Travis?"

He nodded. "Sherry?"

She pulled out a chair at right angles to his and sat down theatrically. "How nice of you to invite me." She glanced around the room in a way Lew could only interpret as an attempt to see who might be watching her.

"Thanks for coming."

She turned back to him and smiled broadly, then leaned in toward him, exposing the vast reaches of her bosom. She placed one elbow on the table, leaned forward with her chin on her palm, and looked directly at him from a distance that made Lew aware of his personal space.

"You're a *reporter?*" she said, making it sound like a romantic calling.

Lew nodded.

"How *interesting*. Tell me about it." She continued to stare at him with wide eyes from point blank range.

Lew leaned back a bit. "What would you like to know?"

"Everything."

At that moment Molly appeared and approached their table with menus and water. She glanced at Lew, then the young woman.

"Hi, Lew. You're usually here with your fellow language murderers. You have new company."

Lew nodded. "Molly, this is Sherry. Sherry, Molly."

Sherry reached out her ring-laden hand, wrist bent at a dramatic angle, and said, "Good to *meet* you, Molly."

Molly nodded back, not taking her hand, as she was still putting down the menus and water. "Hi. Would you two like to hear the specials?"

Appearing slightly miffed, Sherry leaned back and waited. Lew said, "I'm going to have the usual, Molly, just a tuna sandwich on whole wheat toast with the works. And a cup of coffee, black."

"Don't even have to write that one down," Molly said, looking to Sherry.

"Do you have burgers?" she asked.

"Not as such, but I have a nice meatloaf; I could cobble together something close."

Sherry frowned. "Well, okay. Never had that before, but I'll give it a try. On white bread, with mayonnaise and catsup?"

Molly started jotting. "Fries?"

"Sure."

"Sweet potato or regular?"

"Regular."

"Small or large?"

Sherry glanced at Lew.

"Whatever you like," he said.

"Large."

"Beverage?"

"Do you have milkshakes?"

"No. Just coffee, sodas, and beer."

"A Budweiser."

Molly jotted that down and headed off to the kitchen through the swinging door.

Sherry returned her gaze to Lew. "This is *so* nice of you."

"Shall we get started?"

"Sure." Big smile.

"So maybe the best place to start is with what I already know from reading the paper. Your encounters with Mr. Campbell?"

The smile turned into a frown. "Awful man."

"Can you add anything to what was in the paper?"

"Just that the whole thing was frightening. He's a lecherous old man."

"Why did you…spend time with him?"

"He insisted. Wouldn't leave me alone."

"This was at school?"

"Wherever. School. His house."

"You went to his house?"

"Well, everybody did. He invited all kinds of girls over there."

"No boys?"

"Yeah. There were some boys too."

"At the same time?"

"Yeah. He said it was to offer extra help."

"Did he offer extra help?"

"Well, yeah. He'd go over stuff with you."

"Like?"

"Whatever you needed help with. It was different for different kids."

"But then this led to…?"

Her expression turned dark. "He'd make me stay after everyone else left. That's when he'd put the moves on me."

"The moves?"

"I probably don't need to spell it out."

"No, I'm curious. Exactly what did he do?"

"Well, you know. He'd invite me to sit on the couch next to him. Put his arm around me. Pretend he was trying to show me something in the book."

"And?"

She leaned back, an expression of indignity. "Before you knew it he'd be… trying to make a move on me."

"Why didn't you leave?"

She frowned. "Well" …she hesitated… "how could I?"

"Why couldn't you?"

"Well…I didn't know what he might do."

"Like?"

"I don't know. He was a dirty old man."

"You were afraid of him?"

"*Yes*. This huge athletic man."

"I thought you said he was old."

"Well, he was pretty old. But he was still big and strong."

"Would he say anything while making these advances?"

"Yeah."

"Like?"

"Well, like the tape I gave the police. Suggestive stuff."

Lew kept his voice low and even, as though he were sympathetic. "One example?"

She hesitated, then stopped and leaned back, looking at him. "Hey, this isn't the kind of questions I thought you were going to ask. You said it was about the problems young women face in the world today."

"Isn't this one they often face?"

"Well, yes. But…"

"You know Mr. Campbell is being accused of murdering Trixie

Lawson?"

She nodded.

"Were you afraid he might hurt you?"

She looked out into the room, as though assessing what to say, then back. "Kinda."

"That sounds scary, Sherry." Still his voice was quiet and sympathetic.

She nodded.

Molly arrived with their drinks and set them on the table. Lew nodded his thanks. He reached for his coffee, blew on it lightly, took a sip. He said nothing more, just looked out into the room, waiting.

Silences are awkward. This one became painfully so. He continued to look away from Sherry.

Finally, she said, "Aren't you going to ask me anything more?"

He looked back at her. "Maybe something a little different."

"What do you mean?"

"I learned that the pictures you sent purporting to show Mr. Campbell in states of undress were taken while he was resting in his hammock in the back yard."

She frowned, looked aside, then back, scowling.

"And that the tape with his voice was taken from a modern version of *Romeo and Juliet*, apparently recorded in class." He watched her reaction.

She scowled at him in apparent confusion. "Why would you say that?"

"Isn't it true?"

"Well...." She shrugged.

"Do you realize you have put Mr. Campbell in a dangerous position? Your story adds to evidence that he was possibly Trixie Lawson's murderer. Which he may be, I don't know. But why would you want to submit false evidence to the police?"

"I didn't..."

"Should he be convicted of her murder, it could result in his execution. Capital punishment is still legal in California. Why would you want to put someone else's life in jeopardy?"

She took in a breath, her eyes darting back and forth, out into the room and back at Lew.

"Were you angry at him for some reason, Sherry? Like because he gave you a D minus in English?"

"How did you know that?"

"I'm an investigative reporter. I try to gather evidence about any story I'm working on. It's in the school's records."

"Well, that doesn't prove I lied."

"No, it doesn't. But along with the fake pictures and tape, it makes it look likely."

"I...I..."

His tone was still quiet and controlled. He looked at her with a thoughtful expression. "Do you want to tell me the truth?"

She scowled, looked out into the room again, then back. Took a sip of her beer.

Lew waited.

She took another sip. A different look entered her eyes.

Lew felt something on his knee. A hand. Ever so lightly. She was watching him intently.

He didn't react. The hand moved up, slowly, toward his crotch.

He looked away, then back toward her, lifting his phone from beneath the table. He spoke into it. "Let it be recorded that the hand you just saw on my knee and thigh belongs to Sherry Wingate."

She bolted back in her chair. He pointed his phone toward her. "This is Sherry Wingate." He kept the phone aimed at her, recording her reaction.

At that moment Molly emerged from the kitchen with a tuna sandwich in one hand and the cobbled-together hamburger and fries in the other. Sherry took one glance at her and lurched up, kicking her chair out behind her so violently it tipped over, and bolted for the door. Lew continued to record her until she disappeared.

As she rushed through the door she almost collided with a big man about to enter the restaurant, who turned and stared at her as she ran down the street. Then he stepped in and looked around the restaurant, his expression confused about what had just transpired.

Other customers had been watching the theatrics for the last few moments: Sherry's abrupt stand, the tipped-over chair, her rush to the door. They were now staring at Lew.

He waved to them. "Show's over. Sorry for the disturbance."

Molly set the plates on the table, glancing at the chair that had been knocked over. Lew got up and set it straight. "Sorry," he said.

"She had a little emergency. She won't be having lunch today."

"Want me to wrap it up?"

Lew waffled for a moment. "Leave it for now. The fries look pretty good."

"Okaay." She left shaking her head.

A shadow appeared over the table. Lew looked up. The big man who had just entered the café was standing there looking down at him. He was about six feet four inches tall and weighed well over two hundred pounds. He wore a fedora. He was glancing back and forth between Lew and the front door.

"Emmett! To what do I owe this pleasure?"

Emmett was an old friend of Lew's. He'd worked in real estate most of his life but was now semi-retired, just taking clients he already knew. He was a handsome man for his age, single, but always hoping lady luck would hit his number. Somehow it never seemed to happen.

"Your lucky day, I guess," Emmett said, in answer to Lew's question. He glanced at the meatloaf sandwich and fries. "You order two lunches?"

"Oh. It was for the young lady who just left."

"She was with *you*?"

Lew nodded.

Emmett frowned. "*She* was with *you*?" he repeated, as though he couldn't get this through his head.

Lew nodded again.

"Well, it looks like you had your usual effect on women." He glanced again at the front door.

Lew smiled.

"On what possible pretext did you lure that gorgeous young thing to have lunch with you? She's... how should I put it? A bit out of your league."

"I invited her to help me with an article for the paper."

Emmett frowned, glancing down at the table. "She coming back?"

"No. Why?"

"What are you going to do with that?" He was staring at her food.

Lew pushed Sherry's chair out with his foot, nodded for Emmett to sit down. "Have at it."

"Really?"

"Yeah. On me."

Shrugging, Emmett squeezed his large frame onto the chair and took a big bite out of the meatloaf sandwich. Speaking in a muffled voice he said, "What, she didn't view you as a legitimate journalist?"

"Apparently not."

"So she's smart as well as beautiful."

Lew nodded.

"You have her number?"

"Yeah."

"Why don't you let *me* give it a shot. I kind of have a way with the ladies."

Lew smiled. "I know what a lady killer you are, Emmett. I don't think it would be fair to her. She wouldn't stand a chance."

Emmett shrugged in agreement. "Yeah, you're probably right." He stuffed some French fries into his mouth. "That Bud hers?"

"Have at it."

He slurped down a big slug, took another bite of the sandwich, and said through a mouthful of food, "You know, you're not as bad a guy as I'm always saying." He threw Lew a sideways glance.

"Thanks, Emmett."

An Old Cedar Bungalow

Lew left Old Blue in the driveway and headed for the back door. As he neared there was a sudden movement off to one side. Slightly startled, he glanced that way. There was a sizable black animal making a beeline for him.

"Earl! You hiding over there in the grass?"

An abrupt "meow".

"You come over for a pet?" He leaned down and reached out to give him a stroke.

Earl let out what might be described as an annoyed meow.

"*Earl*? Surely you're not seeking anything more than affection?"

A short, punchy "meow". With a stare at the back door.

"Oh! You're cold. Sure, let's get inside."

He opened the screen door, then the old wooden door, and held it for Earl.

A brief "meow", as in, 'About time'.

Lew followed Earl through the doors and closed them behind him.

Another short, forceful "meow", as in 'Now'.

Lew reached down and rubbed behind Earl's ears. A brief, softer "meow", as in, 'That's nice. Now let's get on with it.'

Lew went into the kitchen. Earl followed him and sat down in front of the cupboard where his kibble resided, staring up at it.

"Oh, did you want something?"

Earl glanced at him, then back at the cupboard.

"You know, you're entirely predictable, Earl. Do you ever think about anything besides your stomach?"

No response, just more staring at the cupboard.

Lew sighed. "Okay. But it's not dinner time yet. Just a snack." He pulled down the bag of kibble and sprinkled a little in Earl's food dish.

That was the end of the conversation, as the usual crunching ensued.

***

Tired from his adventure at Molly's, and enjoying a full stomach from the tuna sandwich, Lew felt himself getting sleepy. He wandered into his living room and lay down. In a moment Earl trotted in and hopped up next to him, licking his lips. He began to give himself a bath as Lew felt his eyelids growing heavy.

The next thing he knew he was emerging from a dream. Only slowly did he let himself return to full consciousness, enjoying the sense of rest the nap had provided. He pulled out his cell phone and glanced at the time: almost three pm. Earl was sound asleep by his side. He put the phone back in his pocket and gently edged away from Earl, sitting up. He rubbed his eyes, feeling a sense of renewal. Naps were one of the nice things about old age. Rediscovered from one's earliest years on the planet.

He got up quietly, leaving Earl to continue his nap, and went out to the kitchen. He put some water in the teakettle and turned on the only burner where the electric sparker still worked. The others required a match to light. He got out a coffee cup, plastic cone, filter, and bag of Peet's coffee. He waited for the steam to begin wafting from the teakettle, poured hot water into the cone, waited for it to seep through, repeated this a second time. Then he took the cup with him to the den, blowing on it lightly as he took the first sip.

Having gotten the satisfaction he'd sought from puncturing Sherry Wingate's story, Lew sat back down in front of his computer, returning to the quandary he'd been facing before lunch. The pictures of Hyde's boots, and his boot prints from the murder scene, were still up on the screen. It constituted clear evidence Hyde had been at the scene of the murder. Should he go to the police with this? He decided no: they already had a warrant out for Hyde's arrest. There seemed little point until they found him and brought him in.

His eye kept going over the boot prints. He scrolled back to the other pictures of boot prints he'd taken, the ones nearer the police tape, trying to distinguish them from one another. Once again there was nothing he could clearly identify. He scrolled to those further out from the tape, then enlarged the picture where they began to be identifiable. He got a magnifying glass out of his desk and held it up to the screen.

With the help of the enlargement and the magnifying glass he noticed something new. The first boot print that was clear enough to identify—Hyde's—looked like it had been made over another print. The front half was well defined, the back half was smushed a bit. He moved the magnifying glass around the outline of the print, first to one side and then the other. It seemed clear: Hyde's was on top of the other one.

He repeated the exercise with another print of Hyde's. The same pattern emerged. Hyde's boot print was made on top of another one.

He leaned back, contemplating what was implied by the fact that Hyde's prints were made after the others. It seemed obvious: Hyde had been there after whoever had left the others. Whether they were the killer's or the cops, he was apparently the last person at that spot. Which suggested that perhaps he'd gone up at some point after her body had been found and removed. But why?

The phone rang. He pulled his phone out of his pocket and glanced at its screen.

"Tim. To what do I owe this pleasure?"

"Glad to hear you feel that way. Haven't been quite sure of late."

"Apologies if I've been difficult. You'll understand better in about forty years. Being cantankerous is a requirement of old age."

"You're not *that* old, Lew."

"You trying to take away my excuse for being cantankerous?"

"No. Sorry."

"So, what's up?"

"Got a call from Tony just now. Thought you'd want to know."

"Okay."

"Hendrik Hyde is in police custody."

"What?"

"He returned to Sienna early this afternoon. The police watching his house arrested him before he even had time to go inside."

"You're kidding."

"Surprised me too."

"Is he being pleasant and cooperative?"

Tim chuckled. "Tony said they were thinking of getting earmuffs to block out the racket. He's threatening to file complaints left and right. I must admit, sometimes I have genuine sympathy for our guys in blue. They have to put up with a lot in their quest for justice."

"So what does that imply, Tim? If Hyde just showed up, apparently he *wasn't* trying to hide from them?"

"Yeah. I don't know what to make of it."

"Did you ask Tony that?"

"He's as surprised as we are."

"Well, while you're here, you might be interested in something *I* just put together." Lew briefly sketched his analysis of the boot prints and his deduction about when Hyde was at the scene of the murder.

"Really? He turns up voluntarily, and now you're saying he was only at the murder scene after the fact? That's two things in his favor," Tim said.

"Yeah, it's hard to keep up with. I think I'll go take another nap, see what else unfolds."

"*Another* nap? You've already had one?"

"It's part of my conditioning routine."

"For?"

"Being cantankerous."

A brief pause. "Bye, Lew."

"Bye, Tim. Thanks."

343 Chestnut Street

Lew had barely hung up when his phone rang again. He glanced at the screen. This number seemed vaguely familiar. It came to him.

"Hi, Peggie. What's up?"

"Can you come over here again?"

"What for? Don wouldn't talk to me."

"He says he will."

"Really?"

"I think he's gotten to the breaking point. I heard him crying during the night. I'm really worried about him."

"And he says he'll talk to me?"

"He said it through tears. Coughing and gulping. If he doesn't get this out it's going to kill him."

"Okay, Peggie. I'm willing to try. When did you have in mind?"

"The sooner the better."

"Okay. I'll be there in a bit."

***

Lew pulled up in Old Blue, parked, and walked up to the Thompson's front door. As he approached, the door swung open. Peggie held it for him as he stepped in. He glanced around. There was Don, at the far end of the living room, in the same chair as last time, staring straight ahead.

"I'm not going to say a thing," Peggie said, loud enough so Don could hear. "I'll be in back if you need me."

Lew walked over to the chair opposite Don's and looked at him, again amazed by the man's size. He spoke gently. "Peggie said you'd like to talk to me?"

Don looked at him. His eyes were moist and his breathing

uneven, as though he was struggling to maintain his composure. He nodded.

Lew sat down slowly and leaned back. "Same rules as before, Don? You just tell me whatever you want. I won't ask questions? And it won't go any further than between us. That okay?"

He nodded.

Lew said nothing more, just waited.

Don swallowed, closed his eyes, took in a deep breath, let it out. "I think I have to tell someone," he said.

"Okay."

Another deep breath. "About that night."

Lew nodded.

He looked up at the ceiling, then at Lew. "I didn't mean to do it; I just couldn't stop myself."

Lew waited.

"I was angry. Really angry."

Lew waited.

"He drove me crazy."

"Mr Campbell?"

Don nodded.

"Because?"

"He did bad things."

"Like?"

"He had those students over. A lot. Those young women?"

Lew nodded.

"And they'd be in there for hours."

Lew waited.

Don looked at him, his expression pleading. "They were innocent. Those young people."

Lew nodded.

"That was not right."

Lew waited.

"That night I just couldn't stand it anymore. I had to do something."

Lew waited.

"I saw him leave."

Lew raised his eyebrows. "You saw Mr. Campbell leave?"

Don nodded. "Yes. He left about nine pm."

"Oh. How?"

"A car picked him up."

"So he was gone that night?"

"Yes. But I still had to do something."

"Okay."

"So when I couldn't sleep, I got up. I went out to our shed. I got something out. And I went over there."

"With something from your shed?"

He nodded. "That's when I did it."

Lew cocked his head. "Did what, Don?"

He closed his eyes. Looked away. Bit his lip. "I trimmed his hedge."

Lew said nothing for several moments, trying to take this in. Finally, he said, "You trimmed Mr. Campbell's hedge?"

Don nodded, beginning to sob. "His yard is a mess. He doesn't do anything to take care of it. I work hard to keep ours looking good. It's not fair. I know I shouldn't have. I know it's not my property. But I couldn't stop myself. He has no respect for anything. Not those kids. Not his yard. I just couldn't stop myself."

"Is that how you got scratched, Don?"

Between sobs he gasped, "Yes. The hedge has thorns. It was hard to see. I deserved it. I shouldn't have done it."

"So you scratched yourself trimming his hedge?"

He nodded, rears running down his cheeks. "I know I'll go to hell. I know that was a bad thing. I just couldn't stop."

Lew felt his own eyes moisten. He was at a loss for what to say. He waited until the sobs softened and Don began to regain composure.

"This is what you couldn't tell Peggie, Don?"

He nodded, his expression one of misery. "God will be my judge. I know that. It's what I deserve."

"You know, Don, however guilty you feel, from a legal standpoint this isn't a serious crime. I don't think the police would care much at all."

"It's not the police I care about. It's God. He is my judge."

Lew nodded, waiting a moment to say more. "Do you think, now that you've told me, you could tell Peggie?"

He rubbed his face, looked at Lew through reddened eyes.

"Maybe."

"Shall I get her?"

He sighed, then nodded.

Lew got up and walked to the other end of the living room. He called softly. "Peggie?"

She emerged from the back, her expression a mix of concern and confusion.

"I think Don can talk with you now," Lew said.

"What did he say?"

"I told him I wouldn't share it with anyone," Lew said. "But I think he'll tell you now."

"Okay." She glanced at Don, then back at Lew. "Thanks, Lew. I can't tell you…"

"You're going to have some work to do," he said. "But probably not what you think. Good luck."

He glanced back at Don, who was still trying to dry his face, as Lew opened the door and left.

The Sienna Police Station

At Tim's request, Tony had agreed on still another meeting at the police station to bring everyone up to date on developments. Lew arrived at precisely nine am, the agreed-upon time. He parked across the street from the station, got out of Old Blue, and crossed the street.

As he opened the door to the reception area in front, he heard shouting coming from somewhere in back, an angry male voice.

"You're going to pay big time for this, you pathetic losers! You think you can lock up Hendrik Hyde, you've got another think coming! I'll sue your asses all the way to hell! You'll wish you lived on another planet by the time I'm done with you, you fucking cocksuckers!"

Lew glanced at Ros. "He sounds upset."

She grimaced. "It's been going on since I got here a half-hour ago. It never stops."

"You can't muzzle him?"

"If it were up to me…"

"We meeting the usual place?"

She nodded. Lew headed for the conference room, the shouting growing louder as he neared.

"I'll ship your filthy souls to hell, you goddam bastards! You're going to rot in hell for all of eternity! You think I can't do it, you're going to…"

Lew entered the conference room and closed the door behind him. Fortunately, the room was well insulated and drowned out most of the shouting. Everyone else was already there. A cardboard urn of coffee and box of donuts sat in the middle of the table. They nodded to him as he sat down, everyone except John Christiansen, who stared at the table with an irritated expression. Looking at his watch, he spoke first. "Nice to see you, Travis. Now let's get this damn show on the road."

Lew shrugged, then poured himself a cup of coffee and reached for a donut. "Lovely to see you, John. Thanks for the goodies."

"Those came from me, Lew," Violet said softly.

"Ah." He looked at the donut. "Chocolate glazed. Good choice."

She glanced toward Christiansen, a subtle suggestion not to push his buttons too hard.

Lew leaned back, taking a bite of the donut, waiting.

Tony said, "It seems we have some things we need to update. As I suspect you have already discerned, we now have Hendrik Hyde in custody, charged with the theft of half a million dollars."

"Good work," Lew said. "Interesting that he chose to return to Sienna."

"We've tried to interrogate him," Tony said, "but he won't talk. Well, that is to say he won't answer our questions. Says to talk to his lawyer." He glanced in the direction of the cells in back where they could still faintly hear the shouting.

"Seems to be going around," Lew said.

Tony nodded darkly. "Yeah. Campbell still hasn't told us anything either. We're starting to worry about him. He hasn't eaten a thing since he arrived. He seems to be on a hunger strike."

"Any idea why?"

"Nope. But it isn't helping our progress in unraveling this thing."

"So where are you?" Lew said.

"We'd like to charge both of them with murder. There is good evidence they both killed Trixie Lawson. But of course that's not possible." He sighed.

Tim spoke. "John, where are *you* on this? Do you have a theory about which of them did it?"

John shook his head, scowling. "Like Tony said, we'd like to lock them both up for a good long time. About the only thing we've got tied up is Hyde's charge of grand theft."

"And that one looks firm, doesn't it?" Tim said.

"His lawyers will try to get him off, of course. Circumstantial evidence and all. And they're good. He's got the funds to pay them anything they want. But the evidence is clear and damning. We've got the motive, the opportunity, and pretty much open and shut evidence he took the million dollars."

"Did you get any of that back?" Lew asked.

"We're still counting the damn bills to get an exact figure. That's a lot of bills. It looks like it's at least mostly there," Tony said. "Certainly enough to return everything donors contributed.

"Good."

"So, that's about it on our end," John growled. "You got anything for us?"

Tim nodded to Lew.

John rolled his eyes. "Okay, Travis, what brainstorm have you come up with now?"

"No brainstorms. But I have done some more analysis. Not sure yet what it means."

"What kind of analysis?"

"As you know, I took pictures of boot prints and tire tracks up there in the forest. We've already talked about the ATV and tracking that back to Hyde's place." He paused. "I also took pictures around where Trixie Lawson's body was found."

"And?" John said darkly.

"As you doubtless know, there are a lot of boot prints in that area. Inside of where you have the yellow tape, and outside it."

"We couldn't make much sense of them," Tony said. "They were kind of all smushed together."

"I had the same problem," Lew said. "But I also took pictures outside that area, out where I found that cigarette stub under the log."

"Yeah?" John said skeptically.

"As you'll recall, when we were here yesterday, Violet took some pictures of the boots you found in Hyde's place."

A glimmer of interest entered Christiansen's eyes.

"It turned out that those boots are a perfect match for the prints around that log."

John's expression changed to genuine interest. "Hyde's prints?"

Lew nodded.

"You sure?"

"I'll be happy to show you when we leave. If you don't trust our pictures, you can make the comparison from the boots themselves."

"So you're saying you think Hyde is the murderer?" Tony said.

John spoke sarcastically. "Of course that's what he's saying, Tony."

Tony glanced at Lew for confirmation.

"Maybe, maybe not," Lew said.

"What do you mean?" John said.

"I had a hard time figuring out exactly where Hyde's prints emerged from the mishmash around the taped area. But I spent quite a while trying, and I'm pretty sure they're on top of other prints at that point."

John scowled. "So what are you saying?"

"If his prints are on top of the others it means he was there after they were."

"So…you're saying he was there *after* the murder occurred?"

"Probably. Since your officers were there getting the body around two weeks after her death, it suggests it was even after that."

"But you're not sure?"

"I don't know exactly where your officers walked. But there's another clue that I think helps."

They waited.

"When Violet took the pictures of Hyde's boots she noticed fresh needles and dirt in the treads. Suggesting he'd been there relatively recently."

"So we *can't* pin it on Hyde? Goddam it, Travis, why do you have to ruin it every time it looks like we've got it wrapped up?"

Tony spoke quietly. "I think he's right, John. If his boot prints were on top of the others, and they had fresh stuff in the treads, it probably means he was up there later than anyone else."

John looked off to the side, rolling his eyes. "Goddamn it."

"Why would he do that?" Tony asked.

"No idea," Lew said.

Looking at John, Tony said, "That may not be a bad thing, boss. Doesn't it point the finger more clearly at Campbell?"

John's expression brightened. "Jesus, Tony, you're right. If we can clear Hyde from the murder, then it *has* to be Campbell!" He glanced around the table for confirmation.

They were all looking at him, unsure how to react.

"Let's go have a look at the damn boots and tie this sucker down!" For the first time he sounded genuinely pleased.

***

John led Tony and Lew back to the evidence locker. This required them to walk past the cells. Hyde was standing just inside the bars, glaring at them as they passed. Lew was surprised by his size. He was only about five feet six inches tall, and slight of build. But he certainly had a healthy set of lungs. Lew also noticed Campbell lying on his bed as they passed, still in a fetal position facing the wall, his pillow wrapped around his head.

"You're going to be sued so far into the ground you'll wind up in China!" Hyde yelled at them as they passed by. "I'll see your asses burning in hell before this is over. You goddamned…"

They entered the evidence locker, closing the door behind them. Tony reached up and took down Hyde's boots, held them out to John.

John looked at the bottom, noticing the fresh soil and needles in the treads. He held them up to his nose. He looked at Lew. "You're right, Travis, they have fresh stuff in the treads." He held them up to his nose again. "They even have a little woodsy aroma." He handed them to Tony for confirmation, who repeated the examination and nodded in agreement.

"Okay. Let's see your damn pictures, Travis," John said.

Lew pulled out his phone and brought the clearest pictures he had of Hyde's boot prints in the forest. He held the phone next to the boot bottoms. Tony and John both leaned in and studied them.

After a moment, Tony said, "I see what you mean. John, do you see it?"

John nodded. "Yeah."

They looked at each other. "So…" John said, "…it must be Campbell. Right?"

Tony looked at him and shrugged. "I can't argue with you."

John turned to Lew. "I have to hand it to you, Travis. That's good work."

Lew shrugged. "Thanks."

John reached out his hand to shake and Lew obliged.

"Let's go back and tell the others we've got our man," John said.

Tony put the boots back on the shelf and they headed back

toward the conference room, walking past the cells again. Where, blessedly, Hyde had finally stopped shouting. He was slumped morosely on his bed. He glanced at the three of them with a nasty look as they passed.

Just then Ros entered from the front with a man in a suit following. They stopped to let her and the man pass. She approached Campbell's cell.

John muttered to Lew, "Goddam lawyer. He filed a suit yesterday to get access to Campbell. We had no choice. But now that we've got the goods on him, it's not going to help."

They started back for the conference room, Lew trailing the two officers. He glanced back at Ros and the lawyer. She said something to Campbell, who rolled to his back and glanced out at her. His face changed expression, his eyes widening into a look of surprise. Then a smile. The lawyer nodded to him. Campbell sat up as Ros reached to open the cell door and nodded back.

"You coming, Lew?" John and Tony had stopped, were looking at him.

"Yeah. Sorry."

***

The two officers and Lew returned to the conference room. John spoke first. "I believe we finally have this thing wrapped up," he said with a tone of relief. "And I have to give credit to Travis here."

The three *Sentinel* people looked at him with surprise, then at Lew, who shrugged.

"Those pictures should do the trick. The prints are a definite match with Hyde's boots. And they clearly show his prints on the top of others. He must have been up there at some point *after* the murder occurred. So it has to be Campbell."

John turned to Lew. "Can you send those to us before you leave?"

"Sure. What's the easiest way?"

John looked at Tony. "Maybe just leave them with Ros when you leave? And we'll need a statement from you about when and where you got them."

"Okay."

No one said anything for a few moments. Finally, Tim said, "So, are we done here?"

"I think so," John said expansively. "It's great to have this kind of teamwork. You guys deserve a lot of credit."

The four of them stood and headed for the door. As they started down the hallway to the front Harve leaned over and whispered to Lew, "Did you drug him? He sounds like he's on Prozac."

Lew smiled. "I think he's just relieved to think this nightmare is finally over."

"Aren't you?" Harve said.

Lew shrugged. They reached the reception area and Lew stepped over to Ros's desk to transfer the pictures of the boot prints. The others left, nodding to him as they did so.

Lew explained the situation to Ros and asked her the easiest way to make the transfer.

"Airdrop?"

He nodded knowingly. "You want to do it?"

"Sure." She took his phone, hit a few keys, and picked up her own. As she did so the front door opened and a woman stepped through. She glanced around the room, then started toward Ros's desk. Ros nodded to her. "I'll be with you in just a moment, ma'am."

She finished the transfer and handed Lew his phone. "Thanks."

"No problem."

Ros turned to the woman as Lew pocketed his phone and started for the door, glancing at her as he did so. She was not young, but she was still quite attractive. He stopped and stared at her for a moment. Had he met her somewhere? She seemed somehow familiar. She glanced back at him. Embarrassed, Lew nodded in a friendly way. She didn't return the gesture. Apparently she didn't recognize *him*. He was turning back toward the front door to leave when he noticed the lawyer who had been talking with Campbell emerge from the back. He nodded to the woman, smiling, and she smiled and nodded back.

Contemplating this exchange, Lew turned, pushed through the door, and headed across the street to where Old Blue sat faithfully waiting for him. It continued to bug him: where had he seen that woman before? And who was the man she smiled at?

Molly's Cafe

The four of them sat around a table at Molly's having lunch. It had been Tim's idea, and he'd even offered to pay for lunch. He thought they ought to talk, partly to celebrate what finally seemed like a case that had been solved, and partly to decide how much they could report in the paper and how they should handle writing it.

Tim had ordered a Rueben sandwich, Harve the meatloaf special, Violet a caesar salad, and Lew his usual tuna sandwich. They were waiting for their orders to arrive.

"That was a nice piece of work," Tim said to Lew. "Taking those pictures and figuring out that Hyde's boot prints were on top of the others."

"Thanks, boss."

"I think we're all a little amazed," Harve said.

Lew flashed him a look. "You mean at what genius it took?"

"That you actually managed to put John into a good mood. I haven't seen him that happy in weeks."

"He's been under a lot of pressure," Violet said. "He's only human."

Sometimes it's a little hard to tell," Harve said.

"I hope it lasts," Lew said.

All three looked at him. "What does that mean?" Tim said.

"I can't seem to get comfortable with the conclusion they've reached," Lew said.

"You still think Hyde is the culprit?" Harve said.

"I don't know. It's occurred to me that just because Hyde's boot prints were made there after the others, outside the area where the others were, doesn't mean they couldn't have been there earlier, mixed in with the others."

"Eww. Like he went back to the scene of the crime?" Harve said. "Wow."

"But that's not the only thing. Hyde is a thoroughly despicable human being, and I think they've got him dead to rights on grand theft. But whatever the evidence from the boot prints, I'm skeptical that he murdered Trixie Lawson."

"Why?" Tim asked.

"A couple reasons," Lew said. "One is how happy he seemed to have her bestowing her 'favors' on him, at least the way you described them in the bar, Harve."

"She was all over him, and he seemed to be drinking it in," Harve said.

"Why would a man who is divorced and as far as we can tell pretty much friendless want to kill an attractive young woman who seems to enjoy his company?"

"It's not entirely clear to me she was 'enjoying his company', as you put it Lew. She may have been playing up to him for the support he could provide."

"Perhaps. But I'm not sure that changes anything. Why would he care. He's got money to burn. Exchanging what for him was a little pocket change for something he likely needed would seem like a pretty good deal."

"What about being exposed," Violet said.

"Why would he care about that? Being exposed that you're seeing a young attractive woman? That's something most men would want to show off, not hide."

"Still, he's a contemptible man," she said. "Stealing half a million dollars he doesn't need from people who can't afford it?"

"Yes, he's vile. No argument there. But that's different than being a murderer. Now that I've seen him, I'm even more skeptical he could be the murderer."

"What do you mean?" Tim said.

"I had to pass his cell at the station to get to the evidence locker and got my first look at him. He's short and slight of build. Zane told me Trixie Lawson had been a good basketball player, which usually implies height and athleticism. It seems unlikely to me a man his age with his build could physically overcome a young healthy woman bigger than him. And one last thing: the autopsy showed the likelihood that Trixie Lawson had been raped. Why would he rape a woman who by all appearances was already sleeping with him?"

"Well, then, if Hyde didn't murder her, Campbell must have. That's exactly where our friends in blue have come out. Why are you uncomfortable with that?"

"I'm not sure Campbell did it either," Lew said.

"Wouldn't he have had to, if it wasn't Hyde?" Harve said.

"We don't have any other candidates, no. From that standpoint it seems pretty clear. There's just something…"

"The evidence is pretty damning," Tim said. "The timing of his disappearance? How do you explain that?"

"I don't know."

"And just the fact he did disappear. That sure looks like a man trying to escape capture."

Lew nodded.

"What about the bloody tissue found on his front sidewalk?" Harve said. "The one that matched his blood type?"

"I don't think that adds anything," Lew said.

"Why not?"

"Two reasons. First, there were clear signs of a struggle up there in the forest. What would blood on his front sidewalk have to do with that?"

"I don't know. Maybe they struggled there, he somehow got control of her but got scratched in the process, he took her up there to do her in, and she worked herself free and put up a fight?"

"Think about that, Harve. How would Robert Campbell, who's sixty-two years old, get a mile up a trail with a young athletic woman who was still conscious and could put up a fight?"

"Then how do you explain the bloody tissue?"

"You're going to have to trust me on that one. There is another explanation."

They frowned. "What are you talking about?" Tim said.

"I promised the person whose blood it is I wouldn't say anything to anyone else."

"So, you know who it is and you're not telling us?" Tim said.

"Sorry. Maybe I'll be able to at some point. Just trust me, I know how that got there, it's not Campbell's blood, and it has nothing to do with him or the murder."

"Okaay, Lew," Tim said, the skepticism evident.

"If you don't think he's guilty, why won't Campbell talk now?" Harve said.

Lew sighed. "I don't know that either. That's bothering me. I just have a sense there's something else going on."

"Seems like guilty behavior to me," Tim said. "Especially now that he's got a lawyer on the case."

Lew nodded. "Yeah, it does. He's hiding something. I'm just not sure…"

"What would it take to convince you?" Violet said.

"I don't know."

Molly appeared carrying all four lunches, one in each hand and another resting on each arm. "You guys seem awfully focused," she said. "Got a hot story you're working on?"

"We're thinking of a series of articles on little-known eating treasures in town," Tim said. "But we can't think of any."

Molly stared at him. "You know, that corned beef smelled suspect to me, but it's all I had. I think it's probably okay. Enjoy your lunch, Tim."

Tim smiled. "You're incorrigible, Molly."

"Helps with a certain class of clientele."

"How's the tuna?" Lew said.

"You got any wisecracks?"

Lew put his hands up defensively. "I say only the nicest things about this place. In fact, Emmett loved that meatloaf sandwich."

"Tuna's fine." She turned and headed back to the kitchen.

Lew took a bite out of the tuna sandwich, held it up. "Delicious," he said.

One-eleven Preston Place

Lew had just finished cleaning up the dishes from a simple dinner of home-made minestrone soup and a caesar salad. He started the dish washer and walked back into Violet's living room, where she was sipping on a glass of wine. Lew's third glass of gin and tonic sat on the coffee table.

"So you had lunch with Emmett? How's he doing?"

"Actually, my plan was to have lunch with Sherry Wingate, but for some reason she decided to leave before her entre arrived. Emmitt just happened to show up at an opportune time."

"Sherry Wingate? Why?"

"I needed to see her squirm when I started picking apart her claim of having that affair with Campbell. I don't do well with liars."

"So, Lew, if you don't think Campbell is the culprit, who do you think is?"

Lew sighed. "I'm not sure he isn't. It just bothers me that he won't talk. He does act like a guilty man who got caught. But he also acts like a man who is thoroughly depressed."

"Who else could it be?" she asked.

"I don't know. Why don't you help me think about it?"

"Okay."

They both sat there quietly for several moments. Finally Violet said, "How about Hyde's thugs?"

"I don't think it's either Hyde or his thugs, for the reasons we already talked about. They're basically one and the same; his thugs just follow his orders."

"Well, you said his boot prints were on top of others, but you couldn't identify the others. Could they have been his thugs? Maybe he was just there to supervise? Or maybe he went up there afterward to make sure they didn't leave any clues."

"That's a good theory. But I don't think that's it."

"Why not?"

"For the same reason I don't think he did it himself. I just don't see any compelling reason for him to want to kill Trixie Lawson. He had nothing to gain."

"Then why do you think he went up there afterward?"

"Maybe nostalgia?"

"Hendrik Hyde? Nostalgia?"

"I know it sounds a little far-fetched. But he didn't have any love in his life, and she was apparently providing it. Maybe he just wanted to see the place where she was killed because he had a sentimental need to say goodbye."

"Jeez, Lew. You're being awfully generous to a scumbag."

"Even scumbags have feelings."

"All right. Let's assume you're right. Who else could it be?"

"One thought I've had is your friend at the café."

"*Crystal*?" Her tone was incredulous.

"From what you've said it sounds like she had a thing for Rob Campbell. Maybe she was jealous of Trixie Lawson, a pretty young thing who apparently he was concerned about. Hadn't someone said he seemed kind of lost since he'd retired? That he seemed to miss the students, to feel a gap in his life.

"He came to that café every morning. Maybe that was to have regular contact with others? Which he apparently had with Crystal. Maybe she felt she had a special connection with him? Maybe there was something going on there more than a casual link with a customer who was always nice to her? They *are* around the same age."

"How would a woman that old kill a healthy, athletic woman less than half her age?"

"Craft and guile? Maybe she somehow lured her up there and had a weapon of some sort with her."

"Like?"

Lew shrugged. "A baton?"

"Like British bobbies use? A nightstick? You think Crystal could have bashed in Trixie Lawson's head with a nightstick?" She sounded skeptical.

"I admit it doesn't seem likely. But the body was too far gone for them to be able to find much evidence, so who knows what might have happened? A sharp blow to a critical spot."

"Couldn't they see that in the autopsy if her skull had been fractured?"

"It would have had to be something less obvious than that. Like a sharp blow to the back of her neck."

"I'm going to give that one a probability rating of about one on a scale of ten. Highly unlikely." She looked at Lew. "Any other ideas?"

He sighed. "How about his brother James?"

"James, who lives in Florida? Isn't that kind of a long ways away to commit murder? And why? His brother?"

"There are airplanes."

"You're suggesting he hopped a plane, flew out here, went for a hike in the Tahoe National Forest with Trixie Lawson, did her in, and flew back to Florida undetected?"

"Okay, it's a stretch."

"What would be *his* motive? Don't murderers have to have a motive?"

"Maybe *he* was jealous."

"Of?"

"His brother's good looks and appeal with women?"

"He's a married man."

"That doesn't change a man's attraction to pretty young women."

"Wouldn't he be more likely to kill his brother than his brother's girlfriend?"

"I don't know. It's just a wild guess." Lew sighed, with a look of discouragement.

"Really, Lew, you're grasping at straws. That doesn't even get a one on my scale."

"Okay. Here's another one. How about Sherry Wingate?"

"The young woman who accused him of having an affair with *her*?"

Lew nodded. "Maybe she was jealous of Trixie Lawson."

"For what reason?"

"Well, Campbell obviously cared about Lawson. Which he apparently didn't about her, since he gave her a D minus in English.

Maybe she not only resented the grade but had tried her wiles on Campbell and been rejected. And resented the fact he was so solicitous of Trixie Lawson."

"Well, I suppose that might account for a motive. What about an opportunity and the ability?"

"Good question. Like we've said, Lawson was young, sizable, and athletic. Sherry Wingate wasn't particularly big."

"And why would the two of them be up there in the forest? On what possible pretense could Sherry Wingate have lured her up there?"

Lew slowly shook his head, rubbing his face. "Yeah. You're right. It's a stretch."

She nodded. "A two at best."

"So who do *you* think did it?" he said.

"I'm still suspicious of Hyde. He's such a turd. And if he wanted to do her in, for whatever reason, wouldn't he have his thugs do the deed? We don't know anything about their boot prints."

"I suppose."

"I'd give that about a five on my scale compared with your wild theories," she said.

"You might have a point. Although there's still the motive issue. Why would Hyde *want* her dead?"

"Okay, then it's got to be Robert Campbell. It all adds up. He might not have been involved with Sherry Wingate—who apparently is a pretty loathsome human being herself—but that doesn't mean he wasn't involved with Trixie Lawson, who by all accounts was a thoroughly sympathetic young lady. He was lonely, no longer teaching. She was still coming to him for support. She was homeless so he was concerned about her. Maybe letting her stay with him on occasion. What's going to happen in that situation? An attractive young woman who looks up to this thoughtful, supportive man, who is sixty-plus and lonely? Get real. They're going to sleep together."

She continued. "But then for some reason he decided he had to end it. Maybe she threatened to expose him, figured it was a way to get the money she desperately needed to escape her homeless plight. Or maybe he just felt so guilty for taking advantage of a former student he went off the deep end and decided to do her in. It was the only way he could squelch his guilt. So he took her on a hike, and totally against her expectations, did the deed. He'd shrewdly arranged for his escape, flew off into the wild blue yonder, and against what he thought was all odds, got caught. And now he's feeling so much guilt—or maybe just such regret that his plan failed—he can't talk about it."

"That's a good theory. I can't really argue with you," Lew said.

"It's way more likely than your wild-ass theories about Crystal or James or Sherry. More like an eight or nine on my ten-point scale."

Lew nodded. "Maybe. I'm still uneasy. I just have a sense there are more dots I'm not connecting. But your points are good ones. And there is the fact that…have I mentioned lately how smart you are?"

This time Violet just shot him a scathing look. And leaned over and kissed him on the forehead.

An Old Cedar Bungalow

Lew was sitting on his couch, working on his third cup of coffee, Earl curled up at his side. He'd gotten up early, having had trouble sleeping, and left a note for Violet, who was still sleeping. He'd been greeted at the back door by Earl, who despite the early hour was expecting breakfast. Lew had complied, then put on a pot of coffee. He wasn't hungry. He was frustrated.

He kept going over every clue he could think of. Every tidbit of information. Especially the ones he lacked. Violet's reasoning had been sound about Robert Campbell. But he couldn't shake his gut feeling, given all the things he didn't know. Where had he spent those three weeks before he showed up at his brother's house? If he were trying to dodge the law, why would he go there when it was perhaps the only place the cops might be waiting for him? Why was he behaving the way he was now, curled up in a fetal position and refusing to say anything? Who was the lawyer trying to represent him, and the woman who apparently knew that lawyer? There were just too many things he still didn't know.

He worked to go back over every bit of information he did know. Campbell had arranged a flight to New York on September third, spent two nights before in a motel in Sacramento, and left his pickup at home. Did that tell him anything? Parking at airports was expensive. So perhaps he knew he'd be gone for a while? If he wasn't dodging the law, what was he doing? And why New York City? What was there in New York City that had drawn him? Was it just a place where he could get lost? But if he wanted to get lost, why would he show up in Port Le Claire, Florida?

Maybe he wasn't trying to dodge the law. Maybe something had drawn him to New York. He didn't know anything about Campbell's personal life or possible contacts there. All he knew about were his links to some obscure town in Ohio, near Cleveland, where he'd grown up. And hadn't been back to, according to James, since their parents had died twenty years ago. He did have that email exchange going with his old girlfriend there. Could that be anything?

Something stuck in his mind about Cleveland. What had Zane told him about Campbell's flight to New York? It had a layover in Cleveland. Had that been for a reason? Had he arranged to talk to someone in Cleveland on his way through? He would have had to leave the airport security area to do that; visitors can't get through the security check without a reservation. Or had someone join him there, someone who was flying on to New York with him? Or maybe something had happened there that caused him to stay?

Was it possible he hadn't even gone to New York, just stayed in Cleveland? You could do that, just get off a plane on a layover and not get back on. Sometimes it was even cheaper. Would a flight to New York be less expensive than a flight to Cleveland? A lot of flights went to New York, a lot fewer to Cleveland. Maybe it was an expensive place to fly to?

Lew let this line of reasoning play out. If he had stopped in Cleveland, either briefly or for a longer time, why hadn't he told James about it? Zane had told him that the only alert Jim had that Rob was coming for a visit was one earlier that suggested he *might* be coming for a visit sometime in the not-too-distant future. Like he didn't really know. Might something have happened in Cleveland that had caused him to want to see James? Maybe he'd anticipated a possible visit and whatever had happened in Cleveland had confirmed it?

He felt stuck. All this was just speculation. Was there anything firm he could tie it to?

Lew decided to turn his attention to the present. Why was Robert behaving the way he was, refusing to say anything, like he was guilty? Is that why he was going to visit James, to confess to his big brother the awful thing he'd done, get James's sympathy, or perhaps his advice? But how did that explain the three-week gap between when he left Sienna and went to Port Le Claire?

And who was the lawyer trying to represent him? Who, incidentally, seemed quite determined. And that woman he'd seen as he was leaving the police station, who apparently knew the lawyer. There *was* something about her that rang a bell. He took another slug of coffee, trying to connect all the dots.

Earl hopped up on the couch, licking his lips from breakfast. Lew unconsciously reached down and began rubbing behind Earl's ears. The predictable purr began. He sighed, envious.

While still petting Earl, out of the blue it came to him. That picture he'd seen in Campbell's desk drawer! The hot babe in the skimpy dress. That was the woman he'd seen at the police station! A little younger in the picture, but the resemblance was clear. It had been Donna at the police station! Dressed quite differently. Looking considerably more demure. But the right age, and the right degree of attractiveness. It was her! Donna had followed him all the way out here.

But how had she learned about his arrest? He'd been under police guard the whole time since he'd been arrested in Port Le Claire. Who else knew that Rob had been arrested? As far as he knew, Donna didn't know anyone in Sienna other than Rob. Then the obvious answer hit him: James. James must have contacted her.

Another thought burst upon him: *she* must be the one who had hired the lawyer. They had seemed to know each other; those nods he'd noticed as he was leaving the police station. His old high-school sweetheart come to his rescue. But had she come to rescue him because she knew he was innocent? Or because she knew he was guilty? Either seemed possible.

Regardless, Rob must have seen her in Cleveland on his way through. So that was perhaps where he'd spent those three weeks. But why three weeks? What had motivated him to stay that long? Maybe he'd confessed to her and sought *her* support? And despite the heinous crime, she still had enough sympathy for him, or perhaps attraction to him, that she'd decided to try to help? Which would explain the lawyer.

Did that explain his behavior now? Why he wouldn't talk? Maybe he *was* guilty? So the lawyer was there just to get the best deal he could when Campbell was tried for murder? That made sense.

Except that it put Lew back in the place he was having trouble accepting: Robert Campbell being guilty of murdering one of his old students. A troubled young woman who had probably come to him because she needed help. In which case he was worse than Hyde. Taking advantage of someone to get their money was one thing. Killing them was quite another. Was there anything in Robert Campbell's background to suggest he was capable of such an act?

Whatever the answers to all these questions, this felt like progress. It could explain a number of things. But not everything. In particular, not the most important thing: was Robert Campbell innocent or guilty? It didn't look good. But might there be reasons for his staying in Ohio other than confessing his guilt to Donna and seeking her help? Or for his unwillingness to talk?

Offices of the Sienna Sentinel

Lew had called still another meeting of his colleagues. He wanted to share with them his new thoughts on all this. And he wanted any help they could offer on how to answer the questions he still had.

They sat around the usual conference table, sipping on coffee from the office. No one had brought any donuts.

"So, what's on the agenda?" Tim asked.

"Two things," Lew said. "What I think I've figured out. And what I haven't."

"Fire away."

Lew sketched his 'ah ha' moment regarding the woman he'd seen at the police station, and how she had probably learned about Campbell's arrest from James. Also, the fact that she was an old high school girlfriend who had re-established contact with Campbell, and that they'd been exchanging emails for the last year. And that she must be the person who had hired the lawyer to defend Campbell, since they appeared to know each other. And, finally, that it seemed possible Campbell had spent the three weeks he'd been missing with her in Alloro, Ohio.

"You been holding out on us, old man?" Harve said. "I don't remember you mentioning any of this previously."

"I didn't want to overwhelm you with information," Lew said. "Some people get flustered when you do that."

"This does sound pretty relevant," Tim said. "How do you know about their emails?"

"You really want to know?"

"Oh, god." He rolled his eyes.

"So now that you've shared what appears to be a sizable body of information you've been withholding, where does it leave us?"

Violet said, not without sarcasm.

Lew sighed. "Okay, there are still several unanswered questions. One that comes to mind is why he refuses to talk. At all. Or, apparently, eat."

"You don't think being charged with murder explains that?"

"Maybe."

"What else could it be?"

"I'm not sure. But it looks to me like he's depressed. Really depressed."

"Are those two things incompatible?"

"No. But it seems extreme."

"We know he's a bit of a strange bird. Never getting married. Never telling anyone what he's done summers. Having students stay over at his house. Who knows what goes on in that head?"

"Okay, here's another tidbit I should share," Lew said.

"More secret stuff?" Harve said with a note of false alarm.

"This just happened. It was when I was coming back from showing John and Tony the match between Hyde's boot prints and the pictures I'd taken. We had to walk past the jail cells on the way back."

"Was Hyde still in fine form?"

"Fortunately, he'd finally shut up. But as we walked past, Campbell's lawyer was just arriving. Ros was letting him in to talk with Campbell."

"Was he actually going to talk to him?"

"I don't know, but he did seem to know the lawyer. He perked up when he saw him, even smiled."

"At his lawyer? Who smiles at their lawyer?" Harve said.

"Exactly. It was like he knew the guy."

"Maybe he'd hired him."

"How *could* he have. He'd been in police custody since the moment he'd been arrested."

"Well, maybe his old girlfriend had. Donna."

"That was my assumption."

"So maybe he was an old classmate of theirs."

"Not possible. He was younger. I'd put him somewhere in his forties."

"Okay, so we don't know who his lawyer is," Tim said. "You

said there were several unanswered questions. What are the others?"

"The biggest one is the most important," Lew said.

They waited.

"Is he innocent or guilty? It seems to me his behavior could be explained either way. He'd be depressed if he'd been caught and was about to be charged with murder, if was guilty. He'd be just as depressed if he'd been caught and was about to be charged with murder, if he wasn't guilty."

The three of them looked at him, frowning. Finally Harve spoke. "I believe you have narrowed it down admirably, Sherlock. Leaving us pretty much where we started."

"Well, ask yourselves this question: If he's *not* guilty, who could be?" Lew said.

"You must have thought about this," Tim said. "Who do *you* think it could be?"

Lew looked at Violet. "Actually, we've put some thought into this, kicked around the possibilities."

"And?"

"We have no idea."

Offices of the Sienna Sentinel

They sat around the table looking at each other. No one spoke for some time.

Finally Tim said, "It seems to me the weight of evidence is still on Campbell being the culprit."

"Why?" Lew said.

"For exactly the reason none of us knows what to say. There are no other credible candidates."

"Perhaps."

"What do you mean, perhaps?" Tim stared at him.

"Well, humor me. Let's think through that. I agree, assuming we can eliminate Hyde, Campbell looks like the guy. But let's have a thought experiment."

"What's a thought experiment?"

"It's how Einstein figured out the theory of relativity. He just sat around thinking, putting together all the relevant information he had," Lew said.

"Okay, Einstein. What have you got?"

Lew glanced at Violet. "Want to start?"

"Not particularly."

Lew frowned. "Indulge me."

"Well, let's eliminate the most cockamamie one first. You suggested it might be his brother, James." She rolled her eyes.

"Okay. James. Suppose he and Donna are in cahoots. It could mean they're trying to frame Robert so they're free to pursue their own romance. Which would explain why James didn't warn Robert about his house being staked out—assuming he even knew about it, which is unclear. It would also put a different color on what that lawyer is up to."

"What sense does that make?" Tim asked. "We know Donna and

Robert had a high school romance; there's no evidence James was ever involved. He's married, and apparently reasonably happily. And he's the one who helped Donna track down Robert when she wanted to get back in touch with him.

"I'm just trying not to jump to any premature conclusions. It's certainly a long shot. As Violet put it, probably the most cockamamie. But I wouldn't put the chances at zero."

"Not much above it," Violet said. "I agree with Tim. You've said there are things in Robert and Donna's emails that indicate they were close in high school. It feels to me more like a romance that for some reason went off the rails in high school but left some lingering positive feelings. And that she sought him out after her husband died, based on those feelings. James was just a conduit to that end."

"Okay," Lew said. "Let's put the James theory on the back burner. Who else?"

"Well, you also have that cockamamie theory about Sherry," Violet said.

"Sherry Wingate?" Tim said.

"Yeah, the young woman who falsely claimed she'd had an affair with Campbell," Lew said. He proceeded to go through the points he'd made with Violet, in particular her possible jealousy of Trixie Lawson's close relationship with Campbell.

"Also a very long shot," Violet said. "Even given her shady personality, that's a serious stretch. Among other things, I don't know how she could have done it. Trixie Lawson was a large, athletic young woman. Sherry Wingate doesn't appear to be either of those."

Tim nodded. "Agreed. What else you got, Lew?"

"Crystal?"

"The waitress at the café?" he said, skeptically.

Lew nodded, glancing at Violet. She scowled back, then said "Why don't you share your wild theory on that one, Lew?"

"Okay." He proceeded to explain how Crystal and Robert had what appeared to be a close friendship. They saw each other every morning at the café, had done so ever since he'd retired. And she appeared to be quite taken with him. Plus they were about the same age.

"Suppose we give you all that, Lew," Tim said. "Why would she want to kill Trixie Lawson?"

"Jealousy? He was apparently close to the young woman. Maybe Crystal saw her as competition?"

"She'd have to be a little nuts to go that far, wouldn't she?"

"Yes. Do we know she isn't?"

"Doesn't that raise the same question we did about Sherry Wingate," Tim said. "She's much older and less athletic. How could she possibly have done it? And why on earth would Lawson agree to go with her on a hike in the first place?"

Violet stared at Lew with an expression suggesting these were all points he really had no way to counter.

Lew was nodding. "All good points, Tim." He glanced at Violet, who was still staring at him skeptically. "But not necessarily completely convincing ones. The mere fact we don't know the answers to them doesn't necessarily rule them out."

"Do you have even a wildly unlikely counter for any of those objections?" Violet asked.

"Well, as a café waitress she must be quite experienced in dealing with people of all ages, and all personalities. Meaning she's also skilled at understanding people's motivations. Maybe they both just like to hike. And both were concerned about Robert Campbell being missing. She might have distracted Lawson long enough to clobber her over the head—or perhaps her neck—with something."

Lew glanced questioningly at Violet, like he was assessing to what degree she was buying any of this. She was just shaking her head. Then he glanced at Harve, who shrugged. "Seems far-fetched, Lew. But I don't have a better idea. Seems like we've gone through all the possibilities. Who's left? Someone unknown to us?"

"There's a fruitful line of thought," Tim said. "Let's focus on the complete unknown."

No one said anything for several moments. Finally Tim spoke: "How about Phil Palmer? His old teaching buddy."

Harve said, "Really? The guy who noticed he was missing? Alerted the cops? Who he taught with for forty years? His closest friend?" He frowned at Tim.

"Is it something he'd be capable of?" Lew asked, looking at Harve. "Isn't he as old as Campbell?"

"Yes, and he's not very healthy, has diabetes and arthritis. Plus he's overweight."

"How big is he?" Tim asked.

"Six three, six-four. Probably two-forty or two-fifty."

"Could he even make it up a trail like that?" Violet asked.

Harve shrugged. "Feels like a push. He'd have to be seriously motivated."

"He's married, isn't he?" Violet said.

"Yeah. Although now that you mention it, I'm not sure whether that would make him less or more likely to be the culprit. His wife seems less than affectionate."

"What do you mean?" Lew asked.

Harve described her appearance, how she'd greeted him at the door, and the way she'd spoken to Phil.

"So maybe he lusted after young women?" Violet said. "Most men do, don't they?"

"Don't blame us," Harve said. "That's the way we're engineered. Isn't it true of women also?"

Violet smiled ironically. "Good point, Harve. We just have to make do with the best we can come up with."

Lew ignored her. "Didn't you mention he sometimes went hiking with Campbell?"

"As a matter of fact, yes. He said Campbell sometimes invited him along."

"Do you know where they would go?"

"He said the trail where Lawson's body was found was one of Campbell's favorites," Harve said. "That Pembrook Trail."

Lew stared at him, not speaking. For several moments.

"What? Did I say something wrong?"

"Didn't you just say, 'the trail where Lawson's body was found'?" Lew said pointedly.

Harve looked at him quizzically. "Yeah."

"How did he know what trail that was?"

"Haven't we talked about that?"

"With John and Tony. Who asked us to keep it quiet."

Harve spoke slowly. "Yeah."

"Have you read that name anywhere?" Lew asked.

Harve frowned. "What are you saying?"

"The police were clear: They didn't want just anyone going up there out of curiosity and mucking up the boot prints further. They asked us not to put it in the paper. I had to pry it out of them. So how did Phil Palmer know where her body was found?"

Harve, Tim, and Violet all sat there staring at Lew.

Two-Thirty-Seven Chestnut Street

Lew and Harve pulled up in front of Phil Palmer's house.

"I can't believe you're doing this, Lew. This is a job for the cops, not us," Harve said.

"You said he's an old man with lots of physical problems. What could he possibly do? I want the satisfaction of seeing his face when we confront him," Lew said.

Harve rolled his eyes. "I need to have my head examined."

"Where's your sense of adventure, Harve?"

"Same place my sense of survival is. Somewhere else."

Lew opened the car door and stepped out. "Okay, I can do this alone if you'd prefer."

Harve reluctantly opened his door and got out, shaking his head. He followed Lew up the sidewalk to the front door. Lew knocked.

After a moment Palmer's wife opened the door. She stared out at them maliciously. "Goddam it. Didn't Phil tell you not to come back?"

Harve just stood there, said nothing.

She glanced at Lew. "Who the hell are you?"

He held out his hand. "Lew Travis. Good to meet you."

"Go away." She scowled at him.

"We just need a word with your hubby."

"My *hubby*?"

"The man of the house?"

She scoffed, rolling her eyes. "You'll have to look elsewhere for that."

"What does that mean?"

"There's no one worthy of the name living here." The scorn dripped.

Lew glanced at Harve, in a gesture of recognition concerning what Harve had reported about the nature of their relationship. He took a breath. "Well, whatever his gender status, might it be possible to have a word with him?"

"What for?"

"We'd like to explain it to *him*, if that would be all right."

She turned and yelled back into the house. "Hey, scumbag, there's someone here to see you." She stepped back into the foyer as they waited.

After a few moments Phil Palmer came to the door, a dour expression on his face. He gave Harve a hard look. "I've told you everything I'm going to."

"Hello, Mr. Palmer," Lew said, holding out his hand.

Phil switched his gaze to Lew. "You bringing sidekicks with you now, Harvey?"

"Mr. Travis is a colleague at the newspaper," Harve said.

"Which means you can both get the hell out of here."

"This will only take a moment, Mr. Palmer," Lew said.

Palmer stared at him malevolently.

"Or we could do this at the police station if you'd prefer."

Palmer scowled. "What does that mean?"

"You're going to be charged with the murder of Trixie Lawson either way. We just thought it would be more pleasant for you if we did it here."

Harve cast Lew a sidewise glance, a look of doubt. Phil glanced back at Harve. Then at his wife.

"You'll be treated respectfully by the police," Lew said. "Everyone in this country is innocent until proven guilty."

Palmer cocked his head a bit in an inquiring expression.

"It may be some time before there is even a formal charge, and if needed, a trial."

Palmer stared at Lew. "What if I refuse to go?"

"Well, as I said, we can leave it up to the police if you'd prefer."

"But you said I'd be treated respectfully if I go with you?"

Lew nodded.

Give me a minute. He partially closed the door and turned to his wife. Several moments passed. At which point Mrs. Palmer reappeared. Holding a gun. Pointed at Lew. She spoke one word: "Leave."

Lew put up his hands, took a step back. "Yes, ma'am."

Harve also took a step back, nudged Lew, and they started back toward the car.

The door clicked shut. A moment passed. And there was a deafening blast.

They stood there, stunned, looking at each other. Not moving. Until there was the sound of a door reopening.

They glanced back in unison.

Mrs. Palmer stood there, the gun at her side. "I thought I'd save the public the cost of holding a trial. The son-of-a-bitch was as guilty as sin. He didn't deserve to be treated respectfully. He deserved a long, slow, torturous death. But I didn't have the patience. Would you do me the favor of letting the police know?"

"Okay," Harve gulped.

She closed the door quietly.

At that moment a police car pulled up in front of the house. John Christiansen and Tony Gonzales got out.

Two-Thirty-Seven Chestnut Street

Christiansen and Gonzales walked up the sidewalk to where Lew and Harve were standing.

"What are you doing here?" Lew asked.

"What are *you* doing here?" John responded. "This is a police matter."

"How did you know about it?"

"Your colleagues. Apparently they have more sense than you do."

Lew shrugged. "I suppose that's possible."

"So have you spoken to Mr. Palmer yet?"

Lew nodded.

"Okay, now it's our turn."

Lew hesitated. "Unfortunately, that won't be possible."

"Why the hell not."

"He's no longer here."

"Where did he go?" John said suspiciously.

Lew glanced at Harve, who shrugged a 'don't ask me' look back. "He's gone to see someone," Lew said.

"Who?"

"His maker."

"*What?*"

"We didn't actually see him die. But all evidence would point that way."

"What evidence?"

"The gunshot."

"*What* gunshot?"

"The one his wife just ran through him," Lew said.

"What the hell are you talking about, Travis?"

"Let's go see," Lew said, nodding toward the front door.

***

Tony had called the coroner's office, which had sent men over to pick up Palmer's body. Tony and John were sitting in the living room with Lew, Harve, and Mrs. Palmer. She was explaining what had happened.

John said, "You're *sure* he killed Trixie Lawson?"

"It took me a while to get it out of the son-of-a-bitch. He's an obstreperous old bastard."

"Was," Lew corrected her.

She nodded. "Was."

"So what exactly did he say?"

She took a breath. "This young woman came to him because she was worried about Robert Campbell. She was homeless and apparently Campbell had been trying to help her. But she hadn't been able to find him the evening before and thought my husband might know where he was."

"Go on."

"He told her Rob had said he was going for a hike the day before and must have gotten lost up there in the forest. He volunteered to go with her to look for him."

"And?"

"That was a cock and bull story. He just wanted to get her alone up there. When he got back a few hours later he was a mess. He could barely talk. He just said there had been a terrible accident."

"And?"

"He didn't tell me anything more for three days. He barely slept the whole time. Finally he got so exhausted his defenses broke down and I got it out of him. He saw this attractive young woman at his door seeking his help and his desire overcame him. He'd probably dreamt about something like that for a long time. He made up the story about Campbell going hiking to lure her up there, then at some point turned on her and wrestled her to the ground. She fought back, but he was able to overcome her. He said he choked her to death, and then had his way with her."

"*After* he'd killed her?"

She nodded, letting out a disgusted guttural. "It's beyond

appalling. I didn't even want him around the house, but he didn't have anywhere else to go and begged me to let him stay. I've been on the verge of turning him in for three weeks. When these two showed up" …she nodded toward Lew and Harve… "and knew the story, it was just too much. Especially when they said he'd be treated respectfully by you guys. Respect was the last thing he deserved. So I shot the bastard. I hope it saved you some trouble."

John and Tony sat there with their mouths slightly agape. Finally John spoke. "Well, Mrs. Palmer, while we understand your behavior, I'm afraid we have no choice but to charge you with murder. As terrible as your husband was, you did shoot him to death."

"That's fine. Lock me up. I expected as much. At least I'm rid of the vermin."

"We can probably plead extenuating circumstances and keep your sentence to a minimum," Tony added.

She turned to Lew and Harve. "How did you guys figure out he was guilty?"

"Harve asked him in his last visit what trails Mr. Campbell liked to hike, and he said the one where Miss Lawson's body was found," Lew said. "That was not public information. There was only one way he could have known."

She nodded. "Logical deduction. Aren't you the guy who's solved other crimes around here?"

Lew shrugged. "A couple. Keeps me off the streets."

She looked at John and Tony. "Why didn't you guys figure it out?"

They glanced at each other. Finally John spoke: "We were inundated with clues, Mrs. Palmer. We were following them up as fast as we could. We would have figured it out if we'd had more time."

She rolled her eyes, not responding.

"We'll need to get a full description of your husband's crime, and a confession from you."

"I already confessed. I shot the son-of-a-bitch."

"Yes, but we'll need to go through an official process to certify all this."

She rolled her eyes again. "Damn bureaucracy."

The Sienna Police Station

Lew and Harve had asked John if they could accompany them to the police station to meet Robert Campbell, now that he would be freed. They'd spent so much time thinking about him they wanted to actually meet him.

John had reluctantly complied, while insisting they would have to go through the official procedures for his release. They had contacted Tim and Violet on the way in case they wanted to be there. All four of them were sitting around the conference table at the police station, waiting for Campbell's official release.

While they were waiting Harve described the events at the Palmer house, with particular mention of a certain gun. He had just finished the part where Mrs. Palmer had come to the door pointing it at Lew.

Tim and Violet looked at Lew, shaking their heads. "You are out of your mind," Violet said. "You're lucky you weren't shot."

"She had no reason to shoot me," he said. "She had another target in mind."

"Yes, but you had no way of knowing that."

He shrugged.

"Weren't you afraid?" Tim asked.

Again he shrugged.

"If you weren't, what was that 'Yes, ma'am' you uttered?" Harve said.

"I believe that's the correct response when a woman is pointing a gun at you and giving orders."

"I'm surprised you had *that* much sense," Violet said.

"Hey, I'm seventy-two years old. If I can't take some chances now, when will I be able to?"

"You're going to be lucky to make it to seventy-three the way you're going," she said.

The door to the conference room opened and Tony ushered in an attractive older woman and a fortyish man dressed in a suit. The woman looked around the table.

"Hi, Donna," Lew said.

She stared at him. "Who are you? And how do you know my name?"

"Lew Travis." He nodded at the empty chairs in an invitation to sit down.

She eyed him skeptically as she reached for the younger man's hand and led him around the end of the table. They each pulled out chairs and sat down.

"So who *are* you?" she said.

"A reporter for the local paper. These are my colleagues." He introduced Tim, Harve, and Violet.

"You're writing a story and Rob hasn't even been officially released yet?" she said in an annoyed tone.

Lew shook his head. "No. No story. We're just here because we've been trying to untangle this case for the last week and a half, and having spent a lot of time thinking about Mr. Campbell we wanted to actually meet him. Especially now that we know he's innocent."

"I thought that's what the police had been doing."

"They helped."

She looked at him quizzically.

He turned his attention to the man. "And this must be the attorney you hired to defend Mr. Campbell?"

She glanced at the man. "Sort of."

Lew reached out his hand to shake. "Lew Travis."

The man reached back and shook Lew's hand. "David Livingston."

"You're an attorney?"

He nodded.

"How did you happen to get involved in this case?" Lew asked.

He glanced at the woman, nodding.

"So you must have known each other already?" Lew said.

He nodded. "Can I ask you a question?"

"Sure."

"Why did *you* get involved?"

"It was kind of a big deal around here," Lew said. "We don't have a lot of crime in Sienna. And the cops didn't seem to be getting anywhere."

"Did you think Mr. Campbell was guilty?"

"We didn't know. We were trying to figure that out when Mr. Palmer's involvement became evident."

"The *police* seem to have been convinced Mr. Campbell was the guilty party."

Lew nodded. "We don't always agree with them. We were still trying to unravel it all."

"And you figured out it wasn't Mr. Campbell?"

"We just weren't sure it was. Until it became clear who it was."

"Well, it's good to know someone was able to clear his name," Livingston said.

"Did you know Mr. Campbell before you got involved in the case?" Lew asked.

"For a little while, yes. Not all that long."

Just then the doorknob clicked. Tony pushed the door open for Robert Campbell to come in. He looked around the little assemblage with a confused expression.

Donna stood and rushed around the table to embrace him. "Thank God!" she said in a trembling voice as she clung to him.

He held her, continuing to look at the others in confusion. Until his eye landed on the lawyer. Who stood and came around the table, giving Rob a warm embrace also.

"Hi, Dad."

Molly's Café

Lew was halfway through his tuna sandwich, Tim the same with his Reuben, Harve was munching on his jerry-rigged hamburger and fries, and Violet was just starting in on her Cobb salad.

"Well, I can see why you remembered who that woman was," Tim said to Lew. "She's still a knockout."

"It took me a while. I should have figured it out sooner. I think the emails a certain accomplice came up with provided the critical clues. That helped me add two and two."

"Did you *have* to mention that?" Tim said.

"Sorry."

Tim rolled his eyes. "If you have to give any depositions in this case, will you keep my name a long way away from his?"

"Not a problem, Tim. He doesn't want his name involved any more than you do." Lew took another bite of his sandwich.

"What do you think is going to happen to Hyde?" Violet asked.

"Whatever it is, it won't be enough," Lew said. "Unfortunately the maximum sentence in California for grand theft felony is three years in prison and a ten-thousand-dollar fine. I'm pretty sure he'll get the maximum given the circumstances and the amount involved."

"You're right," she said. "Not nearly enough."

"The best part is they were able to recover the full million and can return what was contributed to the people who gave it."

"Still not enough."

"What about Mrs. Palmer?" Harve asked.

"Tony told me he's pretty sure they'll charge her with manslaughter, not murder," Lew said. "And there's a fair amount of leeway in the sentencing based on the circumstances. He thinks she'll probably spend six months in county jail and then be on probation for some period."

"Sounds a lot fairer than what Hyde will get," Violet said scornfully. "That guy should be taken out behind the barn and shot."

"*Violet*. That's not very feminine."

"Feminine is *exactly* what it is," she said.

"What about Campbell, Donna, and their son?" Harve asked.

Lew smiled. "Looks like a happy ending."

"Did you know that was their son?"

Lew shook his head. "No clue. I was as shocked as you. The last email that Donna sent Campbell mentioned there was something serious she needed to discuss with him. This must have been it. Given David's age, the only explanation is he's a son she had by Rob that he never knew about, apparently when it became clear Campbell wasn't ready to get married when they were in high school. She must have just handled it on her own and never told him. Which also explains why his last name is Livingston."

"Which also explains how she found an attorney," Lew continued. "He must have become a lawyer when he grew up. So Donna didn't have to *hire* him to defend Campbell, he was doing it for his own father."

"Whom he'd never known." Violet said. "Although he said he had for a little while."

"That must be how Campbell spent the three weeks in Ohio when no one knew where he was," Lew said. "He must have met Donna on his layover in Cleveland, at which time she revealed the son she'd had by him. So he spent that time reuniting with her and getting to know David."

"Any idea what their plans are now?"

"If I'm any judge of what we saw at the police station, I don't think there's much doubt they'll be together."

"It's amazing Rob never got married," Violet said. "It's like he was waiting for her his whole life."

"Any idea why Campbell refused to talk after he was arrested?" Harve asked.

"I suspect some of it was guilt for leaving Donna and never learning she was pregnant with his child," Lew said. "He was a troubled young man at that point and apparently not ready for such a responsibility. He obviously loved kids, spent his entire adult life trying to help them, and it must have plagued him that he'd missed seeing his own son growing up. Plus now that he'd finally learned about this, he doubtless wanted to make up for lost time. Which was being destroyed by a false charge of murder. Who wouldn't be depressed?"

"I have a question that still bothers me," Harve said. "Palmer told me repeatedly that Campbell mysteriously disappeared every summer and would never talk about what he did. The only clue was that he always returned with a great tan. Any idea what he was doing?"

"That's another tidbit my unfailing Internet guru helped with," Lew said, glancing at Tim. "There were email exchanges between Campbell and a summer camp near Cleveland where he apparently volunteered his time every summer. He'd been a lifeguard there when he was young and knew the people who ran the place."

"Why would he want to keep that a secret?" Harve said.

I'm only guessing, but I have to wonder if it didn't give him a chance to visit Alloro and check on Donna. He probably didn't want anyone to know about that, even James. Plus he *really* didn't want *her* to find out. He didn't want to do anything to disrupt her marriage."

"What makes you think all that?"

"That picture he kept in his desk drawer looked like it had been handled a lot. It was worn and even torn a bit on one corner. Why would you keep a picture of an old girlfriend around, and take it out and look at it frequently, if it was someone you'd completely forgotten about?"

They all nodded.

"According to some of the emails my *consistently* dependable source provided," Lew said, glancing again at Tim, "he was reluctant to have her visit him out here. Which might be the case if he was still in love with her but afraid she wouldn't find him as attractive as she did when he was a handsome athletic young man. Or that she'd somehow disapprove of his life here."

"Men are *so* insecure." Violet said.

"Do you think he knew she had a son?" Harve asked.

"No idea. But he wouldn't have known he was the father regardless" Lew said.

"Well, Lew, I hate to admit it, but I suspect you're right about that," Tim said. "It would explain why he never got married. He never stopped loving his first love."

Violet smiled at the three of them. "Have I mentioned how smart you guys are?" She glanced at Lew. This time *he* shot *her* a scornful look.

"So apparently all those rumors about him taking advantage of high school girls were false?" Tim said. "Just unsubstantiated rumors?"

"There is not one shred of evidence he ever had any but the best motives," Lew said. "He had a lot of trouble making it through adolescence himself and apparently just wanted to help others with that phase of life."

"I have a question that still bothers *me*," Violet said. "What was he doing on September second, the first day he didn't pick up his newspaper, the day before he was scheduled to fly to New York."

"I don't have an answer for that one," Lew said. "Maybe he wanted to spend some time in Sacramento before flying east? Maybe he wanted to get something nice for Donna, knowing he was going to see her in Cleveland? Maybe he was just restless and needed to get out of town for a day. If we get a chance to talk to him, we can ask him."

"So all that timeline stuff was just nonsense?" Harve said. "Even though you spent a lot of time focusing us on it, like you thought it was significant."

"Hey, nobody's perfect. We were grasping for whatever clues we could think of at that point."

"You mean like asking me to talk to Crystal, who turned out to have nothing to do with this whole thing?" Violet said.

"She did provide evidence he was a good man."

"Actually, I went back down there again and happened to talk to her fellow waitress, someone named Velma," Violet said. "She told me Crystal had gone off the rails for a while, thought she had some kind of unique channel of communication with Campbell. Kind of sad, actually. Velma said she's recovered now, sad that she didn't wind up with him, but happy he was found innocent, which she claimed she knew all along."

"He's obviously an appealing guy," Harve said. "Palmer told me a couple of the women teachers at the high school felt the same way."

"But none of it mattered to him," Violet said, "because he was still in love with his high school sweetheart. I guess first loves never really leave you."

"*I* have a question," Tim said, looking at Lew. "Does this mean we're finally going to get a story out of you? Something we can actually publish?"

Lew frowned. "Jeez, I don't know, Tim."

"Well, you should have lots of time on your hands now that this thing is behind us."

"Yeah, but I've got a lot of other things I've let slip that I need to deal with."

"*What* other things have you let slip that you need to deal with?" Violet said skeptically.

"For openers, washing some dishes."

Acknowledgements

I'd like to thank the following people for their thoughtful reviews and helpful feedback. First, Elizabeth Compton, who, despite caring for two small children and working part-time, carefully read the draft and provided her usual insightful feedback and suggestions. Jay Egan, an old friend, whose care with grammar and wording, shrewd insights, and unique wit caught a number of potential glitches and inconsistencies, and added color as always. Bruce Lester, a remarkably well-read friend, who provided numerous thoughtful and helpful insights. And Steve Compton, a new reviewer, who suggested a variety of helpful edits to smooth wording and tone.

Let me also acknowledge that any errors of fact or blunders of judgment are purely my own.